You've Found Her

You've Found Her

A Novel By

Lynn Gregory

You've Found Her
A Novel
By Lynn Gregory

Copyright 2024 by Lynn Gregory

Published by Woods Pond Publishing Group

ISBN:979-8-9915597-0-6
Printed in the United States of America

Other fiction by Lynn Gregory:

The Other Side of a Tapestry (2021)
So Much for Walls (2022)

Table of Contents

Prologue: January 1986

Al Watson was not entirely surprised to hear that one of Pete Addison's kids had been trying to track him down. When he heard Pete had passed away last summer, he sent his condolences. There was no reason not to observe a common courtesy. But he was surprised the call came from Pete's youngest daughter, Teri. He hadn't seen her since she was a small child and never really got to know her. *She must be in her mid-thirties by now.* He was glad he had thought of that before dialing and reaching someone with an adult woman's voice.

"Hello, Teri, this is Al Watson returning your call. It's been a long time. I'm sorry to hear of your father's death."

"Thank you, Al, and thank you for returning my call. It took me a while to locate you. I presume you've returned to England. I have fond memories of your jeep when I was a child in Argentina."

"Ah yes, I loved that old jalopy."

"But I'm sure you're wondering why I called. I'm searching for a woman who worked for my parents when we lived in Buenos Aires. Her name was Ofelia. I believe she was involved with the business you and my parents were also engaged in. She apparently disappeared in 1978, and no one knows where she is or whether she's even alive."

Al thought for a moment, then smiled to himself. This could help him solve a current problem. At least it was worth a shot.

Teri heard a drawer open and the sound of shuffling paper.

"Try this number. Ask for Brigid."

Teri wrote down the information.

"Thank you, Al, this means a lot to me."

"You're welcome. Please give my regards to your brothers and sister."

Her hands shaking, Teri looked up the telephone exchange and turned to Marissa. "It looks like Ofelia is in Northern Ireland. Wouldn't you know she would find another place where people are fighting each other—what is it called—The Troubles?"

Marissa smiled at her newfound sister. "Are you ready to make this call?"

"I've probably been ready my whole life, and for the first time, I don't feel alone."

Teri dialed the number and heard a woman's voice speaking English with a slight Spanish accent, "Hello, this is Brigid."

Teri cleared her throat.

"Hello Brigid. My name is Teresa Addison. My sister Marissa Lozado and I are here together, hoping to speak with Ofelia. Can you help us locate her?"

Her words were greeted with silence that seemed to last forever. Then she heard a clear voice at the other end of the line say, "You've Found Her."

PART 1

September 2 - September 20, 1986

Chapter 1

Teri's eyes were glued to the window as her jet zoomed upward through the clouds. She enjoyed experiencing a plane's ascent as it left behind what looked like a fluffy white mattress. The vision allowed her to imagine jumping through the window and bouncing on the cloud's infinite softness. Of course, she knew it was an illusion, and the clouds were composed of water crystals, but it didn't interfere with her enjoyment. Yet, even in the clouds of her wildest imagination, nothing would ever match her experience flying through the Andes Mountains between Argentina and Chile in 1953, before there were passenger jets. They had flown so close to the snow-covered mountain peaks that her six-year-old mind believed she could reach through the window to grab enough snow to make a snowball. The magic of that moment had been broken when her mother, Susan Addison, looked at her closely and said, in a serious voice, "You do not love Evita." It would take years for her to understand the significance of that moment, the moment that marked the end of the life she had known as an Argentine child up till then.

Now, thirty-three years later, this flight was taking Teri to Ireland, where she would spend a few weeks getting to know her recently discovered birth mother and sister. Eight months had passed since Teri and her twin Marissa discovered they were sisters, the daughters of a woman named Ofelia Cruz, who was currently living under the name Brigid Alvarez in Northern Ireland. Prior to that, they had not known of one another's existence or that Ofelia was their mother.

In Teri's case, Ofelia had served as her American family's live-in maid when they resided in Buenos Aires. In retrospect, Teri realized Ofelia was the adult in the household who raised and nurtured her. When she was six years old, the family left Argentina and moved to the United States. It was an abrupt move followed by no further contact with Ofelia. In the beginning, a puzzled Teri had missed Ofelia terribly, but as the years went by, her memories faded, replaced primarily with curiosity without satisfaction. When asked, her parents always changed the subject, so she gave up asking.

Marissa grew up in a small rural town in Buenos Aires Province called Punta Lapiz where she knew Ofelia as her mother's cousin, a kind relative who visited occasionally but seemed to have a secret life. When Ofelia came by, she always made Marissa feel special with gifts and attention, but she sadly disappeared from Argentina in 1978 during the presidential administration of Jorge Rafael Videla. Videla's administration spanned the years 1976 through 1981, a violent era called Argentina's "Dirty War," in which his perceived enemies, called *Desaparecidos,* were systematically kidnapped and murdered. Rumor had it that 30,000 people disappeared, and when they lost Ofelia, Marissa and the rest of her family assumed she was one of its victims. Although uncertain as to why Ofelia would have been chosen for such a fate, Marissa wasn't completely surprised by the thought of the mysterious Ofelia being engaged in anti-Videla activities.

During the eight months since they first met, Teri and Marissa had made an effort to get to know one another as well as the long distance between their homes in New York State and Buenos Aires Province would allow. The trip to Ireland was their first opportunity to actually be with Ofelia, who the twins hoped would help them understand how they came to be and who their father was.

Soon after the plane crossed the cloud threshold, the sky turned black, and the lights went out inside the cabin, leaving Teri alone with her thoughts. She couldn't help but be nervous anticipating the first face-to-face visit with her mother. All she knew was that she really wanted it to work out.

Transitioning her brain between logic and emotion had often been a challenge as Teri was equally drawn to both. At some level, she saw her ability to control her reactions as the key to making sense of her crazy life story. *I need to flip my brain away from its tendency to over-analyze. This trip is going to require me to open myself up to these complicated relationships and keep my heart open instead of shutting down when things don't go my way. It's time to come up with a logical plan.*

Turning on her overhead light, Teri pulled a small notebook from her bag and began to write.

First, I want to get to know Ofelia and Marissa and become mutually comfortable with them. I also want to learn more about their lives.

What else? I want to find out what Ofelia is doing in Ireland and what she was doing in Argentina.

I hope she'll tell us about her past life and our family history in general. Maybe we can get her to explain her decision to give Marissa and me up when we were born.

Despite her attempt to be cool, calm, and objective by writing things down, just writing the words that she was given up by her birth mother hurt. Teri felt a lump in her throat, and her eyes began to tear up. Wondering if she would hear what Ofelia had to say without breaking down, she decided to take deep breaths and focus on how they felt, a technique she had successfully employed in the past when she was feeling anxious.

This helped, and she went back to her writing.

I hope she will tell us about our biological father. Is that too much to expect?

Teri lifted her head to think about that question and noticed for the first time that her seatmate, a woman with large blue eyes and stylishly combed salt and pepper hair, was looking at her. Teri couldn't read her expression but assumed she was annoyed by the light.

"I'm sorry. am I keeping you awake? I can turn off the light."

The woman smiled, "That's not a problem. I have a hard time sleeping on planes, and it's going to be a long night."

Relieved, Teri smiled back. "I'm a little wired too. Are you traveling to Ireland for business or pleasure? By the way, I'm Teri."

"It's nice to meet you, Teri. I'm Grace. Believe it or not, I'm going to Ireland to follow up on a flirtation."

"What fun. Will you be staying in Dublin or traveling around?"

"I'll be in Dublin for a week. I'm doing this on a whim; hoping it turns out to be as fun as it sounds. I guess I'm a bit nervous. That may be why I haven't been able to relax."

"Have you been to Ireland before?"

"I attended Trinity College a hundred years ago. My husband passed away last year, and I decided to cheer myself up by attending a college reunion. I hadn't been back for a long time, but when he died, I was at a loss. I can't tell you the order of things, only that the reunion invitation arrived in the mail and I decided to go. I just wanted to be around strangers who weren't feeling sorry for me. Surprisingly, I almost immediately ran into a fellow I dated once or twice all those years ago, and we hit it off. He lives in Ireland and invited me for a visit, so here I am."

"I'm sorry for your loss, but what a great story! I hope it turns out for you."

"Thank you. So, what about you?"

"I'm on my way to meet with my mother and sister in Northern Ireland."

"Oh, is your family from here? You seem very American."

"I was born in Argentina where my American parents were working. I lived there until we moved to the United States when I was six. I've lived in the States ever since."

"I thought you said you were going to Ireland to visit your mother and sister."

"Long story short, I grew up in a family that wasn't really mine and just discovered my real mother and twin sister this past January. They're both Argentine."

"This is even more interesting. How did you come to discover them?"

Teri laughed and shifted in her seat. "It really is a long story, but honestly, a lot of fates had to come together. It began when I discovered old communications between my American mother and my birth mother that led me to travel to Argentina. Other pieces started to come together when I reconnected with a childhood friend; then, a major coincidence when Jack, my significant other, came upon my twin sister Marissa in his search for a research project. My sister and I look a lot alike; we're probably identical twins, so you can imagine how surprised he was to meet her!"

"This sounds like a soap opera! Did he end up doing the study? What's that about?"

"Marissa is involved in creating a religious movement of sorts. I don't know much about it, but can tell you it involves integrating indigenous spiritual practices and beliefs. And yes, he recently returned from observing their practices and is hopefully writing up what he found as we speak."

"She sounds like an interesting woman. It must be fascinating for you to meet a person who looks like you and shares your genetic structure but has lived a totally different life. Have you found some things in common you wouldn't expect in a person who grew up in a different culture?"

"That's a huge question I'm interested in exploring, but I really haven't spent much time with her so far. I think there's more to our differences than growing up in different countries."

Teri paused and searched Grace's face to see if she was simply being polite or might be interested in going deeper. She decided to take a chance.

"Have you ever heard of a third-culture kid?"

Surprisingly, Grace didn't skip a beat. "As a matter of fact, I recently ran across that concept. My parents were in the diplomatic corps, and I spent my childhood in three foreign countries: Libya, Japan, and England. Third-culture kids are children like myself who had childhood experiences in cultures different from the ones their parents knew. I haven't followed up yet, but I have heard there are groups out there where third-culture kids can share their life experiences. So far, I have the impression it's all very loosey-goosey."

Grace paused and looked at Teri with increased interest. "Are you a fellow third-culture kid?"

"I think I am, but I also have an academic interest in the topic. I teach Anthropology at a small college in upstate New York and am working towards my doctorate. I've finished all of the requirements except my dissertation and am thinking about studying the impact of the third-culture kid experience on people."

"That's really interesting. What's your angle on the topic?"

"I wish I could tell you, but I don't know yet. My experience has been almost totally emotional, so I've had a hard time putting it in words, let alone on paper. To make it a reasonable social science research topic, I need to sort some things out."

"If you want, I'd be happy to stay in touch and talk with you about my life. It might be helpful to see what we have in common."

"Thank you, that would be great!"

After chatting for a few more minutes, Grace yawned and said, "I think I need to close my eyes to see if I can rest a bit before we land. I want to look as good as I can for my friend!"

"Good idea. Talking with you has helped me turn down the volume of stuff running around my brain, so I just may be ready to sleep now too."

Teri reached up and turned off her light.

It seemed like only a few moments later; lights appeared suddenly in the plane's cabin while stewardesses hustled to wake everyone up in time to serve breakfast before the flight was to descend. Teri and Grace shared a little more about their lives and exchanged contact information.

Looking at her new acquaintance, Teri wondered how Grace could have been so perfectly named. She was small, but willowy and gave the impression of someone who was completely comfortable in her own skin. This almost flew in the face of Teri's expectations regarding the complicated effects of being a third-culture kid, and she, once again, wondered if she would ever understand her own experience, let alone the whole phenomenon. But maybe Grace became graceful because of her name, not the other way around. As she thought about that, Teri told herself to stop it. *Why do I always have to complicate simple things? Grace has her name because that's the name her parents chose for her, period.*

As they walked into the Dublin Airport, Grace became increasingly distracted as she looked for Chris, the man she would be visiting. He was, in fact, right at the gate holding a bouquet of roses with a large smile on his face. It was clear he was as excited about seeing Grace as she was about him. After a brief introduction, Teri left them and followed the signs to the baggage claim area. Marissa's plane had arrived from Buenos Aires the previous day. She and Teri had made arrangements to meet at a nearby bed and breakfast.

Teri was glad to attend to the tasks of collecting her luggage and renting a car before meeting up with Marissa. Although she looked forward to spending time with her twin, she had to keep in mind that they were strangers who had, oddly, shared their mother's womb thirty-nine years previously.

Chapter 2

Teri was grateful to learn the bed and breakfast was only a few miles from the airport. With everything else going on, she hadn't thought about the fact that she had to drive the rental car on the wrong side of the road with a stick shift.

Relieved to get out of the car, Teri found Marissa sitting in a rocking chair on the front porch of the house, reading a book. While she had met Marissa once before, it was still a shock to see her face on another person's body. Seemingly identical, they were both tall and slim with dark brown eyes and naturally curly hair. But from Teri's point of view, their facial expressions and body postures reflected different personalities.

Despite the commonality of their origins, just about every other part of their lives had been notably different, and Teri found herself somewhat intimidated by Marissa in general. Unlike Teri, who, until recently, had been living the life of a nomadic student, Marissa came across as a mature adult who was a leader in her community. Teri had never thought of herself as an outgoing person; yet she was often incapable of holding back when she had something to say, and was certain that lack of self-control was written all over her face. In contrast, her twin spoke thoughtfully in a quiet voice. Teri envied that. It had the effect of making people pay close attention because they figured whatever Marissa was thinking must be profound. At that moment, Teri's perception of Marissa as a serious person was reinforced by the fact that she was reading *Euphoria on the Rocks,* a book of wisdom and poetry by their mutual friend Charlie Elliot.

Marissa led Teri into the house, introduced her to their hostess, and escorted her to her room.

"Would you like to freshen up? Our hostess has offered a late breakfast if you're interested."

"That would be great. Breakfast on the plane was small and full of sugar. I could definitely use something more nutritious."

"I will tell her. Eggs? Pancakes?"

"I would love scrambled eggs, juice, coffee with cream, and maybe a croissant if available. Otherwise, whatever, but no meat. I'm vegetarian."

"Oh, right, I think we may have shared that information. I, too, don't eat animal flesh."

Teri smiled, "Perhaps it goes with being twins?"

Marissa smiled back, "I don't recall that about Ofelia, but then again, she grew up at a time in Argentina when beef dominated every diet. I ate meat all through my childhood and only changed late in life when there was more choice."

"Actually, that's true of me too. My parents always fed us meat, both in Argentina and the U.S. Even when I changed my diet, it was difficult to find restaurants with food I could eat. It's getting better in the States now."

"In Argentina as well." Marissa walked to the door. "See you in the dining room."

At breakfast, they continued with pleasant small talk as Teri settled in. Both women needed to build up to sharing hopes for their visit with each other as well as their mother.

Teri said, "I noticed you're reading Charlie Elliot's book. What do you think of it?"

"I find it enlightening. I had read it before I met Charlie when he and your Jack came to my house to talk about studying our spiritual practices, but speaking with him inspired me to revisit the book."

A warm feeling climbed through Teri's chest when she heard Marissa refer to Jack as 'hers.' She was also proud to have brought Charlie into Marissa's life.

"Charlie is a very special man. I guess you got to know him better when he and Jack were observing your practice earlier this year. Have you seen him recently?"

"No, but we have stayed in touch by mail. He has totally enriched my understanding of the connections between nature and spirit. I've learned so much from him. But tell me, how is Jack? Has he finished the report? Is he still working for the Nevarez Foundation?" Marissa paused, "Pardon me for asking so many questions. You two are still together, right?"

Teri laughed, "No problem. Yes, we are still a couple. He's doing well, and is very busy. At the moment, he's caring for our dog and two cats while I'm here in Ireland. It's my impression that the Foundation folks like what he's done so far. He would probably enjoy having a full-time position there, but we shall see."

"I have no doubt his report will be accurate. I'm not sure it's due to his own Native American background, but he had no difficulty understanding our beliefs. He is a member of the North American Chippewa tribe, correct?"

"Yes, but writing in English for the Foundation is a translation process where meaning can be lost or at least distorted. He cares deeply about getting it right."

"I know. Like Charlie, Jack is a good person. You are a lucky woman, Teri."

"I couldn't agree more."

After a pause, Marissa changed the subject. "This is my first visit to the British Isles, actually my first time away from South America. I'm wondering if you would be interested in visiting a prehistoric site on our way to Ofelia's home in Northern Ireland. There's a site not far from here I would love to see. It's called New Grange."

"I've heard of it, a Celtic version of Stonehenge?"

"I'm not sure, but it is quite old, and I've heard the tour is short and interesting. I suspect Charlie Elliot would find it interesting as well. Like Stonehenge, it is believed to have been a place of both science and religion. And it's not far out of our way, just an hour or so from here."

"Absolutely, let's go. By the way, will you be willing to do some of the driving? I'm not accustomed to driving on the left side of the road."

"I can try. As you know, we drive on the right side of the road in Argentina, but I'm willing to share the discomfort as well as the benefits of having our own rental car."

"Thank you, Marissa. That's a relief! So, what shall we do with the rest of this day? I'm glad we planned an extra night before going to Ofelia. Gives us time to get over our jet lag."

"Our what? I'm sorry, Teri. There are some English words I haven't heard before."

"My apologies. Your English is so good, I forget it's not your native language. Jet lag refers to the effects of flying through different time zones, you know, when you feel more tired than usual. Sometimes it takes a day or so to feel normal."

"Ah, I will remember that. Is it a British Isles term as well as American English?"

"I honestly can't tell you, but I must admit, I'm pleased to be in an English-speaking country. I have no ability to learn other languages and, as I've mentioned before, have completely lost my Spanish."

"Yes, I find it unusual. It sounds like the loss of your native tongue is part of the memory loss regarding your early childhood years in Argentina. I wonder if you could remember more of the experience, the language would come back to you."

"I wonder that too, Marissa. I guess I'm hoping spending time with you and reconnecting with Ofelia will trigger some of those memories. By the way, I think we're going to have to start referring to her as 'Brigid'—at least when we're around her Irish acquaintances."

"This will be an interesting three weeks, won't it? We all have much to do together."

"I couldn't agree more. What do you want to do to relax for the rest of this day?"

"I asked our hostess for ideas, and she suggested we go into downtown Dublin and walk around. There's a bus we can get right on this corner that goes all the way to the Trinity College campus. It's apparently a neighborhood with many good restaurants and places to see."

"Like what?"

"Well, the college library houses the Book of Kells and the famous Long Room. They are both supposed to be spectacular. Maybe we can find a pub for an early dinner later and be back here in time to get a good night's sleep."

"Let's do it! I'm going to change into my most comfortable clothes and shoes. Can we meet in about a half hour?"

As it turned out, everything went as planned. Teri was charmed by the city of Dublin and liked that she and Marissa could relax and focus on seeing the sights as they mentally prepared for their meeting with Ofelia. The bus ride was easy. Teri was happy to use public transportation rather than negotiate the streets with the rental car. It was going to take some time to get used to the driving rules, best not done in a busy city when she was stirred up and tired.

Marissa and Teri were awed by the Book of Kells exhibit and its history. While they knew it was a medieval church document illustrating the four gospels, neither had been aware of its unique history of originally being created by teenaged monks in Scotland who arrived in Dublin via the town of Kells, in the 17th Century. It was also beautifully illustrated and full of symbolism, using animals, including snakes, lions, and peacocks, to represent the resurrection and immortality of Jesus Christ. They followed their visit to the exhibit with a walk through the famous Long Room, where Irish authors over the centuries were celebrated. Both Teri and Marissa were in awe of the fact that it continued to be a working library, even for valuable manuscripts, including Shakespeare's First Folio.

Resting her legs in a nearby pub while they waited for dinner, Teri mused about what they had experienced at Trinity. "What an amazing place to go to college! I met an interesting woman on the plane who attended Trinity many years ago. She was on her way to meet up with a man she had known back then and re-met at a recent college reunion. I must admit, I've kept an eye out for her since we came down here."

"What a lovely story."

"I thought so too. We exchanged contact information. She's the child of diplomats and is interested in the third-culture kid concept."

"What is that?"

"Oh, I'm sorry, I should have spelled that out. Children who spend time living in countries where they don't share the same culture as their parents. In a lot of cases, the parents don't even learn the language, but the children have to go to school and participate in the culture of their friends."

"This sounds like your experience, Teri."

"Yes, and I intend to learn more about it. The woman I met, whose name is Grace, offered to share her story with me. I'm hoping to use this as a topic for my doctoral dissertation."

"That would be fascinating and probably help you to better understand your own experience."

"Yes."

Their conversation was interrupted as a waiter brought them drinks. Teri took a long sip from her glass of the famous Irish beer, Guinness, made a face at its bitterness, and changed the subject. "This is my first time in Europe too. I'm struck by the historical depth people here take for granted compared with the U.S." Looking at Marissa and hoping she wasn't being insulting, she added, "Of course, we know the historical depth is available in the western hemisphere too, but literacy seems to make it more accessible."

"I agree the Book of Kells is an extraordinary artifact and I love seeing how Early Christianity used animal behavior to symbolize its own stories. What saddens me everywhere is how much is lost in both written and oral traditions over time. We have a lot to learn from our ancestors who lived so much closer to nature than most people do these days. I guess that's what I try to do with my spiritual practice."

"I'm looking forward to hearing more about how you bring ancestral knowledge and current understanding of nature together. I don't know how unique it is these days, but the more I study prehistory, the more I'm convinced all human societies have focused on learning what they can about the meaning of life."

"I agree, Teri. As you probably know from what Jack has learned about our spiritual study, the focus on health and balance is hopefully enabling people to live their best lives in the here and now as well."

Teri felt herself relaxing. While she hadn't known what to expect, their conversations had so far made her feel she and Marissa shared important interests. *Is it possible we're enough alike to approach getting to know Ofelia in lockstep?* She decided to test the waters.

"So, Marissa, tomorrow. This is going to be so strange. I mean, neither of us has seen Ofelia for many years, and we never knew who she really was." Teri took a second gulp of Guinness and coughed.

Making a face, she said, "I guess I'm glad I tried the Guinness. I'm in Ireland, after all, but I have to tell you I will never choose it again; it's so bitter."

Marissa laughed out loud, "Then I'm glad you were the official taster. I'm not a fan of alcohol in general. I find it all either too sweet or too bitter. Now I can tell people I don't drink Guinness because my sister told me it tastes bad. But, getting back to tomorrow; like you, I have thought a lot about this and decided it's Ofelia's 'show.' She has to be the leader in how we can be together in our new roles. I've decided to stay quiet until she brings things up."

"I guess I planned to do that too, but knowing me, there will come a time when I'll need my questions answered, and I may not be so quiet anymore."

"I would like us to be on the same page with Ofelia, but I also believe we need to be true to ourselves. I would never judge or try to obstruct your efforts. We probably have different styles and methods and obviously come to this with different past relationships with Ofelia. My greatest wish is that we all come away feeling as comfortable as possible and, hopefully, the ability to move forward as a family. But you can be assured, Teri, I want very much to have you as my dear sister for the rest of my life."

Teri felt her eyes fill with tears. "Thank you for saying that. I feel exactly the same."

***

The following day, they got up early and headed north of Dublin to New Grange. Although only thirty-five miles, it was a daunting drive as neither of the sisters had experience driving on the left side of the road in the right side of the car. However, they both used it as practice, took their time, and stopped frequently to switch seats.

Like the Book of Kells, Teri and Marissa found the New Grange prehistoric site interesting. While they had heard of it and knew it had been built around 3200 BC, earlier than both Stonehenge and the Egyptian pyramids, the simplicity of its presentation was notable. Located in a grassy field populated by contented-looking cows and sheep, the large central monument was part of a complex including other passage tombs, burial mounds and standing stones. At its center is a giant circular stone mound ringed by engraved kerbstones, many of which are covered with megalithic art. A brief tour of its inner stone passageway led them to a chamber where archeologists had found burnt and unburnt human bones. The tour guide said that while no one knows its exact purpose, it is believed to be both scientific and religious because the tunnel system is aligned so the rising sun on the winter solstice shines through a roof box above the entrance and floods the inner chamber. The tour included a simulation of that experience.

As they left New Grange, Teri and Marissa talked about how it felt to be in a place of such deep historical significance. Teri couldn't stop thinking about the level of scientific understanding its creation must have required.

Marissa agreed, "I've been really moved by the places we've visited in the short time we've been in Ireland. It is truly a magical place. I mean, I know we'll never know for sure how this complex was used and what it meant to its people, but it certainly seems to have scientific and religious meaning at the same time."

"I couldn't agree more, and I must admit, I can't get over that we're here with people who may be directly descended from the folks who made this. It's a bit of a shock to the system of an American who lives with such shallow history."

"In some ways, our spiritual group is trying to recapture similar ancient knowledge, and we have the advantage of learning from living descendants of an ancient indigenous South American culture, but it's hard to walk in ancient shoes."

"I'm really interested in how you do it and what you've learned," Teri said.

"Ha Ha! You'll probably have to read Jack's report. I'm too involved to be at all objective. Now, I think we'd better get a move on. It's time to see our mother!"

Teri was disappointed with the way Marissa shut down their conversation about her spiritual work but also understood that they both needed to prepare themselves for the visit with Ofelia.

After a brief lunch, they got into the car and drove straight through to Ofelia's house in County Tyrone, crossing from the Republic of Ireland into Northern Ireland. As they drove through the Common Travel Area between the two nations, Marissa speculated about Ofelia's role in the context of The Troubles that continued to plague Northern Ireland and how and why she ended up in Northern Ireland at all.

Teri nodded, "Hopefully, we'll be finding some of this out, just beginning with her new name and what she's doing here. But it makes sense that she would end up in a part of the United Kingdom given that Al Watson was the agent who helped her to escape Argentina," Noting Marissa's puzzled expression, Teri continued. "Remember Al Watson, the man who gave us Ofelia's contact information? He was working for the British Secret Service. That's how my parents, I mean the Addisons, knew him. They worked together to spy on Juan Perón and his followers. Ofelia was part of their group as well, which was why she lived with my family and pretended to be our live-in maid. And now she is Brigid Alvarez. It will be interesting to see how she introduces and explains us."

Marissa nodded, "Of course. I have much to learn about her life!"

Two hours later, they drove into the small town of Lindo and parked in front of a semi-detached house with a pretty flower garden. Getting out of the car, they walked to the door in tandem and were greeted almost immediately by Ofelia, who, looking at her daughters standing together, burst into tears and threw open her arms. Whatever their resolves to stay in control melted as the three women held each other and sobbed.

Chapter 3

Teri and Marissa couldn't stop crying. Here they were with their mother. Ofelia had been young when Teri last saw her when she was the family maid. Now she looked middle-aged with a bit of gray in her hair. There was definitely a family resemblance; like Marissa and Teri, Ofelia had naturally curly hair that resisted constraint. Teri wasn't sure, but they also seemed to share a similar oval face and nose shape. On the other hand, Ofelia was at least five or six inches shorter than the twins, and Teri was surprised to see her eyes were a vibrant green, not dark brown like hers and Marissa's. The brown eyes and long legs must have come from their father's side.

Knowing Teri and Marissa would have many questions, Ofelia had spent many hours planning their visit. She had worked undercover her entire life and was skilled at reading the people around her with the goal of getting what she wanted from them. There had been many incidences when that skill had saved her from harm, but this was more important. This time she had to find a way to establish honest relationships with her daughters after a lifetime of neglect and deception. As these thoughts ran around her head, Ofelia was shocked to realize all she could do was react to being with these two grown women she had borne. "You are both so beautiful. Thank you for giving me a chance."

Looking at Teri with tears pouring from her eyes, she said, "Teresa, my darling little girl, look at you. I thought I would never see you again! And Marissa. My heart is so full."

While she desperately wanted to bring Marissa and Teri into her current life, Ofelia also feared she would expose them to risk by association. In fact, it had taken a long time to decide how she would introduce them to her Irish acquaintances. Despite their obvious cultural differences, Marissa and Teri were probably identical twins with a strong facial resemblance to their mother. In the end, Ofelia decided to tell the truth; that they were her biological children who had gone their separate ways as adults. The rest was no one else's business.

Within minutes of their arrival, the house was filled with curious neighbors. First, a smiling woman named Bertha with two young children showed up. Ofelia introduced them as her adopted family.

"Please meet my neighbor Bertha and her girls, Meghan and Marnie."

Bertha jumped in, "So grand to meet you two, our Brigid's best-kept secret! We didn't hear about you until recently, but know how lucky you were to have such a proud and loving mother. Brigid has been like a grandmother to my girls, and they adore her. I'm also very grateful for her help." Bertha took a breath. "Oh, sorry, I apologize for blurting all this out. It's such a thrill. And you all look so much alike! It's like seeing three Brigids at once."

Teri and Marissa were happy to smile and not have to say anything further as Bertha and the other neighbors greeted them enthusiastically. Ofelia had clearly established a good life in her neighborhood in Northern Ireland.

When the last neighbor left, Ofelia closed the door and turned to her daughters. "Sorry for the onslaught. Everyone was excited to meet you."

Teri laughed, "It's great seeing you have friendly neighbors, but what have you told them about us?"

"I told them I have twin daughters I haven't seen in a long time. I told them you had both grown up and were living good lives. No one has asked more, and I haven't volunteered more information. People around here are careful to mind their own business. It can be dangerous to reveal too much, so there's no expectation."

Marissa nodded. "We'll get used to thinking of you as Brigid and look forward to learning about your life here. I think I speak for us both when I say we want to be sure we don't say anything that contradicts your story. But, I must ask you, how did you know who each of us is? How could you tell us apart when we came to the door?"

Ofelia looked surprised, "That's an interesting question. It never occurred to me; I just knew. I don't think I can analyze this. As I look at you now, I see that your features are almost identical, but you are each yourself. Now let me show you your bedrooms and give you time to unpack. I'll make some tea. Then we can talk. I know, very British of me, isn't it?"

As they settled into comfortable chairs in the living room, Teri and Marissa digested the fact that Ofelia was in charge and would direct the pace and content of their reunion. Ofelia poured three cups of tea, sat down, and took a sip from hers; then she began to speak.

"I will answer all of your questions, but please, first, tell me how things are going in Argentina. Not the general political stuff, I read the newspapers here. But I'm starved for news about our family."

Marissa said, "My parents, your cousins Sylvita and Raoul, are well and longing to hear news of you. They understand you've been protecting them from harm by your lack of communication, but think of you often. I'm charged with sharing my experiences here when I return. I also know they're anxious to learn when it will be safe for you to come home."

"I miss them terribly but will need to be sure trouble won't follow me to their door. And what about my cousin Che? Is he well?"

"As in the past, I don't see him often, but he always seems the same strong, silent type, a man of few words with a warm heart."

Ofelia nodded, "And you, Teresa. How are the Addisons? It has always saddened me that I had to lose touch with the whole family, especially you, of course. You and I lived with Susan and Pete and their four children for six years. Hard to believe they are all grown up by now."

"Yes, since Susan and Pete died, I haven't had much contact with the boys, but I have stayed in touch with Pat. In fact, she's played an important role in my search for you."

"How so?"

"She was the one who told me about the condolence letter from Al Watson with the return address in London. That's how we ultimately ended up finding you. I have to say, this has been a long journey involving many people you don't know, but there's one significant player you will surely remember, Juan Ignacio Ramón."

"Of course, I remember Juan Ignacio. I worked for his family for several years after you moved to the States. If I recall, you and he were the best of friends as small children. And you've reconnected with him in your search for me. How lovely. How is he doing?"

"He's well, a successful banker. He still lives in the house he grew up in, next door to ours."

"Another person I would love to see again."

"So, tell us about your life here."

"As you know, I'm known as Brigid Alvarez. I have told people I'm a widow; my mother was Irish, my father was Argentine, and I grew up in Argentina, where I met and married my husband, Tomás Alvarez. Tomás died ten years ago, and I decided to move to Ireland. That's the end of my story and all I've told people."

"Was Tomás our father?"

"Yes, that's what they assume, but no one has asked such a specific question."

"Have they asked why you would come to this country in the midst of The Troubles?"

"No, they believe I'm here because my mother was Irish. Brigid was also my mother's name. There are many people with Irish blood in Argentina."

Ofelia leaned back in her chair. "As I mentioned before, people here mind their own business."

"Are you Protestant or Catholic?"

"Excellent question. It matters to people here. I identify as Catholic but get along with all of my neighbors, some of whom are Prods."

Despite her determination not to push, Teri couldn't help herself,

"So, how do you make a living? How do you feed yourself? This is a very nice little house. How do you pay for it?"

Ofelia began shifting in her chair again. "I have a part-time job working for the postal service and help neighbors with child-care, for which I am paid. I also receive a little money from the British government. This is all you need to know."

Ofelia stood up and smiled. "I have some cookies in the kitchen. I actually baked them fresh this morning in your honor. Would you like to try one?"

Teri and Marissa got the message. It was time to step back.

Chapter 4

Ofelia dedicated the next few days to introducing the twins to her life in Ireland and getting them accustomed to thinking of her as Brigid rather than Ofelia. Deeper conversations would necessarily wait for a level of comfort she hoped would evolve as they spent time together. This was complicated by the fact that Ofelia also had to attend to her real business, her role as an agent for the British Secret Service. The moment she heard Teresa's voice on the telephone, she knew her MI6 contact, Al Watson, had set up their reunion. Al never did anything without a specific purpose.

So far, Al had not revealed his reasons for opening that door, but Ofelia knew it had to be something of good size he thought she could help him with. During the years she had lived in Northern Ireland, he'd only called upon her to do small jobs, mostly as a courier between his London office and people working with them around Ireland. It had been a relatively easy life for her. Although she was grateful to Al for saving her life by providing safe passage and a new identity in the United Kingdom, she missed the excitement of her role in the underground in Argentina. While Northern Ireland was in no way a dull place to live during The Troubles, she had never been given a chance to do anything particularly challenging. She had not been asked to live up to her potential or even the good reputation she had earned in Argentina.

While sincerely happy to be reunited with her daughters, Ofelia also hoped this new chain of events meant Al intended to involve her in some interesting work. Although she had been waiting for several months, she wasn't surprised to receive a coded message at the post office, where she worked part-time, on the second day of the twins' visit. The message instructed her to meet with one of his agents at the annual Matchmaker's Festival in the village of Lisdoonvarna along the western coast of the Republic of Ireland. There she would be given more information about her task. As usual, Al gave her no name and said she would be approached by a man she had met there previously.

The timing was perfect (Ofelia was sure Al had seen to that) for her to meet her contact and, at the same time, take Marissa and Teri on a road trip along the west coast of Ireland, culminating in Lisdoonvarna. The timing also worked for Teri and Marissa, who were ready to take a break from Ofelia's quiet life and experience more of the country.

As Ofelia hoped, attending to the drive, beautiful scenery, and scary road twists and turns was a shared experience that served as an icebreaker for the three women. Even crossing the border between Northern Ireland and the Republic at Strabane was seamless. Teri and Marissa enjoyed the puzzled expressions on the faces of the border guards as they examined passports from three different countries, the United Kingdom, Argentina, and the United States, with photos of women who looked so much alike.

As they drove through the countryside, marveling at the number of sheep marked by what looked like bright-colored paint splotches, Ofelia pointed out a variety of places on both sides of the border she hoped to show her daughters before the visit was over. She apologized but explained it was best not to delay their trip south since there were probably many people needing places to sleep near the festival, and she was determined to arrive at a particular bed and breakfast before all of its rooms were taken.

After about four hours on the road, they arrived at the picturesque town of Galway, where they took a break from driving and had lunch outdoors by a canal. While they enjoyed the beautiful autumn weather, Ofelia told them a bit about the Matchmaker's Ball they would be attending.

Teri asked, "Is this a serious event? I mean, it sounds so old-fashioned."

Ofelia laughed, "Well, it really is old-fashioned, but people come for a variety of reasons, only one of which is to meet the perfect mate. And it has a long history, but to this day, thousands of people come from miles around to join in the fun."

Marissa asked, "What is its history?"

"I believe it started back in the 19th Century. The area had long been known for its health-giving mineral springs, and members of the Irish gentry began gathering there every September after the harvest season. At some point, people saw it as an opportunity to find good matches for their children from among the gentry. It was a time when there was a shortage of women and a surplus of bachelor farmers in Ireland, but the festival evolved into an opportunity for singles to meet and enjoy Irish music and dance. In fact, until recently, part of the attraction was an internationally renowned Irish music festival that was held in a nearby town. That part was unfortunately discontinued a couple of years ago, in 1983, when it was the site of a riot during which eight people drowned. However, the matchmaking spirit seems to be alive and well these days."

Teri jumped in, "Wow, it sounds like a college mixer!"

Noticing the puzzled expressions on Ofelia and Marissa's faces, she explained. "You know, a planned event to bring new students together. But where does the matchmaking come in? How do they get older adults from miles around to participate? I mean college freshmen are there to find people to date, but they usually live on a campus where they can follow up. How does this work?"

"Musical performances and dances are currently held throughout September at hotels and other venues all over Lisdoonvarna. A third-generation matchmaker called a *basadoiri* manages the festivities. He gets people to fill out a form. The forms are placed in a famous book that has magical powers. According to tradition, if you place both of your hands on the book and think of love with your eyes closed for seven seconds, you will be married within six to nine months. Don't worry; I'm not trying to find husbands for you two! I only brought you here to get a taste of local Irish culture and have a little fun. I have participated in the festival a few times and, as you can see, did not go home with a husband."

Pushing the matchmaking thing to the back of their minds, Teri and Marissa were charmed by the farmhouse-turned-bed-and-breakfast inn Ofelia had chosen. Arriving in a small town called Oranmore, they pulled into a long driveway and were greeted by several friendly dogs and a smiling woman named Kathleen O'Connor. With a twinkle in her eyes, Kathleen told them her inn was already close to being filled with both men and women in town for the ball, but there were two available rooms if they didn't mind doubling up.

Looking at her daughters, Ofelia asked if they would mind her taking the private room, as she was tired from the ride and needed to nap. When they nodded in the affirmative, she turned to Kathleen and asked, "What time will dinner be served?"

"We serve dinner between six and eight, but you might want to reserve a table. We have a full house; you may not be able to find one for the three of you if you just walk in. On the other hand, some of our guests enjoy sitting with people they don't know since, at this time of the year, they're all going to the Matchmaker's Ball. It gives them a chance to take a look around. We also offer a cocktail hour, nothing fancy, but the bar is open at five."

While Ofelia settled into her room, Teri and Marissa decided to take a walk to get a feel for the countryside. The inn was located on a rural road with little traffic. It felt peaceful, and they both enjoyed the fresh air. When they first walked outside, it was almost shocking how quiet it was, but they were immediately joined by a couple of dogs who followed them into the field. Although the dogs seemed to be allowed to run freely, after around ten minutes, Teri and Marissa became concerned and decided to go back to the house to check with Kathleen to ensure it was alright.

Marissa stayed outside with the dogs while Teri searched for Kathleen and found her working in the kitchen. Kathleen told her she was fine with their taking the dogs along for the walk, but if Teri and Marissa preferred to walk alone, she would put them in the barn until the women were out of site. Teri replied that as long as they didn't run off, she and Marissa would enjoy their company.

Walking through the empty hallway, Teri was surprised to see the back of a man stepping into Ofelia's room. Her first reaction was to hover by the door to make sure there wasn't a problem. Hearing nothing, she went back outside, where she and Marissa continued their walk with the dogs. This was actually the first opportunity they had to speak privately.

"What a beautiful country!" Teri said. "Everyone is so welcoming. I'm looking forward to the rest of this weekend."

Marissa nodded. "I agree. I find this matchmaker's event interesting, but I hope we aren't pressured to do things that make us uncomfortable."

"I know what you mean. I have no interest in being with anyone but Jack, but I've decided to think of it as an ethnographic study. What about you?"

"I think it will be an interesting experience. I have no plans to find my true love here this weekend either."

Teri laughed. As they walked along in silence, Marissa couldn't help noticing how Teri was quietly working on respecting their boundaries. Although Marissa didn't want to hurt Teri's feelings, she was a private person who was unaccustomed to sharing those parts of her life. Secretly, she hoped to come to a place in their relationship where that could happen, but it was going to take a while to change her lifetime habit of keeping her thoughts to herself.

Teri broke the silence. "Oh, Marissa, I haven't told you—I saw something strange when I went back to the house to ask Kathleen about the dogs."

"Something strange?"

"Yes, I saw a man go into Ofelia's room."

"A man? Do you know who it was? Probably someone who works at the inn or maybe she ran into someone she met the last time she was here. Perhaps Ofelia will tell us all about it at dinner."

"Brigid, Brigid…We have to stop thinking of her as Ofelia."

Chapter 5

Teri and Marissa hadn't known what to expect but were quite surprised to hear their mother greeted by the ball's hosts as a celebrity. Apparently, she had previously been selected queen of something or other and attending the ball was a sort of reunion. Within minutes, Brigid was out on the dance floor, participating in an Irish folk dance.

It was a lively crowd with people of all ages wearing everything from ball gowns to jeans and tee shirts. When Teri and Marissa had asked Ofelia what to bring for the occasion; she told them they should dress for comfort because they may end up being there for many long hours.

Watching their mother dancing happily, Teri smiled at Marissa. "Look at her; she's the belle of the ball and seems to know many people here!"

Marissa smiled back, "Did you hear her say the man you saw go into her room wasn't anyone she knows?"

"No, I was wondering about that. I must have been getting another glass of wine when she told you. Did she say why he went to her room?"

"Just that it was a mistake; he thought it was another room. Have you seen him since then?"

"No, but I might have trouble identifying him. I only saw his back."

Teri laughed out loud. "Isn't it funny we're so willing to find meaning in everything she does?"

"Yes, I suppose it's not surprising since she spent her life keeping secrets from us and everyone else."

"I must admit, Marissa, I don't know what I expected when we reconnected with her. But I can tell you for sure, it was nothing like this. What the hell is a Matchmaker's Ball anyway?"

"I think it's what they call it, a place for people to meet and fall in love. And what better way than to dance together?"

Just then, a large man with a wild mop of ginger hair and an equally wild salt and pepper beard stood before the sisters, addressing them with a slight bow. "I hear you are the daughters of the lovely Brigid. You are so alike, yet very different."

The music stopped, and Brigid joined them. "I see you've met my friend Brian. I knew he would find a way."

Brian smiled as if he was in on the joke, but Teri and Marissa couldn't help noticing his face turn slightly pink.

Teri reached out her hand. "It's very nice to meet you, Brian. I'm Teri, and this is my sister Marissa."

"It's nice to meet you as well, Teri. Why do you speak English without a Spanish accent like your mother?"

Teri, Marissa, and Brigid all laughed at once as Brigid answered dismissively, "This would be a very long story, and we're here to dance and have fun."

Brigid was swept away by another dance partner, and Marissa and Teri were approached by someone who thought they should meet the *basadoiri,* the official matchmaker. Marissa went off with him while Brian and Teri continued their conversation.

"Thank you for coming and bringing your mother. I attend the ball every year and have looked forward to the pleasure of her company since we first met a few years ago. I understand it's not always easy for people living in Northern Ireland to make it to Lisdoonvarna."

"We had no difficulty getting through. The officials at the border did seem a bit surprised to see our passports from Argentina and the

U.S. but they were in order, so no problems. I have to ask, how long have you and Brigid known one another? Do you just see each other every September at the annual Matchmaker's Festival here?"

"We met here four years ago when I was elected *Mr.Lisdoonvarna,* and your mother was elected *Queen of the Burren.* These are the official titles for men and women who win the most eligible singles competition. But Brigid always made it clear she was not actually looking for a mate. As she announces, she comes to dance to have fun. So, to answer your question, we do not meet at other times of the year. I don't even know where she lives. It is all very mysterious. Will you dance with me?"

"It would be a pleasure Brian, but I must confess, I'm not here to find a mate either. I am in a very happy relationship in the United States."

"More's the pity. Why are the most beautiful women unavailable? But I would still enjoy the dance. Perhaps the magic of the Matchmaker's Ball will lead you to consider another option."

At the end of the dance, Brian bowed to Teri and excused himself. "I must move on if I am to win another most eligible title." He laughed and disappeared into the crowd.

As she walked to the bar to get a drink, Teri ran into Marissa, who surprised Teri with the news that she had filled out a form and expected to hear from the matchmaker shortly.

"Sounds like fun. I hope you're matched up with someone you like. I'm interested in hearing what questions are on the form. Did the matchmaker also interview you?"

"Yes, I'll tell you all about it when we're in a quieter place. Of course, I have no intention of staying in Ireland, even if I find my perfect match. Can you imagine that being possible with such a different culture? I'm just curious. But the matchmaker did tell me a little more about how this came about. He said that around one hundred fifty years ago, Ireland had a shortage of women because so many were immigrating to the New World, and the farmers had few opportunities to meet marriageable girls. The farmers needed wives to work with them if their farms were to be successful. Interestingly, as the word got out about this event in later years, many Irish-American women returned to attend these events because they were having trouble finding husbands in the New World."

Teri nodded, "I'm just fascinated that it exists. It seems so old-fashioned. I can't wait to hear what Brigid has to say. I wonder how she first got into doing this; coming here in the midst of The Troubles had to be difficult."

"I agree, Teri. It seems like Brigid met some of the same people when she was here a few years ago. And folks like Brian come year after year and have become old friends."

"So, what's the next step with the matchmaker for you?"

"Actually, I think I've already been matched with someone named Mateo."

"Really? Wow, that was quick. What's he like?"

"I haven't met him yet. Apparently, he's also from Argentina, which is probably why we were matched. Our meeting is scheduled for eleven; I should probably head up there soon."

As Marissa left the ballroom, Brigid came up to Teri. "I'm sorry I've been so busy. I hope you and Marissa are enjoying yourselves."

"Oh yes, and you seem to be the belle of the ball!"

Brigid blushed, "I'm surprised to see so many people I met the last time I was here. It has been a fun reunion for me. But where is Marissa?"

"She just went to meet her match. She's been paired with someone; they're meeting as we speak."

"Really?"

"Why are you surprised?"

"Oh, just that she was always a quiet girl. I thought of her as being shy, but of course, she's much older now."

Brigid looked over to where people were dancing and changed the subject. "Excuse me, I love this song."

Returning to the dance floor, Brigid joined a group that was loudly singing Shel Silverstein's *The Unicorn Song* in thick Irish accents. Teri was amused to hear what she knew as an American children's song in a strong Irish lilt.

Then Teri saw Marissa join the singers accompanied by a good-looking man who was obviously the person she'd been matched with. Watching them, Teri couldn't help thinking they looked great together.

At the end of the next dance, Marissa brought her partner to meet Teri. "I told you I'm here with my twin sister. Mateo, I would like you to meet Teri Addison; Teri, this is Mateo Roca."

Mateo responded, "I am doubly charmed."

Teri laughed, "You may end up feeling triply confused before the end of this weekend. Our mother is also here, and there are many people who think the three of us are similar."

"But you do not speak with a Spanish accent."

"True, I live in the United States and have lost my accent. Changing the subject, Marissa, I'm curious. I saw you join the group singing along to the *Unicorn Song*. Where did you learn the words? Was that popular in Argentina?"

"Doesn't everyone know that song? Yes, even in Argentina, it was a big hit in 1968 for a band called *the Irish Rovers*. I believe they were originally from Northern Ireland."

"I never thought about where it was from, except that it was written by Shel Silverstein, the American children's book writer who was also known for his Playboy Magazine cartoons."

"And I didn't know that!"

Mateo looked at the twins curiously, then bowed to Marissa and led her back to the dance floor. Thinking Marissa would have some explaining to do, Teri watched as they walked away from her. Mateo seemed like a pleasant man, probably a little older than Marissa, but there was something familiar she couldn't quite capture. Then it came to her; he reminded her of the man she saw enter Ofelia's room earlier in the day, but she couldn't be sure. She had only seen his back, and even that was a very quick glance.

Unlike Marissa, who had chosen to participate by being matched, Teri fell into her comfortable anthropologist's participant-observer role, which allowed her to be involved but not committed. It allowed her to meet people, dance, and socialize while simultaneously keeping her distance as she presented herself as a curious foreigner, a nosy American who was interested in learning who these people were and their reasons for participating.

Within a few hours, she'd heard the stories of many people and had even come up with a few study ideas she could use for lessons with her students at the college where she taught. One she hadn't anticipated was the relationship between what they wore and their reasons for attending the Matchmaker's events. She was fascinated to learn how few people claimed they were there to find mates, and those wearing both the most and least formal outfits unanimously told her they were only there to have a good time. Another subset of participants were folks she had come to think of as drop-ins, people who simply ran across the festivities and decided to check them out. The serious mate-seekers dressed to signal who they were in the world and were more likely to be interested in meeting someone who appreciated their style and what their clothes said about them.

After a few hours, Teri needed to find a quiet place to regroup and think about what she had learned. Although it was around two in the morning, she felt safe to leave the hotel to walk around the small town by herself. Not the only person wandering the streets, she found a small park where she collapsed on a bench and watched the sky in the moonlight. Teri was ready to go back to the bed and breakfast but didn't want to intrude on Marissa and Brigid's enjoyment and both had shown no signs of slowing down. As she sat quietly, trying to figure out what to do, Brian plopped down on the bench beside her.

"You're looking knackered, Teri. Can I offer you a ride back to your hotel?"

"Oh, thank you, Brian. I was just thinking my mother and sister are more Argentinian than me in this respect. They're accustomed to starting the day later and staying up later. I guess I've spent too much time in the United States."

Brian looked at Teri thoughtfully. "It may also have something to do with the fact that you chose not to participate fully in the evening's festivities. Whenever I've run across you, it appears that you are interviewing people. I almost expected to see you pull out a tape recorder. Your man back home must be very special."

"Was I so obvious? It's just the habit of a social scientist. But you are correct about my man back home. Jack is very special. What about you? I saw you dancing with my mother to great acclaim, I guess because of your past relationship as king and queen. But I haven't heard anything further. Have you failed to find your next queen of the festival?"

Brian laughed, "The night is still young. It's only 2:30, but my offer is still open. I can take a break from dancing and flirting to give you a ride to your hotel."

"I appreciate the offer and may take you up on it, but first, I must find Marissa and Brigid to tell them. I haven't seen either of them for a while."

"I suspect they've gone to one of the other dance venues to hear a different band. C'mon, I'll be coming back and will make sure to let them know your whereabouts."

"Thank you. I am fading. Getting too old for these types of affairs."

"I doubt that, but as I said before, this is not for people who are married; even if only in their hearts." Winking, he added, "But you never know what the little people have in store for you."

"The little people?"

"Have you not heard of the leprechauns, our wee folk with supernatural powers?"

"Ha Ha. I'll take my chances with the little people. Jack is my soulmate."

***

When Teri woke up the following morning, she tiptoed around the room to avoid waking Marissa, who had obviously stayed out very late. She was surprised to find Ofelia already up, sitting at a table in the dining room with her breakfast and a newspaper.

"I'm impressed you're up so early. What time did you get in last night?"

"Probably not long after you. I ran into Brian who told me he had just dropped you back here. But Marissa apparently wasn't ready to end the night then. Is she back in your room yet?"

"Yes, sound asleep."

Ofelia smiled, "It appears she enjoyed the company of the man the matchmaker found for her."

"Yes, what did you think of him?"

"He seems very nice. Imagine finding two people from Argentina in Linsdoonvarna. And another coincidence, I think he may be staying at this bed and breakfast as well."

"Really?"

"I'm not positive, but just as I was lying down for a nap yesterday, a man knocked at my door. I think it may have been him."

Not wanting to reveal her suspicions about Mateo, Teri acted surprised. "Really? What did he say?"

"I don't exactly remember. I was very tired, but basically, he apologized for knocking on the wrong door."

"Did he remember you when Marissa introduced you?"

"I don't think so. Why do you ask?"

Teri was oddly relieved. "No reason. Just being nosy, I guess."

The following day was spent resting and going to the beach and hot springs. In the evening, the three women once again went to the matchmaker's ball, but this time, left early enough to get a good night's sleep. Ofelia wanted to take them south to see the famous Cliffs of Moher before heading back to her house. She was going to have to work the next day at the post office.

Teri was glad to get a break from all of the socializing. As usual, she had found it interesting to hear people's stories and enjoyed the music and dancing, but couldn't help feeling it would have been much more fun if Jack had been there with her. On their way back to Ofelia's house, Teri asked Marissa if she and Mateo had made plans to stay in touch.

Marissa replied nonchalantly that she didn't know. "This weekend was fun, and it would be nice to see him again, but I'll be fine if nothing further comes of it. I have the impression Mateo's work involves a lot of travel."

"What about you, Ofelia? I saw you dancing with Brian. Did any sparks fly between you and your former match?"

Ofelia laughed out loud thinking, *if they only knew it was all business between Brian and me.* "No, I think that would have happened when we were actually brought together a few years ago. Now we're old acquaintances."

"I had a few conversations with him, and as you know, he gave me a ride back to the B and B."

"And what did you think of Brian?"

"He was nice enough and obviously interested in me because I'm your daughter, but he didn't seem like he belonged at a Matchmaker's event."

"How so?"

"I don't know. He was just different from most of the other participants I spoke with. I guess the best way to describe him was that he seemed to be playing a part like he was an actor."

"Interesting."

Chapter 6

September 16, 1986

Dear Jack,

I know I've only been away for a couple of weeks, but I find myself missing you so much. I don't think I realized until now how much I count on sharing my thoughts with you as they come tumbling through my head. It seems like every time I reflect on the past year, I find a new way to react to all of the amazing changes in my life. It's hard to believe I have gained a mother, a sister, and YOU, the love of my life!

So, what have I been doing since I arrived in Ireland? Well, I guess I'm mostly getting to know my mother and sister little by little. I'm hampered by my inability to think in Spanish, which is obviously intuitive for them. Ofelia, oh no, I need to get into the habit of calling her Brigid, which is her name here in Ireland. She is Brigid Alvarez, the child of an Irish mother and an Argentine father.

Brigid and Marissa are both much more comfortable with English than I am with Spanish, but there are times when I can't really participate in their conversations. I've come to believe my inability to move forward with conversational Spanish is a psychological block that was created by the Addisons when they took me away from Argentina at age six and somehow convinced me to abandon my early life and language. This is something I definitely need to work on.

Anyway, here I am with hopes of learning more about my mother and sister and maybe even what brought each of us to this point in our lives. Both are lovely, interesting people, and we are all working on getting along well without pushing too hard. One day at a time, but as you know, patience is not my best virtue!

We just got back from Lisdoonvarna in the Republic of Ireland, where we attended a "matchmaker's" event. And no, I'm not looking for another mate, but it was a truly unique experience. I kinda sorta did a fun little study of people I met there. I'll tell you more about that when I see you. I also learned a few things I didn't know before about Ofelia and Marissa and am once again reinforced with the knowledge that becoming a "family" with them may be a long and winding road, but I still believe, worth the effort.

Ireland is a really beautiful country, on both sides of the border. Although it remains in the midst of The Troubles, news of which dominates the newspapers and television, I have yet to personally experience anything beyond the inconvenience of crossing borders. I've met a lot of friendly people and even learned to be at least slightly comfortable driving on the wrong side of the road in the wrong side of the car! In addition to seeing the sights along the West Coast, we stopped at a few historically interesting places along the way. On this Northern Ireland side, a highlight was visiting WB Yeat's gravestone in the wonderfully named town of Sligo. I just love that name for some reason. Did you know he penned his own epitaph?

Cast a cold Eye

On Life, on Death

Horseman, pass by

I took a photo, it actually gave me the shivers!

I hope all is well in Mariel and Gordon and the cats are behaving for you. Good luck with writing up your data from Marissa's spiritual group study. I look forward to reading it when I get back, if you want my thoughts. I suspect Marissa will be interested in seeing what you came up with as well. I know you did an awesome field research job, but it's always the writing that gets you a permanent position with places like the Nevarez Foundation.

All my love,
Teri

P.S. This question comes out of the blue, but do you know whether Marissa is in a special relationship in Argentina? I know it's none of my business, but she doesn't talk about her personal life. She met and was matched up with a guy here but says she doesn't care if she sees him again. As I said, none of my business, but I can't help being curious.

Chapter 7

Ofelia frowned as she folded the newspaper, set it on top of the coffee table, and said, "These people are idiots! Why have we learned nothing?"

Teri looked at the headline announcing the latest killings. She agreed with her mother that violence had its place in getting people's attention, and sometimes civil disobedience was the only way available to right institutional and culturally accepted wrongs. Yet, to her as an outsider, it seemed like Ireland had become so volatile; even those who agreed on the hoped-for outcomes of equal rights and unification were willing to harm each other over the details.

Ofelia continued her rant. "When I first came here in 1978, it was hard for me to distinguish between Northern and Republic of Ireland folks. Yes, they disagreed about a lot of things, but they seemed alike in the way they walked and talked. I know there's still a lot of tension and anger between the Protestant Unionists and Catholic Republicans. They have a wretched history and have treated each other horribly. No one wants to feel uncomfortable and unable to trust their neighbors." Putting her head in her hands, Ofelia added, "I guess I was just an optimist. I know this is not simply about who wins the argument."

Teri looked at Ofelia, then smiled, thinking she might have found an opening to get the understandably cautious Ofelia to tell her more about herself. "I've often wondered where your optimism, or is it idealism, comes from. It seems like you've never lived in peaceful times. I mean, Argentina was a mess the whole time you lived there, one terrible oppressive government after the other."

"Yes, but my family life was so dysfunctional. I think I spent my childhood searching for community. When I think about it now, it wasn't surprising that I was drawn to people who provided me with a feeling of belonging and a sense of purpose. Back then, in the 1930s and 40s, Communism, Socialism, whatever you want to call it, was the idealist's dream. We believed it was a philosophy that could translate into a system of government that would lift all boats and give everyone a chance to live a healthy, prosperous life. Of course, horrible leaders like Stalin and Mao Tse-Tung turned it into an evil system of governmental oppression, giving it a bad name that stokes fear in people's hearts to this day, but in the beginning, they gave us hope." Ofelia's voice drifted off. She closed her eyes and leaned her head against the back of the sofa.

Teri sat down next to her mother and gently took her hand. She was overcome with feelings of respect for this woman who had fearlessly dedicated her life to making the world a better place. Despite regret at losing precious years, Teri was in awe of her mother's passion and willingness to face danger. Their reunion had been emotional, and while they and Marissa were dedicated to establishing themselves as a family, questions remained unanswered. Ofelia's life story had never been presented in a linear fashion. Teri wanted to make sure she got it straight. Her mother had not only lived through, but been an active participant in an important part of the world's history between 1945 and the present day.

Although she had lived a very different life from Ofelia, Teri shared her optimistic nature and had always hoped the hard lessons of the past could be mined to convince people it was possible to make things better for everyone. To this end, she pursued an academic career in the field of Anthropology and joined a community of thinkers who maintained that positive change could be achieved through knowledge, understanding, rational thought, and cross-cultural communication.

While her own childhood had been complicated by decisions made by Ofelia and the Addisons, she had never actually suffered or been in fear for her life.

Teri said, "I'm interested in learning about what the world was like back then. I want to understand what was going on. I know I can read about it in the history books, but you lived it. I want to hear your story."

Ofelia looked closely at Teri, a tear forming in the corner of her eye. "It's been difficult for me to explain my past actions and decisions to you and Marissa. I have felt a great deal of guilt and sadness for giving you up, giving you away when you were born. I've also feared the danger will come back and cause harm to you and your sister."

Teri stopped her, "Yes, but you, too, have been hurt. We can't deny our feelings but at the same time… I can't speak for Marissa, but for me, knowledge is power. I think it always helps me to learn." Teri faced her mother with a determined smile, "So let me ask you a straightforward question. You talk about how your idealism attracted you to Communism, the idea that Communism was a system of government that would make everyone equal socially and economically and would result in world peace. Yet, you seem to have started out as a big fan of Juan Perón, Argentina's notorious fascist dictator."

"We all had big hopes for Perón. He was the first leader who spoke about the rights of workers, people who had been subjugated and whose basic needs had been ignored forever. He promised to give us a voice. And for me, it was especially important that he had a connection with our indigenous Mapuche community. It was rumored that his mother was Mapuche, and he would do right by her people. As you know, my own grandmother was Mapuche. She spent her entire life in what you would call a reservation. My grandmother, mi abuela, lived in squalor her entire life and was murdered by government troops because she was a powerful member of her community. Abuela was the spiritual leader, the *Machi*. They killed her because she was respected, and they feared she would incite people to reject their control."

"Did that happen before or after Perón was in power?"

"Oh no, this was maybe five years before Perón became el presidente. I was only ten years old, but I remember it as if it was yesterday. The death of my grandmother and the violence of it—the government troops burned her house down. To this day, we don't know if she was already dead or alive at the time. It affected everything in our family."

"I thought she lived far away from you in the southern Pampas."

"She did. I didn't get to see her often, but I remember her overwhelming strength, love, and wisdom. My mother did not have her strength and was never the same. She fell apart, became an alcoholic, and stopped being a mother to me and my brother Tomás. After that, she only cared for her alcohol."

Teri hadn't heard Ofelia speak about this part of her life and wanted her to continue, but knew she had to tread carefully. This was the first time Ofelia had even mentioned the name of her estranged brother. "And your father? Did he help?"

Ofelia's eyes flashed with anger. "My father...I'm not even sure which one he was. There were some men who claimed that title, but no one stayed around long enough. No, my mother was alone except for her brother Ernesto. Thank God for him and his family. They were my family: Tío Ernesto, Tía Cecilia, and my cousins Sylvita and Che. I knew they were the only people I could count on, but I must admit, I always wanted my own mother to be there for me. I spent a lot of time taking care of her and doing what I could to make her happy. I remember being hopeful when Perón became president. I couldn't wait to tell my mother. We had heard he was sympathetic to Mapuche well-being. Perhaps he would avenge my abuela's cruel fate."

Teri watched as her mother closed her eyes. Hoping to continue their conversation later, she placed a pillow under Ofelia's head and left the room.

Unbeknownst to Teri, Ofelia had closed her eyes to avoid the conversation she knew they would eventually have to have. Although her brain was somewhere in a hazy place between awareness and sleep, Ofelia could feel the need her daughters had for the truth, for the answers to their questions. As she drifted off, her mind traveled back to 1945 when she was 15 years old and filled with dreams of a better life.

"Mamá, Mamá. Have you heard? Perón has been released from prison. He has been elected el presidente. Everything is going to be alright. He cares about us, and he has married Evita, who cares even more because she comes from our workers' background. Everything is going to be great!"

Ofelia's mother, Sofia, sprawled out on the bed, looked up, rubbed her eyes and said sleepily, "I'm happy to hear this, Ofelita. Do me a favor, bring me my bottle of whiskey. This calls for a celebration."

"Can we invite Che and Sylvita for dinner instead? Tio Ernesto and Tia Cecilia too?

"Oh, not today, mi hija. I have a terrible headache. Perhaps another day when I feel up to making food."

Sofia laid her head back on the pillow, then lifting it slightly, moaned and said, "Please, my bottle of whiskey. It will help me sleep. I'm sure you can fix yourself and your brother, some rice and beans for supper. There's my good girl."

Mamá, please, wake up, wake up. I don't know where Tomás is. He hasn't been home for weeks. Please, Mamá, don't leave me alone. I'm scared to be alone."

Ofelia woke up shaking. The dream was too real, and she had apparently called for help.

Chapter 8

Hearing Ofelia cry out, Marissa ran into the living room to find her writhing in her sleep on the sofa. She was obviously having a bad dream.

Marissa reached out and gently stroked Ofelia's arm until she opened her eyes and blinked several times.

"A difficult dream?"

Ofelia rubbed her eyes with the back of her hand. "Yes, I was back in my hometown."

"I thought I heard you cry out for Tomás."

Ofelia said, "I think I was looking for him in my dream."

Teri, who had been in the kitchen, came into the room. "Are you alright?"

Having a moment of good feeling; of being cared for by her daughters, Ofelia smiled. "Yes, it was just a dream. It was not just a dream but a memory from my childhood. In my dream, I couldn't find my brother."

"What happened?"

Ofelia looked at Marissa. "Did you know my mother Sofía?

"No, but I heard stories about her."

"What stories?"

"I was young, but what I mostly remember was that she was very beautiful but sick."

"I guess that's a kind way to describe her. My mother was beautiful, and I guess her alcoholism was a sickness. In my dream, I was trying to wake her up to celebrate Perón becoming president, but by that time, it was too late. Her life had been plagued by one disappointment after the other. Alcohol was her only comfort."

"How sad for you. How old were you when she began drinking?"

"I don't remember a time when she didn't drink, but the worst part began when her mother, mi abuela, was murdered. Our home was never the same."

"What about your brother?"

"Tomás was a restless soul and was rarely around by the time I was a young teenager." Tears formed in Ofelia's eyes. "I desperately wanted my family, mother, and brother, but I was alone. I was saved many times by my uncle and aunt and cousins, the part of my family who raised you."

"They are good people. You and I were lucky to have them," Marissa said.

"I agree, we still are. I would not be alive or here today were it not for the help of my cousin Che."

"I've often wondered, does he know where you are now? Have you two been in touch?"

"We have not been in touch, but he may know. In our business, it's important to keep secrets, and although it seems I've been safe these past few years here, one can never be too careful." Ofelia paused as if she had a new thought, "Marissa, have you told them about this visit?"

"Yes, my traveling to Ireland would have been difficult to explain otherwise since Teri found me and you, but I'm certain everyone in our family understands the need to continue to be discreet."

Teri interceded. "I hate to think you're in danger because of my actions. I've always assumed Al Watson put us in contact with you because he felt it was now safe to do so. Did he tell you why he gave us your phone number? Why he thought it was safe enough? Is Al in contact with Che, do you think?"

Ofelia's face shut down. "So many questions, Teresa. You must know there are some things I'm not at liberty to speak about. I won't speak about Al Watson or any of my communications with him, but I will tell you I trust him to protect us from harm."

"Can you tell us more about your mother, our grandmother? I know she disappeared one day, but what was going on then?"

"You have the right to know, but it has been a long time. Some of these memories are painful."

Looking at Teri and Marissa, Ofelia knew she could no longer avoid this conversation. It was time for her to tell them the truth. They had come all the way to Ireland to become her family. If that was going to happen, she needed to be honest with them. Both of her daughters were intelligent women who would see through falseness.

"The dream, the moment I described to you, was real. I was fifteen years old and dealing with a mother who was passed out drunk most of the time. My older brother stayed away from our house, and I was often left alone with her. Then, one day, my mother cleaned herself up and even put on lipstick. It was bright red, I'll never forget. She went out to meet a man. She brought the man home. I think she thought he liked her, but all he did was ogle at me. It was horrible; he kept blocking me from moving and putting his hands on my body. By the end of the evening, my mother was once again thoroughly drunk, and the man was telling her he wanted to marry me. From that day forward, she told me he was very rich, and that I should marry him to save our family. She told me no other man would want to marry me because we were so poor and because I was part indigenous, part Mapuche."

Teri interrupted. "Have I told you that Jack is Native American? He's a member of the Chippewa tribe."

Ofelia looked at Teri. "I didn't know that, Teresa. I didn't mean to be offensive, but you must understand this was a different time.

While we're still experiencing racial prejudice in both North and South America, it's now socially acceptable to be proud of our Mapuche heritage. Back then, it was more complicated." She took a deep breath and went back to her story. "I cannot describe to you how repulsive that man was to me. He was old and ugly, so whenever I had a hint that he would be coming over, I hid or went to my uncle and aunt's house. But my mother persisted. She told me she was going to die if I didn't marry him. That was when I decided it was time for me to leave. So, I went in search of my brother Tomás."

"How did you know where to look for him?"

"I didn't. I began my search by asking my cousin Che if he knew anything about Tomás's activities or whereabouts. He didn't know where he was but had heard Tomás had become part of a gang dedicated to protecting our new president, Juan Perón. I didn't know what that meant then, but Tomás was a big fan of Perón. I figured all I needed to do was find people who were working for El Presidente. I was very innocent. Che knew that, and tried to dissuade me from running off. At the same time, Che knew I had to leave my mother's house, so he made me promise to keep him informed of where I was going and what I was doing. By the way, Che was also a supporter of Perón then. It took us both time and experience to learn he was a fascist and a phony."

"Che took me to a local political meeting, probably to discourage me from pursuing Tomás any further. No girls were there, and from the beginning, the men were rowdy. Some yelled at me to go home to my mother, and others made lewd remarks about my body. Che took me outside and asked if this was what I wanted to do. He was being very brave himself."

"That had to be frightening. What did you do?"

"I can't tell you where I got my courage, but I decided to learn what they were meeting about and take my next steps from there. I guess I was feeling desperate. Che tried to discourage me, but I went outside and listened through an open window."

"What did you learn?"

"Remember, I had no life experience to assess, or even understand, what they were talking about; but the gist of it was that they saw Perón's presidency as an opportunity to have a say in government, to move forward what we would now call a progressive agenda to bring Argentines out of poverty. That certainly appealed to me, so I decided to continue to attend these meetings, even if it meant standing outside and listening through the window."

"Did you find Tomás?"

"No, I just kept going to the meetings and mostly ignoring what the men said to me and about me. I stayed outside at first, then I stepped inside and stood near the door. I think they started thinking of me as a joke, but as I persisted, some of them wondered what I was doing there. For the most part, men in our town thought of young girls as silly, frivolous beings who only cared about clothes and boys. They couldn't figure out why I would keep coming back to a place where people were talking about politics. I guess they just got used to my being there, and I was even asked where I had been once when I missed a meeting." Ofelia smiled at the memory, "It made me feel like I was part of the group. But the big breakthrough took place after a month or two when there was a heated discussion going on, and one of the men said, 'Let's ask Ofelia her opinion.' I had never spoken up before and was shocked to be asked."

"What was it about?"

"I can't remember exactly, but I'm pretty sure it had to do with how a woman would react to something they were planning to do. And

I guess I gave them a good answer because some of the men started including me in their discussions." Ofelia paused and said thoughtfully, "That was when I met Paolo, a meeting that changed my life."

"Paolo?"

"Yes…Paolo was an older man. Of course, everyone there was older than me, but he was probably in his late twenties. He was very handsome and cultured and obviously well-respected by others who attended these meetings, but believe it or not, he was actually interested in my opinion. I had never had that kind of attention from anyone, and I fell deeply in love, as only a fifteen-year-old girl can."

"You were living with your mother? Was she still trying to force you to marry the repulsive suitor?"

"Oh yes, and it was becoming increasingly difficult to be at home at all. I had not found Tomás, still had no idea where he was, and knew if my mother and her disgusting man knew where I was spending time, they would have found a way to lock me up or immediately marry me off, a fate I would've found even more impossible. I began to hope Paolo would take me away from all of that, so when he proposed that I become his mistress, I said yes, even though I was a virgin and knew nothing about such things."

"You became his mistress?"

"Not at first."

"Why not?"

"Well, meanwhile, Che was worrying about me getting involved with Paolo and, to be perfectly honest, the volatile politics of that time. He knew the only thing I cared about more than Paolo was finding Tomás and getting away from my mother. So, he did some exploring and discovered another group of Perón supporters down the Rio de la Plata in Olivos, just outside of Buenos Aires. Olivos was also the location of the presidential palace where Perón and Evita lived. I had never been away from the small town where I grew up, and it seemed like the other side of the world to me, but Che convinced me Tomás was no longer nearby and that we should take a trip down there. I can't tell you how excited I was for the adventure.

"How did you get there?"

"Believe it or not, we took a train. Another first for me."

"This is starting to feel like an adventure novel! Did you find Tomás there?"

"I didn't find him, but I eventually learned what he was doing. Actually, the first thing I learned was that, unlike the group I started with, this group included some women who lived in houses I could only dream of. It was so different from our little town of Punta Lapiz."

Looking at Marissa, Ofelia said, "Punta Lapiz has become a comfortable place to live over the years, but back then, the only people who lived there were impoverished farmworkers. Before Olivos, I had never used a flush toilet in my life. All of the houses in Olivos had indoor plumbing. My involvement with the new group allowed me to experience what I saw as luxurious living."

"In retrospect, I came to realize I was involved with some powerful people; but at the time, I had no way of judging. Anyway, I didn't have to go through all of the steps to be allowed to attend the meetings because I was immediately welcomed by the women. In due time, I began to share my thoughts, and people actually listened!"

"That must have been an amazing experience for you."

"Yes, I was seen as a representative of the rural youth, a constituency the Peronistas wanted to claim. And they liked me because of my big mouth. I had no fear and spoke my mind about what was wrong and how we needed to improve living conditions."

Ofelia smiled at a memory, "That was when they began calling me Anahí."

Marissa reacted, "I never knew that. They must have had a very high opinion of you."

Teri interrupted, "Who, what's an Anahí?"

"Do you remember the tree in Juan Ignacio's backyard with the bright red blossoms?"

"Of course, that was where we buried our treasure box. What does that have to do with your nickname?"

"Of course, you were very young to learn this when you lived in Buenos Aires, but that tree, the *Ceibo,* produces the national flower of Argentina, which is also called *Kapok.* There's a legend that says it was created when a young Guarani Indian girl named Anahí was burned as a witch while defending her people. The trunk of the *Ceibo,* with its flaming red flowers, grew from her burned body and came to symbolize courage and strength in suffering."

"You must have been proud to be associated with a national heroine, but what a sad story. Wait, did you choose to bury our treasure box near the roots of that particular tree for a reason?"

"To tell you the truth, I didn't think of its significance at the time. It was simply the closest tree. But I have to say, I'm enjoying thinking about how some important pieces are coming together. Without the treasure box, it's unlikely we would be here together today."

Marissa said, "The Ceibo also has medicinal properties our group has been exploring."

"Like what?"

"Among other things, its bark is used to treat rheumatism wounds and as a diuretic antispasmodic; its resin can cure intestinal diseases, and its leaves contain camphor properties that help to heal wounds as well as anti-inflammatory properties for tumors."

Teri smiled, "Wow, this is an all-around powerful tree! I love when science and folklore come together like this. So, getting back to your story, Ofelia, it sounds like you were finding a home with the Olivos group."

"Yes, and this new group was different, not only because they were interested in finding ways to make things better for the working people, but they were also watching Perón and Evita to see what they were doing. So, a lot of the time, there was debate, and some people were less than happy with how things were going."

"And you, personally? What was going on? Did you continue to try to find Tomás? How long were you away from home in Olivos? How did you live when you were there?"

"I basically never went back to my mother's house, and I gave up my search for Tomás. I heard about him now and then but never saw him again." Ofelia paused and looked at the floor. "Actually, that's not entirely true. I did see him once when he was doing his thing, harassing people who were trying to get Perón's attention. I think he looked at me and then turned away. We were definitely not on the same team by that time, and the more I learned about what he was doing, the less I was interested in having any part in it. As I mentioned before, he was part of a group of thugs who had volunteered to be bodyguards for Perón."

"Thugs?"

"Yes. They were violent, and the Olivos group was becoming less and less enamored of Perón, a position I came to share. The longer I was with them, the more I lost interest in finding my brother. I stopped missing my home and family because the women in the group took care of me and always treated me kindly. I still don't know exactly why, but they took me into their homes, where I ate and slept. I guess I was a novelty, a fifteen-year-old girl from the country who had things to say, and I also suspect they felt sorry for me when they heard what I told them about my mother and what waited for me if I went back."

"What about Che?"

"Che did go back and forth. His parents understood what was at stake and trusted him to watch out for me. I was fortunate then, and throughout my life, to have Che."

"And then?"

"Well, before I go further, I must tell you I had begun to be a spy for this group. They saw me as being fearless, which was probably true because I was totally naive. But I also trusted them to cover my back, so I was sent around to listen in on what others were saying. Fifteen-year-old girls were never suspected of having the brains to understand serious words. For me, it became great fun."

"What kinds of places did you go where you could spy like that?"

"I answered advertisements for helpers at homes and stores and childcare. These little jobs also provided me with a living, such as it was. I made a little money, listened to what people were saying, and reported back to the group whose members had sent me to those specific places. In the end, it gave me a resume' and skills to be a live-in maid, such as I was for the Addisons."

Teri took a breath. "I thought you did that as part of your undercover work; that the Addisons took me in because they wanted you."

Ofelia smiled at Teri. "Living with you, watching you grow up, was definitely part of the deal. It was the best part as far as I was concerned, and by that time, I had a lot of choices. I was pretty good at what I was doing. I was a good actress."

Then her smile took in both Marissa and Teri. "I hope I'm answering your questions and promise to continue later, but I'm getting hungry. Would you mind if we take a little time to prepare and eat dinner?"

"Of course not. Why don't you take it easy? We can make dinner. What would you like?"

"Something simple, soup, and maybe a green salad."

"Coming up!"

Chapter 9

Sipping from a gourd of after-dinner yerba mate with a contented expression, Ofelia said, "Thank you for giving me a break. I'm refreshed now and ready to continue with my story. I believe I had recently moved to Olivos and was running spying errands for the group?"

Marissa interrupted, "I want to hear about Paolo. Is it possible you are speaking of Paolo Fuentes?"

Ofelia looked at Marissa closely and took another sip. "Yes, Paolo Fuentes. Do you know him?"

"Not personally, but everyone knows about him. He's very rich and powerful. I always thought he was a wealthy landowner who avoided politics."

Teri was fascinated, "You were the mistress of such a man when you were fifteen years old? But wait, I thought you met him at the meeting near your home town. Did you see him after that?"

"As it turned out, he also attended the Olivos meetings sometimes. In the beginning, I occasionally saw him there, but he didn't acknowledge me. I was heartbroken and realized he'd been toying with me when he asked me to be his mistress. And I eventually knew why. The women I stayed with spoke of him with admiration, but it was known that he was married and had children. He was not viewed as a man who cheated on his wife or had mistresses. In any case, I was quite busy and didn't see him often, although I never stopped fantasizing."

"What changed?"

"Everything changed by the end of the first year. I had become known and, I believe, trusted; and the group was becoming increasingly disillusioned with Perón and Evita and his policies."

"Why? How had they changed?"

"I'm not sure Perón and Evita had changed at all, but who they were and what they were doing was being revealed. They came into power promising to be like Robin Hood, taking from the rich and giving to the poor, but it soon became evident that they also stole from the poor. By the end of that year, the Olivos group, as we have been calling them, began to work towards exposing the Peróns and replacing them with good government."

"Where did Paolo Fuentes fit into this? Wasn't he originally aligned with the pro-Perón group?"

"I learned later he was never a fan of Perón, but his prominence enabled him to attend all these meetings, almost as an observer. He didn't want to be known as an advocate for any particular government. He wanted to foster change from the background, which required collecting information without being noticed."

"And that's where you came in?"

Ofelia smiled again, "Yes, that's where I came in. It was my sixteenth birthday and Che, who remained my lifeline to my aunt and uncle, came to see me. My mother was out of the picture at this point. I never saw her again. This makes me sad now, but at the time, all I knew was I wanted to be where I was, with adults who cared about me. Anyway, Che was in and out of all of the under-the-surface political activity, so I saw him in Olivos sometimes, and he kept me and his parents up to date. On my sixteenth birthday, he came to Olivos and brought me a small gift. I think it was a box of chocolates. Some of the people in the meeting saw this and made a little fuss over me turning sixteen. One of those people was Paolo. It was the first time he paid any attention to me in Olivos.

That was the beginning of our closer relationship. I was still madly in love with him, but of course, no one could know."

"Your affair started when you were sixteen?"

"Yes. I know, in retrospect, it was foolish of me, but I was so young, and he was a very attractive and powerful man. I guess he took advantage of my innocence in a way, but he was always kind and never lied to me. He was married with children and he himself was taking a risk by being with me. He always said he felt bad that this was all we would ever have together, these stolen moments. In a way, it was very romantic."

Ofelia gazed out the window for a moment, seemingly lost in a past memory. Then she looked back at her daughters and said, "He used to sing the song *Ojos Verdes* to me."

Teri said, "I don't know that song, but it's sweet that he sang about your green eyes."

Marissa laughed, "Oh, this is much more than sweet, Teri. *Ojos Verdes* is one of our most romantic songs. I believe it was made popular by the famous flamenco singer Miguel de Molina way back in the 1920s. I can understand how this must have charmed you, Ofelia."

"It sounds like he really cared about you, but did anyone else know about your relationship?"

"Che may have known, but we never spoke about it. At the time, I believed no one else knew."

"How long did your relationship last?"

"Well, it was very off and on, but altogether, about two years as lovers."

"How did it end?"

Ofelia became quiet for what seemed like a long time. She didn't look distressed; but was clearly trying to decide how to move forward with her story.

Teri and Marissa were thinking her story was coming close to when they came on the scene, so it didn't surprise them to hear Ofelia choose her words carefully. While they had previously learned from clues Ofelia had shared with Susan Addison that a man named Miguel Martínez was their biological father, neither of them had ever spoken of it with Ofelia, and neither had even directly asked her his name or anything else about him. This was a big moment.

Ofelia cleared her throat, took a sip of her mate, and resumed talking. "My relationship with Paolo didn't exactly end or even start. We met very sporadically, and to be perfectly honest, my life continued as it had been for the most part. I continued being sent out to spy. And as I mentioned before, the group was becoming more and more dedicated to finding ways to get rid of Perón. In retrospect, I believe the "affair" was very one-sided. I was the only one who was in love. I'm sure he knew it and that I would do just about anything to please him, to get him to pay attention to me."

Teri and Marissa listened carefully as Ofelia paused to take another sip of her drink. "He told me our work was becoming serious and that, through his business connections, he had been in contact with people from other countries who would help overthrow Perón's government. He told me because I had such good acting skills, I could play an important role in that effort."

"What did he ask you to do?"

"Basically, Paolo, along with some of the other people in the group, came to me and said they had a special assignment. They had a way of getting me a job providing childcare for an important member of Perón's inner circle, a man named Miguel Martínez, who did financial work for the government. I was honored to be trusted with such an important assignment, and I happily said yes. What I didn't know at the time was that they wanted me to seduce this man so he would share government secrets with me."

"Why did they think he would do that? You were so young!"

"He was seen as a weak-willed man who was in an unhappy marriage with a woman who bullied him. I guess they figured he would be easy to seduce. They saw him as a perfect source of information because he and Perón had been friends for a long time, even before Perón became powerful. Perón trusted him, so he had him spying on other people in his administration he didn't trust so much."

"You were brought in to spy on someone who was spying on someone else?"

"Basically, yes, but I was also being asked to obtain information from an insider. Again, I was honored to be chosen for this task. They were telling me they thought I was smart enough and a good enough actress to be in the room without threatening anyone. And, as you probably know, Perón himself was known to be enamored of young girls—even younger than me—so he would not disapprove or suspect what I was really there for."

Although she had already been told the story of Ofelia's affair with Miguel Martínez, Teri found it shocking to hear the details from her mother's lips. These adults, including a prominent member of Argentine society, were willing to use an innocent child that way, putting her in danger as well as robbing her of any possibility of a normal future. And this was about how she and Marissa came into the world! Teri began feeling overwhelmed by her mother's words. At the same time, she had many questions she hoped Ofelia would answer. She didn't want to overreact or cause Ofelia to stop talking. In an attempt to stay calm, Teri stood up and walked towards the kitchen.

"I need to get a glass of water. Anyone else want something?"

Teri caught Marissa's eye and felt like she was looking into her own soul. Marissa was clearly struggling with the same need to absorb what she was hearing and stay calm. Marissa remained seated and responded, "Thank you, I would also like a glass of water. What about you, Ofelia?"

Ofelia said no; she was still sipping from her mate' gourd.

When Teri walked back into the living room, she was ready to hear more.

"I know those were difficult times, Ofelia, but I must admit it surprises me that you were the one who was chosen to spy on Perón." Teri said.

"Oh, I wasn't the only one in the group who was infiltrating that world. That was basically what we were all trying to do. This is just my particular story."

"How were you introduced to Señor Martínez? How did you get the childcare job?"

"Paolo set it up. He knew the family, and, of course, they had no idea he was working against Perón. I don't know the details, but I think Paolo and his wife were socializing with Miguel and his wife when the subject of childcare help came up. It was known that Miguel's wife had little interest in her children, so Paolo suggested they might want to hire a nanny or some such person. He knew of a young woman who had experience and was looking for a job. I can't tell you exactly how long it was before I was hired, but I know it wasn't long after my sixteenth birthday."

"Did you move into their house then?"

"No. My back story was that I was an orphan living with some distant relatives Paolo knew through business. I occasionally spent the night at Miguel's house when they went away or were out for a long evening, but I usually went back to the homes of my women friends, who, in reality, had become the closest thing I had to relatives at the time."

"What about Che?"

"Che remained my real family, but I did not go back there, even to visit. I was afraid of my mother and what she would do to me."

"Did Che know what you were doing?"

"He knew I was deeply involved with this anti-Perón group and that I was working undercover. He worried about my safety because I was so fearless. He was worried I would get caught because I was willing to try anything. But he never knew exactly what I was doing. He was not an insider and remained on the periphery of the group's activities. He didn't learn what I was up to until I became pregnant."

Ofelia stopped and looked at her daughters. "When I became pregnant with you."

Although she already knew, Teri asked, "How old were you when we were born?"

"I had just turned eighteen."

"You were working for Miguel Martínez then? Is he our father?"

"I think so, but I was also still involved with Paolo on occasion."

Marissa, who had been quietly taking Ofelia's story in, reacted visibly. "Paolo Fuentes could be our father?"

For the first time, tears filled Ofelia's eyes. "Yes. I am so sorry to tell you this way. I was involved with both men. I was still in love with Paolo, but I have to say, Miguel was a kind man. I was in love with both of them as only a young girl can love. You could be proud to have either of them as your father."

"Did either of them know you were pregnant?"

"I don't think so. Early in the pregnancy, I became very sick. I could no longer take care of Miguel's children, so I left the position saying I hoped to return when I became well again. The women from the group I was living with went along with my illness story and the pregnancy did not become known among my colleagues. As usual, Che came to the rescue."

"What did he do?"

"He took me back to his home, to my Tía Cecilia and Tío Ernesto. They took care of me throughout the pregnancy."

"What about your mother? Wasn't she nearby?"

"I never saw her. I really don't know where she was or what she was doing. It was a difficult pregnancy, carrying twins."

This story was becoming surreal to Teri. Ofelia was describing the beginning of her life. She couldn't help asking, "When did you learn you were having twins?"

"I didn't learn there were two of you until you came out of my body. I had been cared for by a local midwife throughout the pregnancy who was sworn to secrecy. She was a family friend who could be trusted to protect my secret, but she was not a sophisticated medical professional. I think she was as surprised as everyone else that there were two of you."

"But you must have been huge carrying two babies!"

Ofelia laughed, "I felt like I was carrying an elephant, but no one thought it unusual. It was such a relief to have you out of my body, but having two really complicated things. You have to understand it was shameful to have a child out of wedlock. As much as everyone adored both of you the minute you were born, your existence had the potential to ruin my life and reputation. I was only eighteen years old, and single, with no ability to raise a child. This may sound selfish, but I loved the work I had been doing and longed to go back to my life. It felt important."

"But, even with one child, you would have been constrained."

"Again, I apologize for my past decisions. We did have a plan for one child. My cousin Sylvita, who was already married, would raise her as her own, so I would still be part of my baby's family and get to see her grow up. We had come up with that plan early on. Sylvita had also been laying low throughout the latter part of my pregnancy so when the baby was born, she could claim it as her own."

Looking at her daughters, Ofelia's voice became louder.

"You need to know, I did not choose one of you over the other at any time, nor did Sylvita. You were identical in so many ways. I wasn't with you very long after you were born."

"So, how did I end up with the Addisons?"

"Believe it or not, it was through Paolo."

"Huh?"

"I went to one of the women who had been protecting me. She suggested I ask Paolo for a way to find a good home for the baby, preferably where I could be part of her life."

"Did Paolo know you were pregnant? Did he suspect the baby was his?"

"I don't know how to answer that question except to say we never spoke about it. We never spoke about the changes in my life, why I wasn't seeing him, anything. When I went to Paolo, it was as if I was anyone in the group who needed this help. We all saw him as someone who could fix things and would be discreet. You must understand; I was desperate. All I could think was if my mother found out, she would force me to marry that horrible man, and he might even reject me or do terrible things to my babies. I guess when I think about it now, I was totally irrational, but in those days, women had few rights, and I was still a child who wanted a life. So, I decided to trust Paolo and the other people in the group to help. I had to. Next thing I knew, I was meeting the Addisons, who kindly accepted me and you, Teresa, into their home. They had just moved to Buenos Aires with a large family, and you were to be their new baby."

Teri closed her eyes, holding back tears she knew wouldn't stop if she let them start.

Ofelia looked at her and kept talking, "I was so happy to be with you those early years. Susan Addison also loved you but allowed me to be as much of a mother as I could. You must remember that she and I were both engaged in undercover work, as was her husband, as well as raising her family."

Then she turned to Marissa and said, "I will always regret not claiming you, both of you, as my own, but I truly believed I provided you with families that would take good care of you. And I was there to watch you grow up, and in your case, Marissa, know you as a relative."

Looking back at Teri, she said, "I never thought I would lose you at such a young age. I didn't anticipate the political changes and national instability that continue to this day in Argentina."

Teri and Marissa watched as Ofelia broke down and began to sob uncontrollably. Overwhelmed, neither Teri nor Marissa was able to say or do anything.

Wiping her tears, Ofelia said, "I need to stop now." She stood up and went to her bedroom.

Chapter 10

Teri finally fell asleep and didn't wake up until past ten. She found Marissa and Ofelia in the kitchen speaking in rapid Spanish. They were speaking too fast for her to understand, and Teri was once again distressed by her inability to communicate in what she believed to be her native language. Undecided, she stood outside of the door until there was a pause, then entered with a forced smile on her face.

"Buenos días."

Marissa walked over and kissed her on the cheek. Then she said, in English, "We're making coffee. Are you interested?"

"Yes, please."

As they sat around the kitchen table, Ofelia smiled at Teri, "We were just talking about how we should spend our last few days together. Unfortunately, today is the only one when I have some free time. Perhaps you would like to drive up to the northern coast? It's very pretty there, and we can visit the Giant's Causeway."

"I've heard of that, what is it exactly?"

"Well, there are two versions, the scientific geological evidence and the traditional mythological history. It's a popular tourist place where you can learn all about both and choose your reality about it."

Thinking this was a perfect metaphor for her life with these people, Teri said, "I would love to go there."

The Giant's Causeway was a lot of fun. A fascinating site along the northern coast of Ireland, it was composed of 40,000 interlocking basalt columns, which had been created by intense volcanic and other geological activity. When they began their walk, Teri and Marissa each chose a different audio guide to listen to along the way. Teri heard the story from the point of view of folklore giant Finn McCool, while Marissa learned its geological history and science. The rock formations lent credence to both points of view as Ofelia and the twins spent the day exploring walkway trails, climbing rocks, and watching the ocean movement as it crashed against the rocks; while at the same time learning the site's traditional Irish folklore explanations for some of the more dramatic geological formations that resembled a Giant's boot, a Wishing Chair, a Camel, Giant's Granny, and an Organ. By the time they returned to the house late in the afternoon, all three women were ready to retreat to their rooms to rest.

Teri fell back into worrying she would be leaving in a few days with too many unanswered questions. Not ready to sleep, she decided to look back at her goals for the visit. Figuring it wouldn't hurt to take a look at her original thoughts, she pulled out her small notebook and began to read. Then she wrote a second letter to Jack.

September 18, 1986

Dear Jack,

Only two more days here, so you probably won't receive this letter until after I get home, which may seem silly, but I need to think some things through, and if I can't have you in front of me, this will have to do. By the way, I can't wait to have you in front of me! I miss you so much!!

I've fallen in love with Ireland, it's a beautiful country with really nice people. I know that sounds weird given the way they're treating each other as The Troubles go on and on. It's interesting that life here seems normal and abnormal at the same time as people agree and disagree and fight and get along. Everyone has a story. But it may just be that I've been so absorbed with my own story, along with Ofelia and Marissa. In any case, we'll be going our separate ways in a few days and I've decided to revisit my goals. Did I tell you I wrote some goals on the plane on my way here?

So, here are the goals as I wrote them:

First, I want to get to know and become mutually comfortable with Ofelia and Marissa. I want to learn more about both of their lives.

What else? I want to find out what Ofelia is doing in Ireland and what she was doing in Argentina.

I hope she'll tell us about her past life and our family history in general. Maybe we can get her to explain her decision to give Marissa and me up when we were born.

Okay, about my progress: number one, so far so good. Of course, I would like to be totally comfortable with my mother and sister, but that will take more time.

The same goes for number two. Oddly, I feel like I've learned more about Ofelia's life than Marissa's, but have decided to think it's just her personality to be a listener and somewhat guarded. Again, I believe I will learn more with time, and we're on a good track.

Number three is interesting. Ofelia has told us what she's doing in Ireland, but I'm quite sure there's more to it than the post office and babysitting for her neighbors. For one thing, what's the scoop with Al Watson and why he helped her get out of Argentina and probably saved her life? And why has she made it clear she will not answer questions about him? She has told us quite a bit about her past life, pretty much up to the time we were born. That's kind of where we stopped. I would love to know more about the work she did with the Addisons and what exactly was going on when it became clear she (and they) would have to leave Argentina. However, I suspect she will never talk about that. I think she believes it would be dangerous even to this day, given the continuing governmental instability. And here's a big one. It sounds like she doesn't know the identity of our biological father. It may not be Miguel Martínez, after all. It may be another guy she was in love with, Paolo something or other. Isn't Paolo an Italian name?

Only a few more days until I see you again. I can't wait! I don't think we have anything in particular planned for the next few days here as Ofelia has to work, but I guess I'm hoping we can get her to talk a bit more about her life.

You may or may not have received this letter by the time I get home, but you can count on hearing it. I love imagining you here as I write. You always help me think better (but I'm actually focusing on how it feels when we're touching each other at the moment…not sure whether I love you more for your mind or your amazing body… gotta stop or it won't get past the censors!)

ALL MY LOVE to YOU (and Gordon, Sherlock and Chomsky)

***

Shortly after Ofelia left for work at the post office the following morning, Marissa received a visitor. To everyone's surprise, Mateo, the man she had been matched with at the Matchmaker's Ball, showed up at the door. He said he was in the area for a conference that would be starting later in the day and decided to take the opportunity to see Marissa before she returned to Argentina. While Marissa had previously said she was indifferent, she was clearly delighted to see him again. Teri was surprised he knew where Ofelia lived but decided not to bring that up.

Teri spent the day by herself. Although she would have enjoyed spending her last full day in Ireland with her sister, she understood and enjoyed seeing Marissa happy. However, she was further disappointed when Mateo offered to take Marissa to the airport the next day. Teri would be on her own driving their rental car to the Dublin Airport.

As they said goodbye the following morning, Teri told Ofelia she appreciated her honesty when she spoke of her past life. With tears in her eyes, Ofelia put her arms around her daughter and hugged her tightly. "My dear little Teresa, this has meant so much to me. I've spent many years thinking about you and hoping you had grown up to be a larger version of the wonderful child I knew all those years ago, and you have. I must admit, in some ways, to my chagrin, when you press me to talk of painful subjects, that beautiful child could be very stubborn and persistent. But you must know that I am very proud to be your mother. I hope we continue to be in each other's lives as much as possible. I know I will try."

Teri drove to the airport with mixed emotions. She truly felt she had connected with her mother and sister emotionally and that it was probably good they had stopped grilling Ofelia for answers when they did. Their last few days allowed them all to breathe and be together in the moment. Yet, Teri was still haunted by the unanswered questions and wondered if she would ever be satisfied with knowing only part of Ofelia's story.

PART 2

September 20 – October 11, 1986

Chapter 11

Teri had been in transit all day, first flying from Dublin to Newark, New Jersey; then driving a rental car three-plus hours to her home in the small town of Mariel, New York. Jack had offered to pick her up at the airport, but she figured it made little sense for him to spend the seven hours on the road the back-and-forth trip would take.

Stepping out of the car, she glanced up at her fifth-floor apartment window and saw Jack's smiling face. It warmed her heart to know he'd been looking out for her arrival. She waved, and he indicated he was on his way down to help with her luggage. Happy to be home, Teri skipped up the steps to the front door of the building. As they embraced, Jack told her how much he had missed her, then picked up her largest bag and began the climb to the fifth floor. As often was the case in their otherwise attractive brick building, the elevator was out of order.

The minute they opened the apartment door, Teri was enthusiastically greeted by their yellow lab/golden retriever, Gordon. The cats, Sherlock and Chomsky, were nowhere to be seen. The commotion had obviously spooked them, but Teri knew it would take very little time before they would show up to demand treats and lap time.

After helping deposit her suitcase and extra bags in the bedroom, Jack went into the kitchen to make dinner, calling out, "I'm making lasagna and a special dessert to celebrate your homecoming."

Teri kicked off her shoes and unpacked her bags, throwing most of their contents into a laundry basket. Then she yelled into the kitchen that she was headed for the shower to get the travel dust off. When she stepped out wrapped in a towel, Jack handed her a glass of wine.

"This is just the first course of your dining pleasure. The lasagna should be ready in about an hour, any ideas about how we should spend the time?"

Teri threw off her towel and climbed onto the bed. Joining her, Jack laughed and said, "Just wait for dessert!"

As they relaxed in the living room with another glass of wine, Teri thought about how much she loved Jack. She had been drawn to his warm and expressive brown eyes even before they became a couple. As she got to know him, she learned those eyes told you all you needed to know about how he was feeling at the moment. Everything about him, especially his typical relaxed, friendly demeanor, promoted trust and comfort, even when he was super focused and concentrating on the many things he cared deeply about. Not only did she find him incredibly attractive, but he was also the best listener she had ever met and always easy to talk to.

Reacting to the big smile on Teri's face as she looked at him, Jack said, "I know you had big goals for your time in Ireland. How are you feeling now?"

"I guess I have mixed feelings. I'm sure you didn't get the last letter I sent where I revisited the goals I came up with on the flight over, did you?"

"Nope."

"I hate to admit this, but a nagging part of me feels like I failed at reconnecting with Ofelia and Marissa; at least to the extent I was hoping."

"How so?"

"I think we were all too careful, too polite. I do think the doors were cracked open and we got Ofelia to tell her life story, at least up until Marissa and I were born. I feel good about that. I think it was hard for her to talk about her unhappy childhood. Reliving that time in her life was obviously painful. While she was telling her story, I mostly felt sad for her and even, at times, scared; but once I was alone on the plane, I came back to realize I still didn't know Ofelia or Marissa, well at all."

Jack seemed a little amused. "Teri, you are one of the few people I've ever known who is truly compassionate but, at the same time, not in the slightest bit interested in participating in the melodramas in other people's lives. You three were together for what, three weeks? How long does it take to begin learning about people when you do an ethnographic study? Isn't a big part of it just about establishing trust so they'll open up to you?"

"Of course, but that's with strangers, not my family!"

"Exactly; with your complicated family history where people were working as undercover spies, for example, would you really expect everyone to open up easily?"

"I guess not, but I do think we all want to feel good about ourselves and each other. I almost feel like Ofelia was more transparent than Marissa."

"Look me in the eye and tell me you would expect Ofelia, with her lifetime of hiding and spying, would be more open than Marissa, who has basically nothing to hide? Don't you think Ofelia is just better at hiding things?"

Teri looked at Jack. "I never thought about it that way. I really do like connecting with people, but I am mostly interested in getting to the big picture, probably too quickly. I'll probably never be a natural listener like you. You know, Jack, I've been thinking that you got to know Marissa better than I do, spending all that time observing her spiritual work and talking to the people around her. Funny, she didn't talk much about that part of her life while we were together, and I never asked. I guess my blind spot was that I deeply wanted her to just be my sister and for Ofelia to just be my mother. I think I put aside Teri, the social anthropologist, completely. Wow!"

"I suspect that didn't happen entirely. You were definitely in study mode when you were at the Matchmaker's events. And I'm willing to bet the therapist in Marissa came out as the three of you interacted with each other. Aren't therapists trained to be quiet and listen?"

"What? Marissa's a therapist?"

"Maybe I'm using the wrong term, but I know she mostly makes her living from counseling people. I think she said that's what she's always done professionally. She doesn't get paid for the religious work."

"I'm stunned! I should have known that. Ever since I got the impression that she's very private, I've avoided asking personal questions. That reminds me, do you know if she's in a relationship?"

"That, I don't know." Jack laughed softly. "It doesn't fall under the kinds of data I'm collecting for my study. But getting back to you, dear anthropologist, the great letter I did receive helped me to be there with you."

Jack paused and brushed aside a lock of hair that had fallen in front of his eye, a gesture Teri always found endearing. Then he continued, "I, for one, am glad you were, at least occasionally, able to put the social scientist part of you aside to get to know Marissa and Ofelia. It seems to me that you did get to know both of them, and one part of them is that they aren't people who are going to spill everything just for the asking." Jack laughed. "If they were, I would question their being related to you!"

Teri laughed, "Of course. Oh, Jack, I've really missed you. I feel like you're the best part of my brain."

"And you're the best part of my life!"

Just then, the timer buzzed loudly and Jack went into the kitchen to take the lasagna out of the oven to settle. By that time, Sherlock and

Chomsky had decided to forgive Teri for her absence and sprawled on her lap and the back of her chair, respectively. Turning on the Carol King *Tapestry* CD, Jack insisted she stay put while he made a salad and prepped his special dessert surprise, a chocolate fondue, reminding her of the previous New Year's Eve, the very first time they had made love. So much had happened since then, but as far as Teri was concerned, her relationship with Jack was the highlight of her time on Earth.

When they finally hit the sheets to sleep, Teri was beyond exhausted. She slept a solid ten hours and woke up the next morning refreshed.

Finding Jack at the kitchen table quietly sipping a cup of coffee, Teri kissed him on the head and began telling him about her plans for the day.

"I need to do laundry and get over to the college to check my mailbox. What's on your agenda? Oh wow, I feel guilty. I never asked how your Nevarez Foundation report is going! Sorry for being such a motormouth; I'm just so happy to be home with you."

Jack looked up and gave her his warmest smile. "Me too, Teri, you've been away too long. But, as far as the report is concerned, I'm feeling a bit discouraged. Writing isn't as easy for me as it is for you. I keep hitting walls where I just can't describe or express the real meanings of things like words and rituals. I'm meeting with the Nevarez team in a couple of days to talk about my progress, and I feel like I'm way behind where I ought to be."

"I'm sorry, Jack. I think there's always a time in our attempts to understand other cultures, and the words they use to describe their beliefs, when we hit walls. There are many things that simply have no equivalent in a different language. Not to diminish your struggle! Maybe you can have a deeper conversation with Marissa. She's pretty fluent in English, much better in English than I am in Spanish. I hate to admit that since Spanish was my first language."

"I totally believe your block with the Spanish language is psychological, but agree I need to go deeper with Marissa. This doesn't just involve Spanish to English translation; it also involves Mapuche that's both blended and not blended with Spanish in her spiritual work. I think I have a lot of sorting to do!"

"Why don't you say exactly what you just told me to the folks at Nevarez? I've always had the sense they're trying to promote deep cross-cultural understanding. Do you think they would support an extension of your field time as well as writing?"

"I'm going to have to ask."

"Have you talked with Charlie about this at all? He's positively otherworldly about spirit and nature. Oh, I'm sorry, I haven't asked. Is he in California?"

"I'm not sure where he is. I've had such a tough time putting my thoughts into words that I haven't even tried to talk with him about the work yet."

Chapter 12

It was a beautiful early autumn day with a New England-ish feel of crisp but not too-cold air. Teri decided to walk the half mile to the college campus. She had spent enough time in the past few days being propelled by fast-moving objects. It was time to get back into her own body and feel her legs!

As she passed familiar houses, gardens, stores, and other local businesses, Teri marveled at how the small town of Mariel had come to feel like home. She knew it wasn't just the familiar fieldstone architecture, but her friends: Jack, Charlie, her closest woman friend Vanessa, and Vanessa's husband Cliff. They had all participated in what they had come to refer to as the Ofelia Mystery Circle. Teri doubted she could ever have discovered her true origins without their collective help. It was like they created a think tank that evolved into a loving community.

What was unusual was that it had happened at all. Teri had spent her adult life with a constant urge to be someplace else, someplace besides wherever she was at the time. When asked why she moved around so often, she joked she was born with "itchy feet." Most people interpreted that to mean she was always in search of new adventures, but when she thought deeply about it, that wasn't it. Instead, she was looking for a place to call home, a place of comfort. Her childhood life and memories had been built on lies and deceptions scripted by Pete and Susan Addison, the people she knew as her parents. Yet, somehow, even as a small child, she was aware there was something missing. For reasons she didn't understand, these parents never quite passed the sniff test.

While they hadn't been unkind, their relationship with her was marked by a palpable emotional distance. In the beginning, Teri had very much wanted them to love her more, but somewhere along the way, she had let go of that desire and begun to reciprocate their indifference. It was okay when she was a small child because she had Ofelia. Ofelia gave her all the love and care she needed. Things simply fell apart when the Addisons moved to the United States, leaving Ofelia behind. After that, Teri had increasingly crawled into herself.

Thinking about the past year was overwhelming. It had been just about a year since Teri discovered a letter, THE letter, from Ofelia to Susan Addison, asking for help and telling her she was in danger. It was postmarked July 1978, three years after Susan had passed away. Susan obviously never saw it.

When Teri first read the letter, she was at the Jersey shore cleaning out the Addison's summer house and enjoying the early autumn weather. But she was unhappy, frustrated, in a relationship that was going nowhere, and simply feeling incapable of moving forward with her life. In many ways, the letter started her on the path to the happier place she was in now. Perhaps it was time for her to let go of her need to know everything, but part of her would never feel satisfied until all of her questions were answered. As she walked, Teri began a conversation with herself and decided to start the day with a meditation visit to Josh Woods, her place of refuge in Mariel.

The minute she stepped into the woods, Teri felt her body relax as all of her senses took in its familiar sights, sounds, and smells. She headed for her favorite log, sat down, and focused on the vibrations of the earth and life scurrying around her until her brain settled into its own flow.

So what now? I know I'm not done, there are still many gaps both in my knowledge regarding what went down and, to be honest, my own self-confidence.

Granted, Ofelia opened up about her past to a point but never got around to what she and the Addisons were doing together in Argentina and what she was doing there after they left in 1953. It's probably my fault for not bringing it up, but we never spoke about the letter and Ofelia's ultimate escape to Ireland. There's so much left to share and learn. Jack's right; it will take time, but how can we keep moving forward long distance?

Okay, I have the rest of this semester while I'm free from teaching to take concrete steps and move forward with my life. First things first, it's time for me to get a move on with my dissertation research. The good news is I probably can start without a grant; I have a lot of money from the house sale and inheritance from the Addisons. I must admit, I'm still floored by the amount they saved and passed on to us, me and their real children. I guess the spy business can be lucrative!

Teri laughed out loud thinking about how her not-real parents made their living. How ironic that she was benefitting. With a new sense of purpose, Teri walked back to the Bateson College campus. As she walked, she found herself remembering Marissa's favorite quote from the Persian poet Rumi "Stop the words now, open the window in the center of your chest and let the spirits fly in and out." This was probably a completely natural way of approaching life for Marissa, but Teri had to work at stuff like that.

In the end, her visit to the college campus was uneventful. Her mail was boring and she didn't run into anyone she was interested in catching up with. Vanessa was on her honeymoon—a month-long Mediterranean cruise, and no one else seemed to notice Teri had been away. However, as she was leaving the campus, she was pleasantly surprised to run into Charlie Elliot, the famous poet and author who had become a dear friend and spent time in Argentina working with Jack while he studied Marissa's spiritual work. They had first met Charlie the previous year when he was a visiting professor at Bateson and became involved with Teri's search for information about Ofelia.

"Hey Charlie, did you give in to Bateson's efforts to keep you teaching here for another year? I thought you were back at your home in California."

"I was, I came this time to give a speech at a conference Bateson is sponsoring. I have no particular plans after that and no, I won't be teaching here this semester, but may do so in the future."

Reaching over to give him a hug, Teri said, "It's great to see you. Can you come over for dinner tonight? I want to tell you all about my time with Marissa and Ofelia in Ireland."

"Absolutely. What time?"

"Anytime. Actually, now would be good. I know Jack wants to catch up with you too. As we speak, he's preparing for a meeting at the Nevarez Foundation with hopes of getting them to support his going back to deepen his understanding of Marissa's group's spiritual beliefs and practices. I'm sure he would appreciate your advice."

"You're offering me an opportunity to learn about two subjects that are high on my interest list. I'll be happy to walk back to your place with you now."

"Great! I'm pretty sure Jack is holed up in his apartment preparing for the Nevarez meeting."

"I thought this was the final meeting where he was to present his findings."

"Yes, the meeting is supposed to be for him to present his findings. But in the process of trying to pull it together in words, Jack has become convinced he came away with important questions he wasn't even thinking about when he was doing his field research. He's hoping to convince Nevarez to support further, deeper research."

"From what I know of Nevarez, going deeper is right up their alley. If I recall, this piece of the study was like an audition for a permanent position with the Foundation. I suspect they'll be impressed with what Jack's learned about what he needs to learn further."

"I guess that's what he's hoping, Charlie, but as you undoubtedly know from your own research experiences, it can be a terribly frustrating part of the process!"

Charlie nodded. "And what about you, Teri? Have you come up with your specific dissertation topic? I know it's going to be about the third-culture kid experience."

"Well, yes and no. I guess I'm a bit slow on the uptake, but I've definitely made a commitment to myself to pull the proposal together in the next few months so I can begin my own data collection. My personal stuff has pretty much taken over the past year, but getting together with Ofelia and Marissa has helped me get over that hump. I think I'm ready to pay more attention to the rest of my life."

"That's great news."

"I have an idea; let's go to Jack's place first, and maybe you two can put your heads together to figure out how to approach Nevarez. I just got back from Ireland yesterday and need to do some laundry."

Teri left Charlie at Jack's door and headed to her own apartment. She and Jack had maintained their separate places in the building even though they went back and forth frequently. This was particularly helpful when one or the other was working long hours and needed to be alone to concentrate.

Jack was pleased to see Charlie. Having spent time in the field with him observing Marissa and her colleagues, Charlie was the one person in the world who had the capacity to help.

Seeing a look of frustration on Jack's face, Charlie went right to the heart of it, "Tell me, in as few words as you can, what you've learned and what else you want to learn."

Jack grunted, "That's the problem. I'm not sure what else there is to learn."

"I understand. Can you think of categories of things you want to learn?"

"Like what?"

"I don't know, maybe things like focusing on the methods Marissa's group uses to help people understand each other and release social tension. I know your original interest was learning how indigenous cultures have affected the larger Argentine methods of political discourse. Maybe revisit that part specifically?"

<h1 style="text-align:center">Chapter 13</h1>

By the time they finished dinner, Teri had given Charlie a synopsis of what she and Marissa learned about their origins from Ofelia, but most of the conversation was focused on Jack's research. To Jack's relief, Charlie helped him come up with a plan to convince the Nevarez Foundation to fund a follow-up visit focused on learning more about Marissa's group's Indigenous conflict resolution methods.

Taking a last sip of coffee, Jack said, "Charlie, if this comes through, is there any chance you could come with me to spend at least a little more time in the field? Your insights are so valuable. And to be perfectly honest, having a big name like yours associated with the project could go a long way towards convincing Nevarez to continue the support."

"Depends on my schedule, Jack. I have some commitments but nothing long-term, mostly speaking engagements. But I would be proud to be part of your research team. Do you want me to come to your meeting?"

Jack laughed out loud, "I love being called a research team! I guess it's all theoretical until we hear what they say this week. I should probably do that meeting alone, but if it's okay with you, I'll tell them you'll be actively working on the project if we get the go-ahead."

Pouring half and half into her coffee cup, Teri turned to Jack. "Have you spoken with Marissa about continuing the on-site data collection? It might be a good idea before you go forward with Nevarez."

"Oh my God, I can't believe I've just assumed she'd be okay with my going back there. Thanks for bringing it up. I definitely need to speak with Marissa—to get her permission. I haven't even shared my findings on the first part with her yet. Is it time to panic?"

Teri laughed, "I can only tell you how pleased she was with what you were doing with her group. She told me everyone loved you, and she felt the questions you asked people were insightful and often helped move their own conversations forward. I don't know exactly what they're about, but have the feeling the members of her congregation are open to evolving as they bring their various belief systems together."

"Open to evolving as they bring their various belief systems together … I like how that sounds. I still need to get a handle on what the various belief systems are and how they're similar and different from one another. Then, maybe I'll be able to hone in on what they do when they run into disagreement."

Teri said, "I think this has much broader potential, even beyond the next phase where you look at how, if at all, these methods have become part of the national culture."

Jack and Charlie laughed. "Teri, you're always ten steps ahead. So far, this is a small but hopefully doable study."

"I know, I know, I can't help myself. I'm a big-picture person. I was always told as a child that my eyes were bigger than my stomach."

"One of your many charms. What do you think? Is it too late to call Marissa tonight?"

Charlie stood up to leave, "I think this is my exit signal. Jack, let me know if I can be of further help. I'll be here for a few days, then heading back to California."

"Will you be here through the weekend? My meeting with Nevarez is on Friday."

"I can do that."

"I hate to bother you, but can you take a look at my written proposal for the extension? I'll try to get it drafted by the end of the day tomorrow. It will only be five pages."

"No problem. I'll be running around most of the day. I can give you a call around four."

"Perfect."

Charlie gave Teri a hug. "Thanks again for dinner. It's great to see you home again. I'm glad to hear your visit with your mother went well, and you learned about her life and reasons for the decisions she made."

Teri smiled. "It was great in a lot of ways. Of course, we still have a lot of questions."

"Like what?"

"I'd like to hear what she has to say about the codes and secret ways she and Susan Addison set up to communicate with each other after we moved to the United States. We never asked about the treasure box Ofelia helped me and Juan Ignacio bury in our backyard when we were children or about the coded clues Ofelia left in the *Mamá* book that enabled us to find her and learn about our relationships. And to this day, I really don't know what the Addisons and Ofelia were actually doing together." Teri took a breath. "If it weren't for all of those pieces, our group would never have had the ability to solve my family mystery."

"Ha Ha! So it continues, the famous Ofelia Mystery Circle. Perhaps there's more for our Circle to uncover. By the way, when are Vanessa and Cliff expected back from their honeymoon cruise? It would be great to catch up with them before I head back to California."

"I'm not sure of the exact day, but think they'll be back sometime next week."

"Let me know. It's starting to look like I'll be motivated to stick around longer than I originally planned."

"Will do. Goodnight, Charlie."

After seeing Charlie to the door, Jack picked up the phone to call Marissa, who said she believed her group would be delighted to spend more time with him and Charlie. She told him she would ask for consensus again but had little doubt that it would be fine. Jack pointed out that he still needed to get the Foundation to approve the follow-up research, but Charlie was willing to be part of the team, which he thought would improve their chances of moving forward.

"That would be excellent. We are all big fans of Charlie's work. I'll meet with the group in a few days and will let you know what they say. Meanwhile, I wish you well with the Foundation. And, if they want to speak with me about what you've done here, I'll be happy to give you a strong recommendation."

"Thank you so much, Marissa. I'll do what I can to move this forward and will keep you informed. Would you like to speak with Teri? She's right here."

"Absolutely."

"Hola Teri. How was your flight? I'm still recovering from jet lag; you see, I remember that term. I hope to see my parents and Che tomorrow if he's available. I'm interested in what they have to add to what we learned from Ofelia."

"My flight was fine," Teri said, "but I'm still wired, so I guess it's from jet lag too. I can't wait to hear what your parents and Che tell you. Please let me know! It's very cool that Jack and Charlie might be able to continue with their research too. I guess we'll have to wait to find out, but meanwhile, I'm thinking about calling Juan Ignacio to see if there's a chance he'll help us meet with Miguel Martinez. If so, I will be traveling your way. Are you interested?"

"Of course. I'll also be asking my parents and Che about Paolo Fuentes."

"This may sound like an odd question, but does anyone know if he's dead or alive?"

"I will explore that question, but I believe I would have heard if he died. Paolo Fuentes is very famous in this part of the country."

"I'll let you know what Juan Ignacio says."

"Thank you."

While Teri said goodbye to Marissa, Jack put on a jacket and grabbed Gordon's leash. Inviting Teri along, he said, "Would you like to take a walk around the block with me and Gordon? I need to come down a little so I can sleep tonight, and I believe Gordon is ready for his evening's constitutional. I will understand if you just want to crash."

"Nope, I absolutely want to take that walk. It's a way to be home with my favorite men. Tomorrow, you write your five-pager all refreshed."

"And what about you? What will you be doing tomorrow?"

"Two things. I need to catch up with my dissertation adviser to talk about third-culture kid ideas. And I need to call Juan Ignacio to see if he'll help Marissa and me connect with Miguel Martínez before it's too late."

Chapter 14

Marissa wasn't surprised to hear Jack might return to learn more about her spiritual work. She was on a long learning curve to gain the wisdom to earn the title of *machi*. When she was being honest with herself, she actually doubted she could ever get there, not having grown up in a Mapuche community. Yet, the other members of her group were content to have a leader who could bring parts of this ancient religion into their lives in modern society. Like Marissa, most were not primarily Indigenous, but they were all attracted to a religion that integrated spirituality with personal health, societal well-being, and the true natural world, and they liked the idea of adopting tenets from one of their homeland's oldest religions.

Happy to be returning home to her quiet life following the intense visit with Ofelia and Teri, Marissa felt it might be a while before she would be ready to return to her usual routines. There was so much to absorb, so much new information about her family's history; not to mention getting used to the idea that Ofelia was her mother and that she had a twin sister who seemed to expect the discovery of their relationship to begin with total openness. She liked Teri but felt uncomfortable when she saw that expectation (or maybe it was just hope) in Teri's eyes. And then there was her growing interest in Mateo. Of course, she wondered if there was any there there. He said he would be back in Argentina at some point, but it was much too early to even think of it as a long-distance relationship. It wasn't really a relationship at all.

Ah, it was nice to be back in her quiet home with her best friend, her Welsh Corgi, Lobito.

Sitting on the sofa cuddling with Lobito, Marissa began to relax and think about things she needed to do to get back on track with her family, her counseling job, and her religious practice. The latter two were on a schedule. She had appointments with clients, many backed up after her three-week hiatus, but thank goodness, would not start for a few days. Same with her religious practice. Family definitely needed to be the first thing on her agenda, but even that could wait for her to settle into her home. Tomorrow was soon enough, and she had many questions for her parents and Uncle Che.

***

Taking her time the following morning, Marissa was ready to reconnect. She began by phoning her mother, Sylvita.

"Hola Mamá. Estoy en mi casa. ¿Cómo estás?"

Sylvita was relieved to hear Marissa's voice.

"You must come here for dinner. When was the last time you ate well, being in a strange country?"

Marissa smiled as she heard her mother being so motherly. She loved being home.

"May I come today?"

"Absolutemente! Ahora?"

Leaving Lobito with a dish of his favorite food, she walked the few blocks to her parents' nearby home, the modest home she had grown up in. Her father, Raoul, stopped pulling weeds from a small flower garden in their front yard to greet her. A man of few words, he told Marissa her mother was waiting in the kitchen.

"I hope you are hungry. Your mother has been preparing your welcome home dinner for several days."

Walking into the house, Marissa inhaled deeply and began salivating as she took in the aroma of her favorite home-cooked meal.

With a big hug, Sylvita said,

"I have made a simple dish of arroz con pollo with a side of vegetable empanadas. Are you ready to eat?"

Marissa nodded as Sylvita continued. "I'm looking forward to hearing all about Ofelia and know you probably have some questions for us, but let's eat first and wait until after dinner to talk. Your Uncle Che will be joining us then. He's the one who can answer your questions."

Happy to hear Che would be part of the conversation, Marissa said, "Thank you, and my favorite foods too. Now, tell me what you've been doing these past few weeks."

"Just wishing the time would pass quickly so we would be together again, Marissita. And hoping you would have a good experience and learn what you wanted to learn."

By the time Che showed up, Marissa and her parents were finishing their meal with a cup of yerba mate. Che settled into a chair with a serious expression on his face. Facing Sylvita and Raoul, he said. "I come with sad news. I just heard our cousin Tomás was murdered."

Sylvita looked at Che, "A sad day for our family, but I can't say I'm surprised. He has lived a dangerous, violent life. Where is he? Can we bring his remains to be buried with our family?"

"He was in prison in Buenos Aires. He was murdered in prison. I will look into whether we can claim his remains."

Che turned back to Marissa, "I'm sorry to begin our reunion with this news. I am very interested in hearing about Ofelia and her life in Ireland."

"How sad! I don't believe I ever met Tomás. If I did, I don't remember him. But Ofelia told us about him. She will be upset to hear this news."

"Yes, but probably not surprised. His entire life has been defined by violent gang activity. Always an eye for an eye with that man. I was afraid to disagree with him even as a child." Che sighed and continued, "I'm not sure it's a good idea to tell Ofelia just now. Let me learn more about the circumstances and whether we can claim his remains. Knowing Ofelia, she'll be motivated to come back for his funeral."

"Ofelia told us she hadn't been in contact with you since she left Argentina eight years ago."

"Es verdad. That is true."

"Our conversation with Ofelia was enlightening for Teri and myself, but there remain many questions. I'm hoping you can help fill in some of the blanks."

"I will try to help you, Marissa, but there may be some things that would be dangerous to share. As you know, while our government has changed more than once, some of the conflicts between factions remain."

"Do you really think Ofelia would be in danger if she returned to Argentina?"

"I honestly don't know. I think the fact that the British Secret Service's Al Watson allowed you and Teresa to visit with Ofelia, where she has been in hiding the past eight years, indicates that he, at least, and perhaps Ofelia as well, believes things are better. I am a small cog in all of this. I didn't even know where she was, and it was believed it was good to keep me ignorant of that. I know you understand that I needed to protect you. And I hate to say this, but I'm not sure you, your sister, and Ofelia are completely out of danger."

Sylvita quietly stepped into the conversation and asked Marissa,

"How is Ofelia doing? I miss her every day and have been worried we would never hear from her. I'm hoping your visit will be the beginning of us all being together again."

"Ofelia seems to be enjoying her life in Northern Ireland and being in Ireland, in general. She lives in a small town, where she has a lovely little house and a close community of neighbors. Later I'll tell you about the Matchmaker's Ball she took us to."

"What does she do for a living?"

"She has two part-time jobs: one at the local post office, the other caring for two little girls. Her identity has, of course, been changed. She is known as Brigid Alvarez, the daughter of an Argentine father and an Irish mother. She introduced us as her daughters and told people our father was a man who passed away named Tomás Alvarez."

Marissa took a long swallow of her mate. "I'm pretty certain she made that name up—all of those names, but it is interesting that she gave our fictitious father her brother's name." Marissa paused and looked at the floor, looked up again, and said, "She told us she wasn't sure whether our real father was Miguel Martínez or Paolo Fuentes."

Sylvita gasped, "Paolo Fuentes?!? The powerful patrón? How would she have known him? And who is Miguel Martínez? She would never talk about her babies' father."

Sylvita and Marissa looked at Che, who had remained quiet. Marissa asked, "Did you know of her relationship with Paolo Fuentes?"

Che cleared his throat. "Paolo Fuentes was involved in some of our political activities. I knew he and Ofelia were acquainted and that he played a role in finding places Ofelia could infiltrate to obtain information. I did not know whether they had a relationship other than that. Paolo's involvement in our political activities was clandestine. None of us wanted his powerful friends to suspect he was working to overthrow the government."

Che paused and cleared his throat again.

"I was led to believe Miguel Martínez was your father, Marissa. I knew Ofelia was working as a nanny for him and his wife when she became pregnant. I also knew part of her job was to become intimate with him to obtain information."

Marissa interrupted, "Did Señor Martínez know of her pregnancy? Did he know she gave birth to twin daughters?"

"I don't know for sure. He was married with children and a strong-willed wife who would have been quite unhappy to hear of the affair. He was also in a vulnerable position in the government during a volatile time. Although he was considered to be a simple bureaucrat, he was known to have a long history with Perón. He greatly benefitted from that relationship but was also obviously endangered by it. As you probably know, his wife and children were murdered, and he has been in hiding for the past eleven years."

"Teri heard this from her childhood friend, the banker Juan Ignacio Ramón." Marissa paused, "Do you know Juan Ignacio?"

"I know him slightly. We met through my friend José who worked with me at the box factory. José was the man who originally connected Teri with Juan Ignacio and started this chain of events. I suppose we should be thanking him for bringing our family together but I just don't wish to be noticed. These remain dangerous times for those of us who are closely associated with the labor movement. Our current president is very unpopular with laborers. While President Alfonsín has been successful at eliminating government corruption, he has not done much to strengthen our economy."

At that moment, Marissa decided it would be best to be discreet and not say anything about Juan Ignacio Ramon's relationship with Miguel, or the fact that he knew where Miguel was in hiding. It was clear the subject of Miguel Martinez could be a risky one to bring up, and she and Teri already had a potential path to meet him.

"Tío, please don't do anything dangerous on our behalf!"

Che smiled. "I will do what I can. So please tell me, Marissa. How is Ofelia doing? Is she well?"

"As I told Mamá, she seems to be happy with her life in Ireland."

"I'm sure she didn't speak with you about any political activity she may be engaged in."

"You are correct, but Teri and I also wonder why Al Watson allowed us to find her there. He claimed to be retired, but the story we heard was that he was doing Teri's father, Peter Addison, a favor by helping Ofelia escape from Argentina and setting her up with a new identity and home in the United Kingdom. I hate to be suspicious, but given their professions, it seems odd that Al or Peter would do such things out of kindness."

"There could be many reasons beyond kindness. Did you get the impression Ofelia was conducting business for the British Secret Service?"

"I have no idea. If she is, she has a good cover there. She appears to be well-established as a middle-aged member of her little community. I mean, she takes care of two little girls! How ironic is that? There are quite a number of people from Argentina living in Ireland, and her cover is that of a woman of mixed parentage, with an Argentine father and Irish mother. That also explains her fluency in English. One of her jobs is with the local post office, which could perhaps provide her with access to useful information, but we heard nothing to indicate she was doing anything beyond what she shared about her current life. Tío, you know more about the world of political intrigue than me. How do you interpret Al Watson and Ofelia opening the door to Teri and my visit? They must have known this also allows our family, as well as you and your cohorts, to learn her whereabouts. Do you believe they feel she is safe now? Do you think she could come home?"

Che began tapping his foot. Marissa wondered if that meant he was uncomfortable with her questions. His response, answering a question with a question, confirmed that suspicion.

"Has she shown interest in coming home, Marissa?"

"She didn't say that specifically, but I can't believe she wouldn't want to. This is her home."

"The Alfonsín administration is now in its third year and seems to be the most stable government we've had in a long time, but I don't know how that affects Ofelia. Our organization, *Personas Por la Verdad*, remains underground and will always be considered communist, anti-Peronist, anti-military, and anti-government, anything that is considered subversive by those in power. In fact, to this day, where one stands on Perón matters."

"Yes, one would think the horrendous dirty war would erase Perón affiliation from consideration. I have mixed feelings about President Alfonsín. He created the National Commission on the Disappearance of Persons, but there are rumors he intends to neutralize this with what's being called a "Full stop law" that would effectively grant amnesty to all acts committed before he was elected president in 1983. This means, of course, the criminal military will be excused from the kidnapping and murder of 30,000 innocent people as part of their dirty war." Marissa paused, "I know I keep asking the same question. What do you think are the implications for Ofelia? There are so many warring factions. Would it be safe for her to come home?"

Che stood up and said, "I honestly can't answer that, Marissa. I promise I will look into all of these questions and would appreciate it if you could keep me up to date on what you learn from your sources as well. Now I must get to work."

He walked out the door.

Marissa asked her mother, "What is his work? I've never known."

"He works for a tango club."

"Really? What does he do there?"

"I believe he is a manager, but he also performs with a small band. In fact, he is its leader; he plays the main instrument, the bandoneon, for the professional dancers and participates in their training."

Chapter 15

Teri was pleasantly surprised when Juan Ignacio called to ask about her visit with Ofelia in Ireland. She'd been planning to call him but was distracted by helping Jack prepare for his meeting with the Nevarez Foundation and her own effort to come up with a plan for her dissertation research. All of a sudden, everything had to take first priority. She had not forgotten the conversation she wanted to have with Juan Ignacio, but it ended up on a back burner. Oddly, his timing turned out to be perfect. Jack was meeting with Nevarez that afternoon, and Teri was home alone with a blank pad of paper in front of her.

"Hola, Juan Ignacio. How lovely to hear your voice."

"And yours, Teri. I was prompted to call you when I heard Marissa had returned from your visit with Ofelia."

"I've been home for about a week and must apologize for not calling you sooner, but it has been crazy around here. However, you picked a great time as I'm alone at the moment and welcoming an opportunity to procrastinate."

Juan Ignacio laughed. "I have been at that place many times. So, tell me, how is Ofelia doing? Did you enjoy your visit? Did you learn her reasons?"

"I'm happy to report she's doing well. She seems to have settled into her life in Northern Ireland comfortably. As for the rest, the answer is yes and no. She answered our questions about her background and reasons for doing the things she did. Well, actually only until our birth, but that was what we were asking her about. Marissa and I believe she was being honest with us. But, after we left, I came to realize I have many more questions."

"Did she talk to you about the treasure box she helped us bury by the Ceibo tree in my backyard when we were small?"

Teri smiled as she responded, "Funny you should mention it. Lately, I've been thinking a lot about our treasure box and its burial place by that tree. I had forgotten its name but have always remembered its magical bright red flowers. We should do something special there."

Juan Ignacio was amused, "Did you remember that the Ceibo is the national flower of Argentina?"

"The national flower is a tree blossom? I did not know that, but I did learn it has personal significance for Ofelia. She told us about its origin story, about the legend that it emerged from the body of a Guarani girl who was being burned at the stake as a witch."

"Oh yes, the story of the courageous Anahí. I grew up hearing about her suffering and bravery along with the medicinal properties of the tree's products, not the least of which is its bark that's not only used in place of cork but also for recreational purposes."

"You mean you can smoke it to get high?"

"Dare I ask, what is its personal significance for Ofelia?"

"Well, apparently, some of the people she was involved with when she was working underground as a teenager gave her the nickname Anahí because she was so fearless."

"From what you've told me, the nickname sounds appropriate. Now I'm feeling that any dedication ceremony to commemorate our treasure box should definitely include Ofelia."

"I agree, Juan Ignacio, I would want Ofelia to be part of it, and hopefully, someday soon, we can all be together in your backyard. But to answer your original question, I never asked Ofelia about the treasure box or the coded letters to Susan Addison or anything else about her life after Marissa and I were born. I think we were questioned out by the end of the visit. I know I didn't start thinking about what I didn't learn specifically until my return flight home. Hopefully, we'll have other opportunities."

"I hope so too. I have a few questions as well. One reason I wanted to speak with you was to ask if you and Marissa are still hoping to meet Miguel Martínez."

Teri's ears perked up. "Yes, definitely. Ofelia confirmed that it's quite possible he is our father."

"Just quite possible? Is there another candidate for this honor?"

"As a matter of fact, there is. And she was apparently never sure. I don't know why, but I lean towards believing our father was Miguel. It sounds like she had a more consistent relationship with him, and the other relationship was more erratic."

"This is very strange for me. I was close to Miguel's family for many years. It's such a small world. I don't recall anyone mentioning Ofelia, even though she had been their nanny. Then again, I wasn't listening for her name when I knew them. Obviously, my relationship with Miguel's son Manuel occurred long after he was a child who might need such services."

Juan Ignacio paused and cleared his throat. "I understand your wanting to have a chance to meet Miguel before it's too late. As I told you before, he is in poor health. His memory goes in and out, but that should make little difference since you never met him before. I can arrange for you to visit with Miguel, but I'm afraid it should happen relatively soon."

"I really appreciate your help, Juan Ignacio. How soon is not too late? How far away is he living? I will need to make travel arrangements that may take time."

"Once you are here, we can get to his hiding place within a few hours. I hesitate to say more until plans are in place. Just give me a time frame that will work for you and Marissa, preferably within the next month."

"Thank you. I'll talk to Marissa and get back to you as soon as I can. Hmmm, maybe I can travel to Argentina with Jack."

"I was going to ask after him. Is he planning a return visit soon?"

"That's what we may find out today. He's currently meeting with the foundation that's been sponsoring his research in an effort to convince them to extend the grant so he can go deeper into his study."

"I would enjoy seeing both of you. Please tell Jack he's welcome to stay over with me as long as he might need."

"Will do. I promise I'll get back to you soon."

Teri put the phone down and tried to plan her next move but found herself incapable of concentrating. So much depended on what Jack would be doing during the next few weeks, and that was totally out of her control.

Turning to Gordon, she said, "Hey, Pup, would you like to take a walk in Josh Woods?"

Gordon was at the door in a flash, and the two of them headed for the woods. Teri decided to drive rather than walk to the park so she would be home when Jack was done with his meeting.

"We'll take the short path, okay with you, Gordon?"

Gordon's helicopter tail told her he would accept any opportunity to spend time in the woods with her. And they were off.

As they walked, Teri was reminded of the many times walking the paths and climbing the rocks in this small part of heaven had helped clear her mind as she experienced just being part of nature. She also recalled a wonderful moment when she first knew Jack. He had come up on her when she was lost in thought, but instead of alarming her by calling out, he walked towards her, singing an old favorite folk song, *The Gypsy Rover*. In her memory, it was a magical moment that characterized his gentle approach to life. She sometimes thought it was the moment she began falling in love with him.

The woods did their job, and by the time Teri and Gordon returned home, Jack was there with a smile on his face. He threw his arms around Teri as she walked into the apartment.

"Nevarez said YES! They will fund another six months in the field, AND they will revisit my needs at that point in time. They told me they truly appreciate where I am in the research and the fact that I have some ideas about what's missing. They're also happy Charlie will be involved. And I quote, 'Charlie Elliot is a world-renowned scholar whose participation will provide prestige to the Foundation as well as contribute to deepening your findings.'"

"This is amazing, wonderful news! Want to go out to dinner to celebrate? On me."

"Sure, where?"

"Your choice, no wait, how about the new Middle Eastern restaurant? I've heard good things about it."

"Let's do it. Then I have to call home and tell my parents the good news. I think they've been doubting the wisdom of my future plans these days."

"I didn't know that. I thought for sure they would be super proud of all you've accomplished."

"Well, they are proud, but I'm not sure they understand that if I'm to be successful in the larger world, I will have to spend time there. Anyway, I'm sure they'll come to understand and accept who I've become or hope to become. And that it may take time for my success to become evident. C'mon, let's get to the restaurant. I'm starving and salivating just thinking about baba ghanoush and fresh pita."

When they arrived home after dinner, it was still early enough for Jack to make the call to his parents. Teri left the room to give him privacy but could tell from the tone of his voice through the wall that things weren't going well. Jack had never really spoken with her about his family, a fact that slightly bothered her because she wanted to think there were no secrets between them. But she felt so comfortable with their relationship that she decided to view it as a cultural difference and not get upset about it. She always figured his family would accept her when they met and saw how happy she and Jack were together despite the fact that she was not of Native American descent. In her fantasy mind, she heard herself pointing out that she had a great-grandmother who was one hundred percent Mapuche, South rather than North American, but nonetheless Indigenous.

Walking into the kitchen where he had been, Teri found Jack worriedly leafing through the Yellow Pages.

"What're you looking for? Can I help?"

"I need to get a flight to Michigan. My father is seriously ill. They were keeping this from me because they 'didn't want to upset me'. I can't believe it, and now he's in the hospital. I need to get home as soon as possible!"

"I'm so sorry, Jack. Did they tell you what's wrong?"

"I couldn't get the details, but it may be kidney failure. I don't know."

"How can I help?"

"Can you drive me to the airport early tomorrow? Now I feel even more guilty that I didn't pick you up when you came back from Ireland, but I need to get there as soon as possible. My mother is not handling this well, and my brother has been useless." Looking at Teri sadly, he added, "My brother has a serious alcohol problem. It sounds like the minute he heard about my father's illness, he went on a bender. No one can find him!"

"Of course, I'll take you. I'm assuming you'll want to fly into Detroit. Let me check to see if you can get that flight out of Ithaca."

Chapter 16

A light was flashing on Teri's answering machine as she walked into her apartment after dropping Jack off at the airport. It was a voicemail message from her friend Vanessa, who had returned from her month-long honeymoon trip in the Mediterranean. Vanessa and her new husband Cliff had been deeply involved in helping Teri figure out the Ofelia mystery. Vanessa had, in fact, been the creator of the Ofelia Mystery Circle where a group of friends put their heads together to read and discover clues and codes Ofelia and Susan Addison had used to communicate. Looking forward to catching up with her friend, Teri sat by the phone and hit redial.

"Hey Nessa! How was the honeymoon? I'm so happy for you and Cliff!"

"It was great, and I promise I'll tell you all about it, but first, I need to hear about your reunion with Ofelia and Marissa. Cliff is also super interested. Can you and Jack come over for dinner tonight?"

"I definitely can, but unfortunately, Jack is on his way to spend time with his family in Michigan. His father is in the hospital, and it sounds like his mother's falling apart."

"So sorry to hear that. What's wrong with his father?"

"Jack didn't get a clear picture of what's wrong. That was one reason he was so anxious to get there, but there's also good news. Yesterday, just before he heard from his mother, he met with the Nevarez Foundation and they committed to supporting more of his research."

"Wow, to deepen the study of Marissa's spiritual group or something else?

"Yes, to deepen the study. I'll tell you all about everything when I come over. What time do you want me?"

"Six-ish?"

"Perfect. That'll give me time to make a few calls I need to attend to."

Hanging up the phone, Teri looked at her cat Sherlock, who was curled up on the other living room chair, and said, "Okay, it's time. Marissa or my dissertation advisor, hmm?"

Sherlock looked at her as if to say *what's the big deal?* and buried her head in her belly.

Teri decided to agree with that attitude. It was time to start the ball rolling with completing her doctoral requirements. It was time to speak to her dissertation advisor, Rosalie Osborne. Feeling a bit anxious, she repeated the mantra, *this is simply a first step.*

Armed with new determination, Teri dialed the number and was rewarded with an immediate response.

"Why Teri Addison, as I live and breathe. How have you been, Stranger?"

"My life HAS been really strange this past year and I totally apologize for dropping our communication. I'm calling today to start things up if I can."

Rosalie laughed, "Not to worry, Teri. You're still within a reasonable timeframe for getting your research moving along. The grapevine here has kept me somewhat up-to-date, so I know about your efforts to locate your birth parents in Argentina. How's that going?"

"The grapevine, huh? Actually, I found my mother and a twin sister I never knew about, so that's been very cool. We're still not sure about our father, but we're working on it."

"Amazing! So, how can I help you?"

"I'm on a break from teaching this semester and hoping to devote some quality time to starting my dissertation research. I know you have nothing from me yet, but I have some ideas about what I want to do, and of course, need your go-ahead. Are you looking for a full-scale proposal up front?"

"That depends on where you are on obtaining funding. If you need to get a grant, your proposal has to fit the granting agency's protocol. I can help you with the formal stuff, so maybe we should start with you passing a clean five-to-ten-page proposal by me. You've done enough professional research to know that they'll be looking for clear goals and research methods."

"I think I can do what I want without external funding. I inherited some money from my parents, I mean the parents who raised me. I'm happy to put together a five-to-ten-page proposal for you, then what?"

"Well, then we find a couple of other people to serve on your dissertation committee, which shouldn't be a problem. Everyone knows you here. They will also have to approve your plans. At some point, you'll need to come out here to Washington to defend the proposal, but let's just get started with the preliminary. If I recall, you want to look into the impact of being a third-culture kid?"

"Wow, you actually remember that! Yes, when we last spoke about it, I had just discovered that it was 'a thing'; but I have since spent more time thinking about it. It's personal for me, but there's not much literature on the subject."

"Well, of course, you'll need to cite what's been done in your proposal. How soon can you have it to me?"

"I'll get started right away. That's the best I can promise, but I'm sure it shouldn't take more than a month. How about the end of October?"

"Perfect. I'll look forward to reading it, and Teri, I'm happy you've been able to find out more about your family background. I always felt you were struggling with something when you were here."

"Thank you. I was, but didn't know why I felt the way I did. I think the third-culture kid part was some of it, but I also spent my whole life living with lies. I believe children have radar about such things."

Saying those words aloud hit Teri in the gut, and she took a deep breath.

Hearing that, Rosalie said, "You know, Teri, you might want to start out by exploring your own experience and how it's affected your life. That would at least give you a baseline to compare with other third-culture kids you interview."

"I guess I've been so busy learning about my family history; I haven't had time to process what it means for me."

"You might want to consider it, Teri. Meanwhile, I'll look forward to your five-pager, and we can move on from there."

Teri got off the phone and immediately switched gears. She had work to do; personal stuff could wait. She would start the proposal tomorrow, but first needed to speak with Marissa about connecting with Miguel Martínez. From what Juan Ignacio said, they shouldn't wait much longer. It sounded like his memory, along with his general health, was deteriorating. The good news was that Juan Ignacio was on board to take them to Miguel's hiding place.

Teri grabbed a can of Coke from the refrigerator and called Marissa who answered the phone immediately, saying, "Can we talk a little later? I have to meet with a client in ten minutes and am running late."

"Sure, what's a good time?"

"How about four this afternoon, my time?"

"Works for me. I'll call you then."

This gave Teri time to take the dog for a brief walk, make and eat a sandwich, and close her eyes for an afternoon nap. She set the alarm for four forty-five and called Marissa back at five on the dot.

"Hola Marissa. How has your homecoming been?"

"Very interesting. I spoke with Che, and he confirmed many things Ofelia told us. He knew Ofelia was acquainted with Paolo Fuentes. Paolo was apparently secretly involved with their underground activities. But Che doesn't seem to have known of their sexual relationship. He has always presumed Miguel was our father."

"I guess we may never know, but one of the reasons I wanted to call you today is to tell you Juan Ignacio has consented to take us to meet with Miguel. He wants to do this soon. Miguel is not well. From what Juan Ignacio says, it also sounds like he has memory issues."

"How sad, but I'm glad he's going to help us meet Miguel. When will you be available to be here? You are, of course, welcome to stay with me. Oh, what news of Jack? Will he be coming back to continue his research?"

"I was just calling to see when you'll be available. I can be there as early as next week. This is important. Oh, so much going on. Jack had a good meeting with the Foundation and will be getting the funding to deepen his research. I'm sure you'll hear from him soon, but he's currently visiting his family in Michigan. His father is in the hospital, so we don't know about his schedule yet."

"I'm sorry to hear that Jack's father is ill. Please tell him I will send white light. As for the visit, next week works for me. Let me know when you need me to be in Buenos Aires to meet with you and Juan Ignacio."

Teri picked up the phone again and made a flight reservation for October 6th, giving herself a little more than a week to both continue settling in after Ireland and preparing to travel to Argentina. Her head was spinning; among other things, she needed to make arrangements for pet care. Jack would probably not be home by then. And she needed to reach Jack and tell him what was going on. Boy, was she looking forward to wine and dinner with Vanessa and Cliff! Perhaps they would help out with Gordon and the cats.

Chapter 17

Finally on the flight to Buenos Aires, Teri counted her blessings over and over. First on her list was gratitude for Vanessa. She had not only helped her come down from all of the current craziness with a lovely dinner and evening of catching up; she had also committed to care for Gordon and the cats and ferried her to the Ithaca Airport for the first leg of her long journey. It was a long uncomfortable experience, trying to sleep for the ten hours sitting between two very large people, both of whom were also obviously uncomfortable in their seats. Teri silently vowed never to travel for that length of time in anything but first-class seats again. Then she remembered her enjoyable conversation with Grace on the way to Ireland and reminded herself to touch base with her while she worked on the third-culture kid study proposal. Thinking about throwing herself into that project gave Teri a smile, and she finally fell asleep for a few hours. Nonetheless, she arrived in Buenos Aires feeling disheveled but pleased to see both Juan Ignacio and Marissa greeting her at the gate. She knew they would take care of her until she regained her "land legs."

Sitting in Juan Ignacio's living room, Teri and Marissa relaxed as they sipped from their mate gourds. Every time she had that opportunity, Teri found herself reliving warm moments of her early life as an Argentine child. Even the aroma of dry yerba mate leaves in the gourd made her feel nostalgic.

Smiling at the twins, Juan Ignacio couldn't help commenting how odd it felt to see two women with such a strong resemblance to each other and their mother Ofelia.

"It's funny that I never thought of your resemblance to Ofelia when we were children, Teresa; nor when we first met last year, but now I see her face in both of you. Of course, I haven't seen Ofelia in a long time, and you and Marissa are obviously very much alike but interestingly different. Anyway, I hope we can determine whether Miguel is your father, but as I have told you, he may not be in a position to be of help."

"Does he know we'll be coming to see him tomorrow?"

"I told him I was bringing visitors, but obviously, no details about who you are and your reasons for wanting to meet him. He may have already forgotten the small part I told him."

The following morning, Teri, Marissa, and Juan Ignacio got up early and began their journey to Miguel's hiding place. Juan Ignacio asked the sisters to ignore the way they were heading. For Teri, that was easy since she didn't know the territory, but Marissa had to shut off her brain. There had never been a time in her life in Argentina when everyone didn't feel the need to be careful and discreet. Every change in government came with one danger or another. All she registered was that they had started their journey heading south and west into the Southern Pampas of Buenos Aires Province.

Along the way, they passed through large and small towns as well as extensive grasslands where they saw herds of grazing horses and cows and fields of giant sunflowers and colorful tulips. The extensive landscapes were dotted with signs for estancias, large estates that had been turned into tourist destinations. After approximately four hours, they stopped in the small city of Tandil for lunch. From there, they drove via several winding roads into the foothills of a small mountain range and followed a narrow road to a gated community enhanced by a terraced garden filled with fruit trees and colorful flowers. It was strikingly quiet, with no human or traffic noise at all, yet they could almost hear the sounds of birds and insects conducting their daily lives. Marissa was enchanted; Teri was curious.

Inside the building, Juan Ignacio was greeted by a woman wearing a deep purple colored suit and high heels named Natalia who proceeded to lead them through various hallways. Although they expected it to be a medical facility, the place felt more like an elegant apartment complex comprised of luxurious living suites. It gave Teri and Marissa a good feeling to think their potential father could be spending his final days in such a lovely place.

The hallways were carpeted and furnished with colorful paintings depicting Argentine themes, including one of the famous 19th-century folk heroes, Gauchito Gil, who was reputed to have been a Robin Hood character who stole from the rich and helped the poor. The residence, whatever its purpose, was welcoming. As she followed Natalia to Miguel's rooms, Teri thought it had the potential to be a cheerful experience, but for the fact that there was no human noise, no sign that people actually lived there.

Stopping at what appeared to be an apartment door with a heavy brass knocker shaped like a hand, Natalia asked the twins to stand back, explaining, "He does not receive many visitors, so it will be best to prepare him for so many of you."

Standing behind the door, they heard her say in a respectful voice, "Buenas noches, Señor Martínez, look who has come to visit you. It is Señor Ramón with some friends."

Miguel greeted Juan Ignacio warmly, then said, "But where is my boy Manuel? You promised you would bring him during your last visit."

Juan Ignacio replied with equal warmth and lied to Miguel without missing a beat, "He was not available to come this time. He sends his regrets with hopes that his work will not prevent him from seeing you again soon. But I have brought some visitors I believe you will enjoy.

I will invite them to join us in a minute, but first, how have you been feeling?"

"I must admit, I have my ups and downs. There are times when I can't remember where I am, which is disturbing. At other times, I am aware I'm in hiding from the government to protect my family from harm. I miss them terribly."

"I understand. With each change in our government, I have renewed hope that your contribution to Argentina's well-being will be recognized."

"Yes, I know you are trying, and I appreciate your help, my boy. So, who are these new visitors? I am in suspense."

Juan Ignacio walked to the door and invited Marissa and Teri to enter the room.

Marissa walked in first. Miguel's reaction was palpable. Standing up to meet her, he said, "Ofelia, how wonderful to see you!" Then he saw Teri and jumped back. "Am I seeing double?"

Looking beseechingly at Juan Ignacio, he said sadly, "I worry about my mental health, but until now, it has been about my memory loss. Now I'm seeing two Ofelias."

Juan Ignacio laughed. "Believe it or not, you are not seeing double. I'd like you to meet Marissa and Teresa, Ofelia's daughters. They look a lot like their mother, don't you think?"

Miguel looked relieved. Then he addressed the twins. "Oh my goodness, you are both so beautiful, just like your mother. Such a treat to meet you. I did not know Ofelia had children. She must be very proud of you."

Teri spoke up first, "It's a pleasure to meet you as well. Do you remember our mother?"

"Of course. It has been a few years since I last saw her. Is she well?"

"Yes, she's fine. She's living in Northern Ireland now."

"I believe I last saw her shortly before I went into hiding. I have often thought about her. Such a lovely girl."

Teri was surprised to hear Ofelia had been in touch with Miguel so recently. She had always assumed their relationship ended when she and Marissa were born. This opened up more questions regarding Ofelia's undercover activities when she worked as the Addison's maid when Teri was growing up in Argentina. Obviously, these questions would have to wait.

After a couple of hours, Natalia knocked on the door and announced that it was time for Señor Martínez to retire for the evening. She told the twins she had prepared guest quarters for their overnight stay, and if they were available, they could visit with Miguel again in the morning before they returned home. As they walked out of the room, Natalia said she hadn't seen Miguel so happy or alert in a long time.

Once alone in their rooms, Teri turned to Marissa, "This place is amazing! It has to be quite expensive. I wonder who's paying for Miguel's stay here."

"I suspect it's Juan Ignacio. He seems to be very fond of Miguel."

"I agree. He's very protective. So, what did you think of Miguel?"

"I find him to be a lovely man. It's hard to imagine him being a close friend of Juan Perón."

"I thought of that as well. But you know what surprised me the most was how tall he is. For some reason, I expected him to be a small man."

"I didn't think of that. Why did you have that impression?"

"I guess because he's been presented to us as being meek in a way, being dominated by both Perón and his wife."

"I understand, but I also believe a lot of people have done things they may not believe in to protect themselves and their families. I have never heard him described as an active fascist."

Teri looked closely at her sister. "It's probably weird of me to associate anything with height anyway. I just had a different image in my mind. He seems to be a kind person, and he is obviously fond of Ofelia. Were you surprised to hear him say he had seen her shortly before he went into hiding? That was eleven years ago."

"Yes. Like you, I assumed their relationship ended before we were born. Now we have another question to ask Ofelia."

"Agreed. Did you come away with any feelings about whether he's our father or not?"

"You know, Teri, I continue to be curious about that and have been thinking about speaking with my college professor about new research in the field of paternity determination."

"Really? I've been wondering if we can compare our blood types. Is there an even more accurate way to measure that relationship now?"

"This is not my area of expertise, but I've read that scientists have been working to develop more finite ways beyond the basic blood typing. Comparing blood types allows them to exclude a man as the biological father, but is not always definitive in a positive way. There is one relatively new test I know about called HLA typing."

"What's different about that? What's an HLA?"

"HLA stands for human leukocyte antigen. It's genetic material, inherited from both parents, found in the white blood cells and is said to be accurate in about 80 percent of all cases."

"That sounds pretty good. I think it's worth pursuing, but how do we get a sample of his blood?"

Marissa laughed. "Great question. We might want to ask Juan Ignacio. But you haven't told me…did YOU get a feel for whether or not he is our father?"

"Not a feel, per se; I'm still in my brain about this. It's just too bizarre to be in search of our biological father, so soon after learning everything I believed about my origins was untrue. My brain tells me he's a decent, nice man who has had a difficult life and is feeling a lot of confusion now. It tells me I could be alright with his being my biological father, AND oddly, I think the fact that he's tall increases those odds in my mind. After all, haven't you wondered why you and I are so much taller than Ofelia? I know our nutrition growing up was probably better than hers, but she has to be four or five inches shorter than you and me."

"I hadn't thought of that, Teri. I know I'm the one with the Biology degree, but I really hadn't thought at all about our physical similarities and differences."

"And I hadn't tapped into my feelings. Interesting how differently you and I process information."

"Maybe the difference is in what matters most to us and what parts of our brains we trust to provide the best information."

"Ha Ha! We could be subjects of an interesting nature vs nurture identical twin study, couldn't we?"

"Perhaps, but we don't even know if we are identical or fraternal. Just because we look alike doesn't mean we're genetically identical."

"Maybe we should find out. When you talk to your professor, would you ask if we can be tested for that too?"

"Yes, of course, we will need to have our blood typed in any case. I wonder if Ofelia would be willing to do the same. Ah Teri, as usual, every time we seek answers, we seem to come up with more questions."

The following morning, after a brief visit with Miguel, Juan Ignacio and the twins set out on their journey back to Buenos Aires. They spoke about their perceptions of Miguel and his health during the trip. As usual, Juan Ignacio was warm and forthcoming with answers to their questions up to a point. Whenever something came too close to the role he played in Miguel's life, he politely diverted to another topic. Ultimately, it became clear he was concerned that no one would inadvertently reveal Miguel's whereabouts or whether he was still alive. Teri couldn't be sure but wondered if Miguel might hold government secrets that could cause harm to powerful people. She wondered if Juan Ignacio was afraid dangerous things would come out of Miguel's mouth without his even being aware, given the fragile state of his mind. In the wake of their previous night's discussion, Teri and Marissa were glad they had decided to hold off bringing up the paternity question until they had more information regarding what would be required of Miguel. They didn't want to scare Juan Ignacio off.

Chapter 18

Marissa had left her car at Juan Ignacio's home in Buenos Aires so the twins spent the night there and drove north to her house in Punta Lapiz the following morning. They were immediately greeted by Lobito and Marissa's mother, Sylvita.

This was only the second time Teri had met Sylvita and found herself looking for a family resemblance. It was strange to think this woman was her mother's first cousin, so she was Teri's first cousin once removed. Although a smaller woman than Ofelia, they looked like they were related and had the same striking green eyes; but it was notable that Sylvita's eyes communicated trust and warmth, while Ofelia's never lost a veneer of cautious observation. Teri couldn't help feeling sorry that her mother had such a sad early life.

Teri was further touched when Sylvita gave her a hug and said she had decided to be sure to see Teri again before she flew back to the United States. Teri and Sylvita did their best to communicate with Marissa's translating assistance and Sylvita invited the twins for dinner the following evening, promising to include Che in the festivities.

Teri was delighted. "I would love to join the family for dinner tomorrow and am very interested in finally meeting Che."

"Buenisimo. I will find him." Turning to Marissa, Sylvita said, "Oh, I forgot to mention you had a gentleman caller yesterday while you were away."

Both Teri and Marissa looked up. While Teri thought she might learn something about Marissa's personal life, Marissa was only thinking and hoping it was Mateo.

Sylvita smiled, "He was very handsome, muy guapo. He said his name was Mateo and that he had met you in Ireland. He left you a note on the living room table. Of course, I didn't read it. It was none of my business."

Looking over at the note, which was in a sealed envelope, Marissa said calmly, "Oh yes, we met him in Ireland, where he was conducting business. How nice of him to come by. I will read the note later."

The following morning, Teri and Marissa reached out to her former professor, Pedro Seguro. Meeting with him together, they told the story of their quest to learn about their origins, a story best shared with the evidence of their twinness before his very eyes. They were careful not to reveal details regarding their parents' identities or reasons for hiding the truth from their daughters. Fortunately, the professor appeared completely focused on the genetic part and proud to speak with them about recent laboratory techniques that allowed scientists to distinguish between different people's DNA.

According to Dr. Seguro, a British geneticist named Sir Alec Jeffreys developed a process of genetic fingerprinting that involved comparing the variable lengths of repetitive DNA found in different individuals. He believed this DNA testing was the most scientifically accurate method to identify relationships between parents and children.

"Are you saying we can obtain this information without a blood sample?"

"Yes. DNA is found in other parts of our bodies. However, this is very new and still in an experimental stage. It is unlikely you would be able to use it for your quest. Your best bet at this point in time is to compare blood samples. You are aware of the HLA typing?"

Marissa and Teri nodded.

"I would recommend you try that. It will probably give you the information you seek."

Thanking the professor for his help, Teri and Marissa decided to find a way to obtain a blood sample from Miguel. Knowing this would require help from Juan Ignacio, they debated the best way to approach him. Teri volunteered to bring up the subject. She had promised to spend her final couple of days in Argentina with Juan Ignacio and thought it a good time to move their plans forward. While he had always been protective of Miguel, he also seemed to want to help Teri and Marissa. Perhaps there was a way to obtain Miguel's genetic information without placing him in danger.

Teri enjoyed the family dinner immensely. She was made to feel like a special guest of honor by Sylvita and Raoul. Che turned out to be quite charming and welcoming, as well. When she first saw him, she had a vague memory of this large man with a gentle manner she had known from the box factory when she was a small child. Thinking about all he had done to protect Ofelia over the years, she could only marvel at how his quiet voice and demeanor disguised such strength and courage, enabling him to accomplish so much in the background.

Teri had come to believe Che played an important role in all that had taken place and knew details he would never share. After all, he had originally introduced Ofelia to her underworld life in Argentina but had always watched out for her. Teri was convinced Che was the one person Ofelia would trust without question.

"I'm pleased to have the opportunity to speak with you at long last, Che. You've been on my mind a great deal during the past year. I have so many questions."

Che repeated what he had told Marissa earlier. "I will happily answer your questions, but there may be some that are still dangerous to discuss."

"Do you believe Ofelia remains in danger?"

"I don't know. I'm always suspicious and believe there are powerful people in this country who would like to hear what she knows and may even see her as a threat to their well-being. I believe caution is in order."

"And you haven't had contact with her since she left Argentina eight years ago, in 1978?"

"That is correct."

"Can you share whether you have a relationship with Al Watson?"

"I've never met the man."

"Let me ask this another way. What role did you play in helping Ofelia leave the country?"

"Only in that I was told there was a plan to save her life, so I did what they asked."

"Who approached you? What did they ask you to do?"

Che was clearly becoming uncomfortable with these questions.

"I'm sorry I can't give you more information than that I facilitated Ofelia's transportation to the first part of her journey. I never saw nor heard about her again. I am not at liberty to say the names of anyone I knew to be involved beyond what I've told you."

Teri smiled at Che. She could see he was starting to shut down, no doubt a well-honed instinctive reaction from his years of secretive radical political activity. She needed to change the tone of their interaction quickly if she was to learn what she wanted from him, but before she could change the subject, Che turned to Sylvita.

"I have located Tomás' remains. I think I can gain custody of them so we can inter him with the rest of our family."

"I'm happy to hear this. I only wish Ofelia was here for the burial. Have you learned any more about whether Ofelia can return to Argentina safely?"

Unsure of what they were talking about, Teri couldn't help interrupting. "Who is Tomás? Is this another relative?"

Marissa said, "Of course you wouldn't have known him. I never remembered him either, but he was Ofelia's brother. He apparently passed away in prison recently."

"Oh yes, now I remember. Ofelia told us she began her involvement with the underground when she went in search of her brother. That was Tomás? I had forgotten his name. How sad. Does she know of his passing?"

Che laughed. "Ofelia has always had sources of information unknown to anyone else, so she could very well have heard. If she knows, it's obviously not from anyone here."

Marissa smiled. "I don't think she knows. That's just my feeling."

Raoul spoke up for the first time, "I believe it's her right to know about her brother's passing. I would want to know."

Sylvita agreed. "I also think she has a right to make her own decision about whether to be at the burial or not. Do you agree, Che?"

Che shifted in his chair again. "I guess I have to have faith that my little cousin has a handle on her own safety these days. She has survived all these years without me taking care of her. I would love to see her again, but will always worry."

Teri said, "It seems to me, from what I've heard, you have dedicated a lot of your life to taking care of her. She's, what, fifty-seven, fifty-eight years old now?"

Che changed the subject. "Teresa, you are in contact with Ofelia. Will you tell her about her brother? I'm not quite sure when I will have custody of Tomás' remains, but will let everyone know as soon as I do. Now I must leave to get to my work. I enjoyed meeting you, Teresa, and am happy you are finally reunited with our family. It's as it should be. Oh, I almost forgot." He reached into his pocket and brought out an envelope he handed to Marissa. "I believe this is rightfully yours."

Surprised, Marissa opened the envelope and took out her Cedula de Identidad, her official Argentine identity paper that included a photograph of her when she was three years old.

Sylvita exclaimed. "Where on earth did you find this? I haven't seen it for years. I thought it was lost forever!"

"Believe it or not, I first saw it last year in a treasure box Juan Ignacio Ramón showed me. I believe it was filled with toys and other items Teresa and Juan Ignacio buried in the back yard when they were young children."

Everyone looked at Teri, who said, "Yes. That was where we found many of the clues Ofelia had left for Susan Addison that ultimately led me to find Marissa and discover that Ofelia was our birth mother. But I don't understand. Why did you take the cedula?"

"I was afraid all of this would be revealed and everyone, Ofelia, and her children, would be endangered. In addition to the photograph, the cedula includes her name, date, and place of birth. Simply from the picture, it's evident that you two are twins. I didn't know what else to do."

Teri sat down. "Please, Che, please stay a little longer. I need to know. You were there. This is about my life, my identity. Please. What can you tell me about the decisions Ofelia made. How did I end up the child of American spies?"

Che sat down. He had never been comfortable explaining or talking at all.

"I will answer as best I can. But I do believe Ofelia is the one you need to ask. As I have already told you, I was not involved in any of the decision-making. They would ask me to do this or that, and if Ofelia said she wanted it, I would go ahead and use my resources to do it. Yes, I did help find a place where she could get the medical care she needed for the birth. None of us knew she would give birth to twins, so when that became evident, there was discussion about what to do. Sylvita had already committed to raising one child as her own and had been pretending to be pregnant during the later months. I honestly cannot tell you who decided to place the second twin, you, with the Americans. When I heard Ofelia would be working at the same home where you were being raised, I was happy for both of you."

"Who were **they**?"

"What?"

"Who asked you to do these things?"

"Sometimes, Ofelia; the rest, I am not at liberty to reveal. There were people who operated secretly, whose lives depended on not being identified. In many cases, some were probably using false names."

"But you knew them. You knew what they were doing. Were they in the government? Were they high-level powerful officials? Who would know American and British spies? Who would place a teenage girl and an infant in their care?"

Teri broke down and began to sob.

Until that point, Marissa, Sylvita, Raoul, and Che had looked at all that occurred as a difficult experience necessitated by their country's broken political system. In the silence that followed Teri's outburst, they were reminded of its serious human toll. Marissa and Sylvita immediately, instinctively, put their arms around Teri. She couldn't stop sobbing. The men stood by helplessly. How did this come to such a disaster?

Chapter 19

Che was dumbstruck. He had always thought of himself and his compadres as the good guys. They had dedicated their lives to working in ways that were often dangerous to themselves to free their country and their people from autocracy and fascism. Yet, how could he look this young woman in the eyes, this woman who shared his blood, and tell her she had spent her life as a pawn in a noble game, a game that was supposed to make things better? What was better?

"I do not know the names of the people who made this decision, Teresa. I do know they were powerful people who had access to, and even relationships with, powerful people from other countries such as the United States and Great Britain. I was a low-level member of this cohort. It was honestly thought best for me to remain ignorant. That has always been the way it works in the underground world. Unlike me, a simple soldier, Ofelia was trusted and recruited for important missions even at a young age. It may have been partly due to her youth, her projected innocence, her obvious intelligence, and, I must be honest, her attractive looks and personality. I don't know, but I do know everyone I worked with held her in high esteem. I tried to stay informed as much as I could to protect her from harm, but I never felt I had any power."

"Che, have you ever known who our father is?"

Che swallowed uncomfortably. "I always assumed it was a member of the Perón government, Miguel Martínez. As part of her work with the underground, Ofelia was placed in his home as a nanny. It was rumored that she was there to become intimate enough with him to learn government secrets."

"Was Miguel involved in the deception around our birth? I know he was a high-level government official at one time."

Marissa looked at Teri. *Hadn't Ofelia told them Miguel never knew about her pregnancy? Was she just double-checking sources?*

"I don't know, Teresa, but I was under the impression that information was kept from Miguel. He was thought to be a weak man who was unhappy in his marriage, a man who might do something foolish and expose Ofelia's work."

"Wait, did Miguel know Ofelia was working undercover, using him to obtain insider information about Perón?"

"Again, I don't know what Miguel thought, but it never came up, so we always figured he was ignorant of her true role."

Marissa looked at Che. "Are you saying Ofelia was the one who made all of this happen—at the age of 17?"

Che looked back at her directly. "I'm saying she wasn't a helpless pawn, but it's very likely high-level individuals were directing her."

"If it wasn't Miguel, who was it?"

"So, we come full circle. I don't know who they were. At that time, Ofelia had developed relationships with several women and men involved with our movement."

"Were you surprised when she ended up with the Addisons? Did you know who they were?"

"You must believe me, Teresa. I never did much more than deliver messages but always looked out for Ofelia. I think, especially because of my family relationship with her, there was an effort to keep me in the dark about what was going on. I was placed at the box factory, around the corner from where you and she lived with the Addisons, specifically to send messages to Ofelia."

"You once gave me a wounded bird in a paper bag. I remember you were very friendly."

"Yes, Teresa. You and I were co-couriers."

"So, you knew who I was."

"Yes"

Che looked at his watch and, once again, walked toward the door. "I must get going, or I will be late for my work. I promise I will let you know when I have possession of Tomás' remains."

Turning again as he opened the door, he addressed Teri, "I believe Ofelia is the only one who can answer your questions. Please give her my love when you next speak."

As the door closed, Sylvita spoke up. "I am feeling guilty for holding on to these secrets for so long. I honestly didn't know what to do and had to trust that Ofelia and Che were dedicated to protecting both of you and our entire family with their secrecy."

Marissa smiled at her mother. "I will never blame you for acting on your good intentions, Mamá."

Teri nodded, getting up. "Nor would I, Sylvita. I'm only happy to have found you. Thank you so much for the dinner. Perhaps I can come by to say goodbye in the morning before I catch a train to Buenos Aires."

As they walked back to her house, Marissa pointed out that Teri had never mentioned the name of Paolo Fuentes.

"I did that on purpose. I know he was a big shot who was involved with Ofelia, but a part of me wants to find out if Miguel is our father before bringing him up. The waters are so muddy already, I didn't want to make Che even more uncomfortable."

Marissa laughed, "I'm sure the muddy waters metaphor is apt. You will see if Juan Ignacio will help us obtain a blood sample from Miguel?"

"Absolutely! I will do what I can to move our research forward."

PART 3

October 12 – October 21, 1986

Chapter 20

As she dropped Teri off at the train station, Marissa took a deep breath. She had to admit she once again felt relieved to be taking a break from Teri's persistent quest for answers. So much had gone down during the past year: discovering and meeting her twin sister, reconnecting with Ofelia, and opening the door to questions about the identity of her father had been exciting, even fun. Jack and Charlie's study of her spiritual group, the questions they asked, and the wisdom they imparted in the process had also helped her to think about things in new ways.

However, she'd been left with little time for reflection regarding how her life had changed and what that would mean going forward. In many ways, she had approached the changes and new information as an observer. There were even times when she had seen all of it as belonging to Teri, her new sister whose life was being totally turned upside-down by these revelations. For Marissa, it had been different. Of course, learning that Ofelia was her birth mother was shocking, but that didn't change who she was or the course of her comfortable life.

Sitting in her favorite chair, sipping a cup of herbal tea and nibbling through a small pile of chocolate-frosted cookies, Marissa focused her thoughts on what mattered most to her and how she would move forward. Central to her world was her spiritual quest, a quest to honor her great-grandmother's Mapuche legacy by integrating indigenous wisdom with other established belief systems. Marissa had not spoken with Teri, nor anyone else, about how much this activity mattered to her. She had not shared how important creating a meaningful spiritual community was to her personal sense of well-being.

Putting down her cup, Marissa looked across the room and saw the note Mateo had left for her. Not at all sure she wanted to go forward with this relationship, she had left the note in its sealed envelope on her living room table. It was probably time to read what he had to say and decide what to do.

Their time together in Ireland had been fun, but Marissa was aware they had met in a bubble where romance was purposely promoted. On the one hand, she was attracted to him; he was muy guapo, as Sylvita had noted, as well as being well-spoken and charming. Yet she was hesitant to bring anyone else into her generally comfortable world, a world she had worked hard to create. As drawn as she was to Mateo, she feared he would turn out to be a distraction. More than one of her past relationships had ended up causing mutual pain, and she had to admit that even when they were pleasurable, it made it difficult for her to concentrate on anything else. She also realized she knew little about Mateo. On the one hand, they seemed intellectually compatible, and he was clearly an accomplished professional. Did he say he was a lawyer? On the other hand, they had not spoken about their spiritual beliefs. What if they were at odds? That would be impossible for her.

All in all, Marissa was unsure whether she wanted to start something new when she was so busy with her own life. Conflicted, she opened the envelope and then replaced the folded note without reading it. Dropping the envelope back onto the table, she decided to sit on it and do nothing. The Universe would provide.

As it turned out, the Universe, in the guise of the handsome Mateo, showed up at her door about an hour later. Seeing him again forced Marissa to let go of the fantasy that she was actually in control of her growing feelings for this man.

Greeting her with a warm smile, Mateo said, "Ah, Marissa, I'm so glad you are here today. I was disappointed when I came by earlier in the week and discovered you were out of town. So soon after you returned from Ireland, it was surprising."

"I had business to conduct in Buenos Aires. I understand you met my mother. Oh, I am being impolite. Please come in."

"I hope I'm not interrupting you."

"No, No. I came home recently and have just begun to catch up."

Mateo smiled, exposing a dimple on his left cheek.

Can this man be more attractive?

"Can I get you a drink, something to eat?"

"Gracias, no. I ate a short time ago. Can we sit?"

"Of course."

Marissa led Mateo into the living room, where they each took a chair. Embarrassed and afraid she was acting like a schoolgirl, Marissa hoped her delight at seeing him didn't show too much. Lobito saved the day as he took a long look at the stranger sitting with his person and leaped into Marissa's lap, all the while staring at Mateo suspiciously. Marissa and Mateo laughed.

"It would appear that you are well protected, Marissa."

"Yes, Lobito is my soulmate. Do you like dogs?"

"I do, and cats as well. I grew up with many pets and loved them all. I don't have any at the moment. My work keeps me traveling quite a lot. It would be unfair to leave them so much. But someday, when and if I settle somewhere, I would definitely want to share my life with a dog, a cat, or both. What about you? Is Lobito your first pet, or did you grow up with them?"

"I've always loved animals and lived with many over the years. I also chose to study animal behavior in college. I think we can learn a lot about living peacefully in nature from other animals."

Mateo looked at Marissa with interest.

"You are a biologist, a scientist? I was under the impression you make your living as a therapist, but are most passionate about the spiritual world."

Marissa laughed, "These are all large topics I can't explain in one or two sentences. But if I must summarize, I'm interested in learning about a variety of sources that will contribute to peace and harmony for all living beings."

"These are noble and intriguing goals."

Marissa laughed again and changed the subject.

"Where are you staying, Mateo? Will you be in Argentina for a while?"

"Yes. At the moment, I'm holed up in a hotel in El Tigre, where I have set up my portable office. Such is the life of the nomad."

"You've never told me exactly what your profession is. Is it very secretive?"

"Not really. I'm an agent for people who hire me to help solve their problems. It's as simple as that. However, my job requires total discretion. I never share either who I serve or what I do for them."

"This is very intriguing … and mysterious. What kind of education and training prepares one for such a position?"

Mateo laughed. "Very clever, my friend, but I'm afraid people who do what I do come from many paths. I think I may have mentioned to you that I have a law degree, but can't say that I practice law. In any case, may I change the subject and invite you out for dinner and dancing later this week, perhaps Friday evening?"

"I would like that."

"If it's alright with you, I will pick you up at seven. I know a nice place in Buenos Aires you might enjoy. They offer a good dinner, a fantastic tango performance, and the opportunity for customers to dance. The music is excellent, as is the atmosphere."

"You've convinced me, Mateo. I look forward to seeing you at seven o'clock on Friday."

***

Despite efforts to attend to other business, Marissa's upcoming date with Mateo dominated her thoughts. The Matchmaker's events notwithstanding (she really had seen them as a fantasy with no connection to reality), it had been a long time since she had gone out on an actual date. In addition, she had to admit she really cared what Mateo thought of her. It was amazing how his coming to her house had affected her. A few minutes prior to seeing him at her door, she had put the note down with no intention of following up. Within minutes, she was both thrilled and terrified at the prospect of actually pursuing a relationship.

After twiddling her thumbs for several hours, Marissa couldn't concentrate on what she would make for dinner, let alone a meaningful relationship with Mateo. In an effort to snap out of it, she laid down on the sofa to nap, but her mind wouldn't let her rest. Although she may have slept off and on, when she finally gave up, her head was buzzing. It seemed like thoughts were ripping through her brain with no ability to settle for an instant. Sitting up, she tried once again to take control. Looking around the room, she noticed Lobito watching her warily. Wondering if she was putting out a weird vibe, she spoke to him gently.

"Wait, Lobito. Come sit with me, and we can have a rational conversation. I'm the counselor. I'm the person who gives everyone else advice. I will come to you for advice on how to deal with this confusion, but it always helps to have you in the room."

Lobito climbed onto the sofa while Marissa made herself a cup of chamomile tea and settled in a chair facing him. She tried to put her feelings into words.

"Work, church, family, home…these are my rocks. How does Mateo fit into what matters to me?"

There were no answers and despite Lobito clearly wanting his person to feel better, this was not helping. Marissa decided to call her oldest childhood friend, Elena Hosta. Elena was the most grounded person Marissa knew, a professional dancer who had spent her adult life in the world of nightclubs where she performed under the name of Betty Yum Yum. During the day, she came home to care for her elderly parents and young children. Marissa could think of no one else she trusted as much to be nonjudgemental. If anyone could help her get her priorities straight, it was Elena.

Elena was happy to hear from Marissa.

"I've been thinking about you and looking forward to hearing all about your adventures in Ireland with your new mother and sister. When did you get back?"

"It's been a few weeks, maybe even a month; so much has been going on, I've lost track of time."

"I've been asking our spiritual group members. They tell me you've been busy with other things these days, so I figured the visit was extended."

"No, it wasn't that. Can you come over for dinner or a long visit this evening? I have a lot to share with you and am hoping to benefit from your advice on a few matters."

"Of course. What time do you want me?"

"Are you free for dinner? If so, come at eight, and we can eat and chat."

"That would be great. See you then…and welcome home mi amiga."

Elena's voice helped Marissa come down to earth. Their conversation reminded her that Elena was not only familiar with the sophisticated social world of Buenos Aires, but she and her dancer friend, Pepper Murphy, had accidentally played a significant role in first connecting Marissa and Teri. She would be interested in hearing all about their visit with Ofelia in Ireland. This conversation could serve two purposes, an opportunity to talk about the Ireland visit, Ofelia and Teri, and get Elena's advice about preparing for her date with Mateo.

A few hours later, Elena was at her door and Marissa was reminded how much she admired her old friend. She remembered that as a child, Elena fell in love with movement and dance and longed to make it her life's work. But to her great disappointment, she did not grow tall and willowy with long shapely dancer's legs. Instead, she was short, muscular, and stocky, with broad shoulders and large hips. While she was recognized to be the most graceful and talented dancer in every venue, her parents and other adults discouraged her from pursuing her dreams, but she never gave up and succeeded in making her living in the entertainment world. From what Marissa could gather, Elena, as Betty Yum Yum, was well-known and well-respected among her professional colleagues.

"May I pour you a glass of wine, Elena?"

"That would be lovely. I've had quite the day with my teenager."

"Oh no. Are you referring to sweet Caroline? It's hard to imagine an easier child. What has she done?"

"She has turned thirteen and decided she should have total control of her comings and goings, and she constantly questions my authority. So, Marissa, I am anxious to hear all of your news, but also have the feeling you called me for a particular reason?"

"You read me well, old friend. There are many important things in my life. Having been away from my family, counseling, and spiritual work, I find myself way behind and overwhelmed with feelings of responsibility."

"But there is something else, isn't there?"

Marissa felt her face begin to flush. "Yes, I'm embarrassed to admit that I have become involved with a man I met in Ireland."

"This is wonderful news, Marissa. Are you in love?"

"Of course not. I hardly know him. His name is Mateo. He is currently in Argentina. He came to my house this morning and invited me to dinner and dance at a tango club in Buenos Aires this weekend. This will sound silly for a woman of thirty-nine, but it's the first time I've been asked on a date for many years, and I don't know what to wear. I thought you could help me."

Elena couldn't help laughing. "Oh, my dear, of course, I will help you choose your outfit, but I think there's more to your anxiety than clothing choices."

"This is very strange for me to say, but I feel intensely drawn to him, and yet, I was ready to ignore him two minutes before he showed up here this morning."

"You said you met in Ireland?"

"Yes, when we were in Ireland, Ofelia took Teri and me to a matchmaker's weekend. An interesting annual event, it takes place each year in a small town in western Ireland during the month of September and is designed to bring people together to find true love. There's actually a matchmaker who surveys and interviews people and matches them up."

"And you chose to participate in this? That doesn't sound like the Marissa I know!"

"I did. I can't tell you what got me to do it. I guess I was just fascinated that such a thing existed and wanted to try it out. In some ways, it felt like I was in another world the whole time with Ofelia and Teri, and this was just part of the bubble."

"And you were matched with this Mateo?"

"Yes. I thought it was because we were both Argentinians, but we had a nice time together. It was relaxing to be with someone from my country who spoke my language. And we were surrounded by many other people doing the same matchmaking thing. It didn't feel strange, but it also felt temporary. I completely believed I would never see him again, that the match was only real in that bubble."

"And then?"

"Well, he came to Ofelia's house in Northern Ireland to see me. I was surprised, but again, didn't see it as a relationship. He travels for his work and told me he had been in Ireland for several months. I was actually more surprised when I heard from him after I came home."

"This morning? Was this the first you heard from him since you returned home?"

"It was the first time I've seen or spoken with him since I returned, but he came by my house last week when I was out of town with Teri and her childhood friend Juan Ignacio. Mamá happened to be here, and he left a note for me."

"Wait, you were with Teri and Juan Ignacio somewhere after you returned from Ireland?"

"There's so much to tell you. But yes. We went to meet a man we thought might be our father."

"Wow, that's big! But can we finish with Mateo first?"

"There's not much else to say. He left a note I didn't read. I thought I was too busy, too far behind in my real life to add Mateo, so I decided to ignore it. I even went so far as to open the envelope, but still didn't read the note."

Elena smiled, "Then he showed up at your door."

"Yes, and now, I feel totally unprepared for this date."

"I'll be happy to help you dress for the ball, Cinderella. You say you're going for dinner at a tango club? Do you know which one?"

"No, only that it's in Buenos Aires."

Chapter 21

Back in Buenos Aires at Juan Ignacio's house, Teri felt the comfort she had always shared with her favorite childhood playmate. Although they had been together with Marissa when Juan Ignacio took them to meet Miguel, this was their first opportunity to be alone.

Since they reconnected as adults, Teri had experienced two versions of Juan Ignacio. Unlike the relaxed, smiling man who sat before her at the moment, he tended to be formal and almost overly polite when other people were around. When they were alone, all of that melted away and was replaced by mutual permission for both openness and privacy without fear or judgment.

Juan Ignacio's first question was about Ofelia. "How does she look? Is she well?"

"She seems fine, but it's hard for me to judge. I only knew her as a young child, followed by no relationship for the next thirty-two years. I have never known her as an adult. All my perceptions relating to Ofelia were those of another person, Teresa the child." Teri gazed thoughtfully out the window, then turned back and continued. "There were times during our visit, especially when Ofelia and Marissa spoke to each other in Spanish when I felt limited in my ability to get the whole picture. Marissa tells me I didn't miss anything and that we came away with the same opinion about how Ofelia is doing these days. I guess I have to trust that."

Juan Ignacio responded thoughtfully, "I understand. Ofelia was a huge part of my childhood, even after you left, but I knew her well into my teen years when she worked for my family, so I probably think of her somewhat differently. But I must ask, do you doubt Marissa?"

"No, not at all. I just find her to be understandably different from me in the way she processes information."

"How so?"

"I'm not sure I can answer that yet. I'm still studying what it means to be a twin." Teri smiled. "Thinking about our differences reinforces my general belief that nature serves as a platform for the variations that come with learning and other life experiences."

"I know you have more questions, but I'm curious as to whether you feel Ofelia was completely honest with you about her past decisions and reasons for her actions."

"Juan Ignacio, I believe she was honest in general, and she was telling us things that were painful for her to remember and share. I also believe we didn't get the whole story. This was partly because we didn't ask about her life after our birth. We were all too emotionally exhausted to absorb more. There may have been other omissions that were none of our business or even had the potential to be dangerous for us to know. I definitely want to learn more, but who knows if or when that will ever happen."

Juan Ignacio shifted in his seat. "I know you don't know the answer to this question, but I wonder, do you think Ofelia believes Miguel is your father?"

"I can't answer that question. I do know she held him in high esteem. She told us we could be proud to have Miguel as our father."

Juan Ignacio shifted again. He was obviously somewhat uncomfortable with the subject. In an effort to help him understand Ofelia's behavior, Teri added, "She was so young, Juan Ignacio! While it seems like she did a lot of bad things and made stupid decisions, you have to understand where she was coming from. She had escaped a seriously dysfunctional home situation and basically found an idealized safe place with these older people who were kind to her. In the process, she became committed to their cause. But we can't forget how young and vulnerable she was."

"I know, I know. I just hate thinking of Miguel as someone who would violate a young girl and make her pregnant. I have adored him since we first met. He was a wonderful father to Manuel and he accepted our relationship from the first day." Tears formed in Juan Ignacio's eyes. "He always protected Manuel from his mother, who treated him abominably from the time he was a young child. She thought he had feminine behavior traits and tortured him. Manuel knew his father was a gentle soul who was taken advantage of, first by Perón and always by his cold, ambitious wife. I guess I just can't imagine him doing the same to a vulnerable girl."

"I suspect we'll never know the whole story, Juan Ignacio. The way I heard it, Ofelia was given that position specifically to seduce Miguel so she could obtain information about Perón and his cronies. If he succumbed, they were both involved in deception. The thing is, I don't care about that. I just want to know who my father is."

"I understand."

"Will you help me do that?"

"I would like to help you, but don't know what I can do."

"I know this is a big ask, but could you help us obtain a blood sample from Miguel?"

Juan Ignacio looked surprised. He paused for a few minutes, then responded slowly.

"I'm not sure I would be able to do that, nor have the right. In any case, I would need to think about it."

Seeing a flash of disappointment on Teri's face, Juan Ignacio added, "I promise I'll get back to you within the next few weeks. I have a lot of things to consider. I'm sure you understand."

"Of course. I don't want to cause trouble for either you or Miguel."

"I know that."

Juan Ignacio smiled and changed the subject. "What would you like to do with the time we have left before you need to return to your home."

"Good question. Would you mind doing a few touristy things?"

"Of course not. What do you have in mind?"

"Well, I've heard good things about La Boca, El Tigre, and the zoo here. I'm especially interested in visiting the zoo where I first met Marissa all those years ago."

"May I suggest you leave your visit to El Tigre for your next time with Marissa? It's much closer to where she lives than here. But I will be happy to take you to the other two. I must warn you; while the La Boca neighborhood is very colorful, it is also a place you must hold onto your belongings. It is a place where petty thievery is common."

"That's too bad. I've only heard about its colorful houses and tango dancers. But I know how to be self-protective."

"Yes, I have great faith that is true."

"Thank you, my friend. And I appreciate you being my tour guide for a day or two before I return to my real life. But one quick question. I know you are friends with Che Delgado, but wonder whether you think he has been completely honest with us about what he knows."

"I actually don't know him well. I met him for the first time when my friend José brought him to meet me because he was afraid opening the door to Ofelia would be dangerous for all of you. But if you want my opinion based on very little contact, he is a dyed-in-the-wool member of a secret subversive organization and operates at a habitually deep level of secrecy. He has obviously been good at this; his survival rate is notable. On the other hand, he cares very much for his cousin Ofelia, and you and Marissa, by extension. I think you can trust him with your life."

"I agree, but that's not my question. What I want to know is if I can trust him to be truthful?"

Juan Ignacio smiled. "That's a good question. I suspect he'll be truthful to the extent that what you don't know won't hurt you. Isn't that an American term?"

"That's what I figured."

"I know it's difficult for you to understand how things have been in Argentina all these years of government instability. Che and I have never known things to be different. We have both survived by being vigilant and staying under the radar."

Juan Ignacio stood up. "It's been a long day. Perhaps tomorrow you can tell me all about what you did in Ireland and Jack's research, and your research plans."

"Then I'd better get a good night's sleep. There is a lot to report about all of these things. And, by the way, we always talk about my life, but never yours. I hope to get you to tell me more about your work in the next couple of days."

Juan Ignacio laughed. "I'm happy to share such information, but it will surely put you to sleep with boredom."

"I doubt that, Juan Ignacio. Buenas Noches."

Chapter 22

Marissa couldn't remember a time when she had so much fun. It was silly fun as Elena helped her choose the perfect outfit for her upcoming date with Mateo, a blue-green silk "party" dress with a big skirt she hadn't worn in many years.

Surprised to hear that Marissa had never been to a tango club, Elena asked, "Didn't you and Mateo first come together at a dance in Ireland? What kind of dance were you doing?"

"Yes. It was a lot of dancing, a mixed bag including Irish folk, rock, and ballroom. There was nothing that required great skill like tango. I can pick up the general steps, but tango seems like flamenco, a whole world unto itself."

"I'm sure Mateo won't expect you to do the tango."

"He won't? I have no idea what it means to attend one of these places."

"You can tell him you haven't learned the tango, and he will think nothing of it. If this is like most places I've worked, you'll have the choice of sticking to being part of the appreciative audience, taking a tango lesson, or just throwing yourself into it when the audience is invited to the dance floor."

"Thank you for explaining that to me. Mateo is a sophisticated man. I want him to be proud of his date."

"He will be proud because he will be escorting the most beautiful woman, wearing the most beautiful outfit in the room. Now, let's find just the right earrings."

The next few days seemed to fly by. With Elena's cheerful help, by the time Mateo arrived to pick her up the following Friday, Marissa was feeling more confident. As they met at her door, his smile reinforced her belief that this would be an enjoyable evening.

Stepping into his car, Marissa asked the name of the tango club and where it was located.

"It's called *Tango y Otra Musica*. It's located somewhere between San Telmo and La Boca. And, yes, it is a long drive."

"I recently drove back and forth to Barrio Buenasuerte with my sister. It always surprises me that Buenos Aires is such a large city."

"It is indeed large. What took you to that barrio? I've always thought of Barrio Buenasuerte as suburban and mostly residential."

"Yes, it is. We were visiting Teri's childhood friend."

"How nice. If I recall, you told me your sister spent her early childhood in Buenos Aires, but you have only recently reconnected with her."

Marissa hesitated. She couldn't exactly remember what she had told Mateo about her family situation when they were in Ireland, but she knew it had been superficial. It was too soon to bring him, or any other stranger, into her confidence at that point. Smiling at the side of his face, she responded,

"Yes, but I want to hear about your family. I know you're originally from Argentina. Are your parents still living in this area?"

"My parents, my sister, and my brother, along with their families, all live in the northwest, many hours from here. That's where I spent my childhood. I grew up on a ranch near Mendoza."

"Ah, wine country."

"We're also known for the best olive oil."

"Is that your family's business?"

"How'd you guess? Now it's my turn to learn about your family."

"I've spent my entire life here in Punta Lapiz. I grew up in a house a few blocks from where I live now."

"But your mother lives in Northern Ireland, and your sister is American? I can't help being confused."

Marissa laughed nervously. "I learned that Brigid and Teri were my mother and sister earlier this year. Prior to that, I knew Brigid as my mother's cousin and had no idea I had a twin sister. The woman you met at my house when I was out of town last week was the woman I knew as my mother growing up. It's a long story, and we're all in the process of getting to know one another."

Mateo smiled and said calmly, "I have all night and would like to get to know you better, but we can certainly save the long story for another time. You must know that I hope to have the opportunity to have many long conversations with you."

"And I with you, Mateo. What else do you wish to know?"

"Well, perhaps you can explain your professional life. I know you work as a therapist but are also dedicated to bringing together a spiritual group that merges various belief systems. I find that fascinating."

"I make my living as a counselor, but am not a therapist, not a certified psychologist. I began working part-time with a social service agency when I was in college and have somehow never left. In the beginning, I was hired to do administrative and clerical work for them. That evolved into running the place, which required stepping in to work in the counseling area more than once. It was never my intention to be a counselor, but here I am after all these years, still giving out advice." Marissa laughed and continued, "It has become my profession, such as it is, but without more educational credentials, I do not qualify to be a therapist per se."

"I hear similar stories from many people and wonder if they are happy about falling into their work. I mean, what would you be doing differently if the fates hadn't stepped in?"

"I have two answers to that question. The first is I don't know. I was a Biology major in college and am still interested in trying to keep up with my field, but I have never chosen a profession that uses that part of my education."

"What's your second answer?"

"That would be my spiritual work. This is my passion and I don't believe I could dedicate as much time to it if my professional life was more consuming. However, I make no money at it, so both are necessary—one to keep my body together, the other for my soul."

"Can you tell me more about it? I know you mentioned bringing together disparate belief systems to, what? create a new religion?"

"I hope I can explain this well. I work with a group of like-minded individuals who are dedicated to creating a community centered around a holistic belief system that integrates all things that make for a good life. Most of us have indigenous ancestors. My great-grandmother was a *Machi*, a member of the Mapuche tribe who served as spiritual leader for her community. Some of the people in my group call me that, but it's not an accurate title for me because a true spiritual leader is not training me, and I, like the rest of my group, want to be true to all of our belief systems, not just Mapuche. What about you, Mateo? Who are your ancestors?"

"All I know is that my family has been in Argentina for a very long time. I believe they originally came here from Spain, but I honestly don't know if they mixed with native South Americans along the way. But your spiritual quest intrigues me. Can I visit one of your group meetings sometime?"

"I would have to clear that with the rest of the group. You must understand; we are in the process of coming to agreement around many issues. Many of us are uncomfortable with outsiders coming in and judging what we're doing."

"I understand, anyway, this evening, we eat, dance and enjoy. And here we are at the club."

"Do you come to this club often?"

"No, this is my first time, but I've heard good things about it, especially about the tango performance and music. And the food is supposed to be very good."

Chapter 23

Marissa was somewhat surprised *Tango y Otra Musica* was so elegant. Not that she had expected it to be dingy, but a dance club sounded like a place where people spent their time drinking and smoking and speaking loudly to hear themselves above the music. On the other hand, Mateo was such a distinguished, well-dressed man; she couldn't imagine his taking her to a place that wasn't nice. After being escorted through a marble-façade entryway, they passed a formal coatroom, beautifully appointed restrooms for ladies and gentlemen, and framed photographs of famous dancers in elaborate costumes.

As they moved into the dining area, Marissa was increasingly grateful for Elena's help getting ready for the date. She had been a little worried her dress was too elaborate for dinner and dancing, but looking around, she saw it was similar in formality to many others in the room, and she was not overdressed. Once seated, she noticed most of the floor space was devoted to comfortably spaced tables and chairs interspersed with waiters in white coats busily moving pushcarts from table to table.

While Mateo said he had not been to this particular club previously, he was clearly familiar with its set-up. Noticing her questioning expression as she gazed around the room, he explained that the performance would take place when they were finished with dinner. He said she would barely notice the process by which the room would be transformed: first to encompass a performance space, followed by an open dance floor where customers could dance with each other or professional dance instructors.

Marissa thought she had never had such good food, beginning with an amazing glass of Malbec she laughingly credited to Mateo's family. Everything was delicious. They even had vegetarian dishes that seemed to be prepared with as much care as the ever-present grass-fed beef. But the best part of it was Mateo and the wonder of the attention he paid to her. It wasn't that she had never had a good time with men she dated, but she had never been so enthralled with their looks, their manners, and their conversation. Was she actually in love? Mateo had also been right about her not noticing as the club staff quietly and efficiently moved things around and opened curtains that had previously been disguised as walls, exposing a large stage and dance space comfortably designed for the professional dancers and their musicians.

The music first got her attention when she heard the shuffling of feet while the small band began tuning instruments. As the audience quieted down, one of the musicians, who was obviously the leader, stood up and introduced the band to the audience. He described each instrument and how its sound blended with the others and provided the performers with a unique vision of their tango movements. He himself played a bandoneón, a type of concertina common in tango music. He then introduced the first set of dancers, three elaborately costumed couples, and sat back down to begin the show.

Like most people growing up in Argentina, Marissa was familiar with tango music and dance. Although it had a deep history in her country, tango had originally been associated with gangsters and brothels. Over the years, it evolved to its current status as a high form of cultural art, not unlike the flamenco in Spain. However, it had been years since Marissa attended a tango performance, let alone one as beautifully choreographed as this one. While the original tango was seen as a declaration of aggressive male sexuality, this performance celebrated both male and female sexuality as expressed by their costumes, facial expressions, and suggestive movements. It was truly exciting to be in the same room. And Marissa was glad Elena had talked her into wearing her beautiful, slightly revealing, blue-green dress. Although it was nowhere near as sexy as the dancers' costumes, she looked forward to feeling pretty while she danced with Mateo.

Somewhere in the middle of his speech, Marissa realized the bandoneón player was Che, her Uncle Che! Gasping in shock, she started to tell Mateo who he was, but had to stop as the performance had begun. There was no opportunity for her to tell him until the performance was over, but it was clear that Che was the leader of the band and the overall Master of Ceremonies.

After the performers took their bows, Che stood up and announced a fifteen-minute break to allow the band to take a breather while the restaurant staff readjusted the dance space for audience participation.

Seeing how happy Marissa looked, Mateo smiled broadly.

"It appears that you enjoyed the performance, Marissa."

"Oh, Mateo, the performance, the food, and your company have all been wonderful. But I must tell you an added surprise. My Tío Che is the bandeneón player!"

"Why didn't you tell me this before?"

"I didn't know until I saw him here. I only learned recently that this is what he does for a living. I've never seen him perform and honestly didn't know the name of the club. What an amazing coincidence! If possible, I will introduce you when the show is over."

"That would be great, but first, it appears the band is ready to play for the rest of us to dance. I'm not very good at tango, but I would love to dance with you again. I have fond memories of our many dances when we first met in Lisdoonvarna. Does that seem as long ago to you as it does to me? Oh, wait. Are you interested in taking a tango lesson? I believe we can do that if you like."

Marissa laughed, "I would love to dance with you again, but I will pass on the tango, especially after seeing the competition. I would still like to introduce you to Che. Perhaps we can connect with him during their next break?"

Mateo approached a waiter and asked if there was a way Marissa could speak with her uncle, a member of the band.

"I can ask, but they are often unwilling to interrupt the flow of their performance." The waiter looked at Marissa and said, "Who is your uncle?"

"Che Delgado, but don't go to any trouble."

By the time she had completed her sentence, the waiter had already walked up to the stage, and within five minutes, Che came to their table with a big smile on his face.

"Marissita, you look so beautiful! Why didn't you tell me you would be here tonight?"

Giving him a hug, Marissa said, "I had no idea where we were going. I was as surprised to see you here as you were, me. But I'm glad we came. Your performance has been amazing. I had no idea we had such a talented musician in our family!"

Mateo stood up when Che came to their table and offered his hand.

"Mateo Roca. I echo Marissa's praise. This has been a wonderful evening, the food, the performance, the company…and he smiled looking at Marissa."

Che smiled back, but a question entered his eyes. "It's nice to meet you, Señor Roca. Are you from Punta Lapiz?"

Marissa laughed as she recognized that Che was going to learn what he could about her escort, even as they first met.

"No, we actually met in Ireland. We were matched at a Matchmaker's Ball. We think it may have been because we are both Argentine, but who knows?"

"Quite a coincidence that you are both here now." Che smiled and continued, "Well, thank you for bringing my little niece to our club. I'm glad to hear you've enjoyed your evening, but I must return to my work. Will you be staying through the rest of the evening? If so, I can perhaps join you for a drink."

Marissa answered, "I would love to, Primo, but I am not accustomed to such a late night. Perhaps another time."

Che nodded and returned to the stage as Marissa and Mateo walked to the coat room and asked a staff member to call for their car.

As they headed out the door, Mateo said, "That was interesting. I somehow got the feeling your uncle was suspicious of my motives towards you. Wait a minute, you say Che is your uncle, then you call him primo. Is he your uncle or your cousin?"

Marissa laughed, "Your feeling was probably accurate. Che is very protective of me and all of the other women in our family. He has never married, so all of his masculine attention is focused on us. But to answer your question, I guess he is both my uncle and my cousin. In actuality, he's my birth mother's cousin, but I grew up knowing him as my uncle, my first mother's brother. We have a long drive home. I will tell you all you need to know about my crazy family. That ought to keep us both awake and alert for the long drive. But before I start, I must ask that you don't share what I am telling you."

"Well, that sounds mysterious."

"I know, and I hate to ask it, but my family history has been una telenovela I only learned about earlier this year. There are still missing pieces and secrets I have no right to divulge. Most importantly, people could be hurt. So, Mateo, I tell you this so you are willing to keep it between us."

Mateo looked closely at Marissa. He was touched by this act of trust and wanted to live up to it.

"Marissa, I'm a private investigator by profession and am practiced in the art of discretion. I would never do anything to harm you."

"I believe you, Mateo."

Mateo reached out and took her hand.

Feeling this was the beginning of something really important, Marissa began, "The two women you met in Ireland are my mother and sister. That's the truth. But, I was raised by another mother who turns out to be my birth mother's cousin, and I didn't meet my sister until this year."

"And Che is your birth mother's cousin?"

"Yes, and my first mother's brother."

"Is it too personal to ask why, and how you discovered this so recently?"

"I can answer the how question easily. My sister Teri, who was raised by Americans who were living in Buenos Aires at the time, discovered it by chance. No, that's not fair. She came upon some questions, did a lot of detective work and found me. And together, we found our mother. As for the why, we learned quite a bit about that from our mother when we were in Ireland. That was perhaps our primary reason for the trip. But I must admit, questions remain. I'm still trying to understand and process this information. It's pretty heavy, as some would say, to learn your life has not been what you thought."

"And your mother gave you up at birth?"

"You understand, thank you. That's the hardest part."

"I understand how painful that must be for you. I didn't get to know either your mother or sister very well when we met in Ireland, but I had the impression you were all fond of each other. Wait, did you know your mother well previously?"

"Not exactly well. She was a remote member of the family I saw occasionally as a child. I knew her as my mother's cousin, but she was very mysterious."

"In what way?"

"She was always very loving, but there were long periods of time when I didn't see her. And then, in 1978, she disappeared, and no one knew where she was. My mother worried about her, but she also seemed to accept the fact that this could happen. I was kept in the dark."

"1978…was that when she went to Ireland?"

"Yes"

"Is it too personal to ask about the secrecy around her move?"

Marissa had been so caught up in their conversation she hadn't noticed that Mateo was pulling into her driveway. For some reason, at that moment, Marissa knew she had reached the limit of her comfort with sharing Ofelia's story. She trusted Mateo and wanted to trust him with her family secrets, but there was still a lot she didn't know about why Ofelia was in Ireland and whether it would be safe for her to return to Argentina. And what she knew was not her business to reveal.

"I hate to stop in the middle of a story, Mateo, but I can tell you, I don't know all of the reasons and feel uncomfortable sharing the ones I do know. I hope you can understand."

Mateo did understand and knew he had hit a wall with Marissa. He had come to care for her and felt a strong urge to tell her the truth about why he was in Ireland and at the Matchmaker's Ball, but before he opened that door, he needed to speak with his client.

"I completely understand and am flattered you've trusted me with such personal information. This has been such a wonderful evening; I wish the evening would never end, but I have to be up early tomorrow to meet with a client." Leaning over to kiss her, Mateo added, "By the way, I totally agree with Che that you are beautiful. I have been very proud to be seen with you on my arm this evening and hope to see you again soon. May I call you tomorrow?"

"Of course. I look forward to hearing from you."

Marissa was happy he wanted to see her again but relieved he didn't assume he could spend the night. She knew she needed to come down to earth before moving forward, but tonight, she would sleep soundly and have happy dreams.

Chapter 24

Marissa woke up the following morning feeling good about her life. She decided to celebrate by walking to the local panadería to pick up a few freshly baked croissants to eat with her coffee. The sun was shining, and she was basking in its warmth, both outside and inside her body. Almost embarrassed, she found herself thinking about the basdoiri's book of magical powers that predicted marriage within six to eight months for those who placed both hands on the book and thought of love with closed eyes for seven seconds. *But, of course, I didn't do that. I wasn't thinking about such things at all at the time. Anyway, it's a silly belief.*

As she entered her house, she said to Lobito, "Hola mi perrito grande. All's right with the world."

She took off her jacket and went into the kitchen to turn on the coffee pot. Humming to herself, she noticed her voicemail machine light was flashing. When she pushed the button, it said,

You have two new messages

But I was only out of the house for ten minutes, she thought.

The first message was from Elena who was curious to hear how her date with Mateo went. She would call back later in the day.

The second message was from Mateo, asking if he could come by to speak with her this morning. His normally calm voice sounded urgent, and Marissa worried that something bad had happened. She dialed the number he left, and he answered the phone immediately.

"Is everything alright? Your message sounded urgent."

"I'm sorry to alarm you, Marissa. This is not an emergency, and I am fine. I have something I want to tell you, and I would like to do it in person as soon as it's convenient for you."

"Of course, Mateo. I'll be here all morning."

"Thank you, I should arrive in about an hour."

Despite his reassurance that he was fine, Marissa was a nervous wreck. She decided to hold off on the coffee so she could share the fresh croissants with him, but nothing could distract her from her thoughts and worries. *What could be so urgent? Was he leaving the country indefinitely or abruptly? Was someone in his family sick or dying? Did he want to end their burgeoning relationship for some other reason? Does he have another lover, a girlfriend, a wife? This is silly. I need to calm down and stop speculating.*

When Mateo arrived 45 minutes later, he found Marissa calmly sitting on the ground in her backyard, chanting and breathing. So engaged in the moment, she was startled when she heard him call her name.

Jumping up, she responded, "Oh, Mateo. I'm so glad to see you. I was going to make a pot of coffee, and I bought some fresh croissants this morning."

As she headed for the kitchen, Mateo stepped in front of her and put his arms around her in a warm hug.

"Please don't go to any trouble for me, but yes, I would love some coffee and a croissant. I have had nothing to eat today and am feeling a bit light-headed."

Once they were settled with their breakfast, Mateo thanked Marissa and cleared his throat: "There's something I need to say to you. I will begin by telling you a true thing. I know we haven't known each other very long, but I have strong feelings for you. You entrusted me with many personal things yesterday evening, and I believe if we are to go forward with the relationship I know I would like to have with you, I must deserve your trust."

Marissa thought to herself, *my meditation will help me get through this, no matter how painful. I am one with the earth and all life forces around me. Nothing can destroy who I am.*

Then she said, "Please go on."

"In a way, I've been lying to you when I act ignorant about your mother. I know she is Ofelia Cruz, not Brigid Alvarez."

"How would you know such a thing?"

"I know because I was sent to Ireland to find her."

"By whom?"

"I can't tell you just yet, Marissa. What I can tell you is that I was hired, in my professional capacity as a private investigator, to locate Ofelia and find out what I could about her current life."

"So, your courtship of me has been a lie."

"No, it started out as a way to learn some things about Ofelia, but it was never about you. I mean, I was not investigating you. When we were matched, I thought it would help me to be around her daughter. It would perhaps give me access to Ofelia herself. As you know, that didn't happen; but my work for the client was accomplished when I located her."

"Are you still working for the client? Are you at liberty to tell me who it might be?"

"No, I am no longer working for them. As I said, it was a fairly simple assignment. I will ask if they have a problem with my telling you who hired me. Given the nature of the request, I don't even know whether they will be following up with Ofelia now they know where she is. It can't hurt to ask, but I am bound to keep it confidential until I have their consent. I hope you understand that it would greatly affect my ability to do my work if it got out that I reveal such information. I've told you this much because I don't want us to have secrets. I would hate for you to learn what I just told you from another source."

Marissa put her head in her hands. She was relieved Mateo wasn't ending their incipient relationship. She was happy he wanted to come clean with her. But now she had something else to worry about. Someone had discovered Ofelia's whereabouts and identity.

Lifting her head, she looked directly into Mateo's eyes,

"Do these people intend to harm my mother, Mateo?"

"I don't believe that is the case. I truly hope I can tell you more after I speak with my client, but I can assure you that the nature of their interest in finding Ofelia would indicate they wish her no harm."

"You know I'll have to tell her about this."

"Yes. And Marissa, I've taken the chance of telling you the truth, hoping it won't destroy our friendship. I promise I'll try to obtain permission to tell you what this has been about and who hired me. I completely understand your need to protect your mother, but am hoping you can trust me enough to take the next step."

"I do believe you, Mateo, but you must know you have put me in an awkward position with respect to my loyalty. What happens if you can't tell me?"

"I honestly don't know. I thought hard about telling you any of this. For me, it was just a job, and meeting you just happened. For me, they were not connected. I thought I could keep them separate but last night, as you began to tell me about your family, I came to realize it's all connected, and I could no longer keep it a secret from you. Having an honest relationship with you is so important."

"I believe what you've told me today, and hope you'll tell me more. But, at the moment, I feel emotionally drained and need to step away.

I'll wait to hear what your client says and, meanwhile, won't repeat what you've told me."

"I understand. I will do so as soon as possible. And Marissa, I am so sorry to cause you distress. I really do care very much."

"So do I."

As Mateo left, Marissa returned to her backyard meditation. This time, instead of seeking help to deal with not knowing what to expect, she needed a way to bring herself back into balance. As she allowed her mind to flow through her entire being, various thoughts ran parallel and crossed one another before they settled into words and complete sentences, two of which gelled. *I believe Mateo is telling me the truth. I can wait to share this information with Ofelia and Teri.*

When she stood up, Marissa was at peace with both of those thoughts, yet couldn't help musing on how odd it felt to be sharing personal feelings with Ofelia and Teri, a mother and sister who were basically new in her life. Although she felt relatively positive about their reunion with Ofelia, she had yet to completely come to terms with Ofelia's lies and life choices. Her feelings about her birth mother remained complex.

The sisters had spoken briefly a few days earlier, so Teri knew about Marissa's date with Mateo and would undoubtedly be interested in hearing how it went. However, she was currently on her way home to the United States. Marissa was relieved to have a few days to wait to hear from Mateo before telling Teri what she had learned.

Chapter 25

Teri arrived home on October 16th, the day before Marissa's date with Mateo. Caught up with her own priorities, she left Marissa a farewell voicemail message, but the sisters had otherwise been out of touch since she heard of the impending date.

During the days following her arrival home, Teri's thoughts were dominated by feelings of frustration because Jack showed no signs of leaving Michigan. While he spoke to her with affection over the phone, he seemed distant and uncertain of his ability to make any plans. As usual, Vanessa helped by getting Teri to focus on her work and accept that Jack needed her to understand his family had to be his first priority at the moment. Not having interacted with them at all made it difficult for Teri to envision Jack in a world where there was anything of equal importance to their life together.

Vanessa laughed, "I know, I know. We create lovely bubbles around ourselves when we're in love. As I have learned the hard way with Cliff, the minute a past relationship where the person feels they have a claim on your loved one enters the picture, the bubble becomes increasingly fragile."

"I get that, but it's still hard. So, how are things with Cliff's daughter Clarissa? Your Mediterranean honeymoon must have been a nice break from that drama."

"It was indeed. And Cliff and I had more than one conversation about balancing us with his family obligations. To be perfectly honest,

Clarissa is fine until she isn't. When she spends time with her mother, it all goes to shit. The other side of it is that she's pre-pubescent and seems to be bubbling with hormones." Vanessa sighed. "I've decided that it's just a few years, and we can handle that, right? Once she's an adult, she'll care more about her own life?"

Teri smiled at her friend, "Thank you for bringing me out of my funk. Not that your troubles make me feel good, but you remind me that we all have shit to deal with. Maybe this is just Jack's and my first test, and my side is about handling it well and not making his life more difficult than it already is. I hereby vow to be a better listener and not bug him either way. In any case, it's time for me to put my head down and take advantage of the rest of this free semester to move my dissertation research forward."

"Atta girl!"

Vanessa looked at her watch. "Speaking of school, I need to get over to the campus for a department meeting in a few, but can you quickly catch me up on your latest foray to Argentina? What did you think of your potential father? Miguel, is that his name?"

"Oh wow. I haven't even had a chance to thank you for caring for Gordon and the cats. I know it was short notice, but greatly appreciated."

"Not a problem, Teri. Now, about Argentina."

"Miguel Martínez…He seems like a nice man who's struggling a bit with memory and other health issues. Marissa and I are hoping to get blood from him to test whether he's genetically related to us."

"How will you do that? I mean, does he know you think he may be your father? Why would he share that information?"

"That's the frustration, Vanessa. We did not discuss paternity, but we WERE introduced to him as Ofelia's daughters. He saw the resemblance immediately and even thought Marissa was Ofelia when we first met. He remembered her fondly. Actually, we were surprised to hear him say he had seen her shortly before he went into hiding. That would have been in 1975. I've always assumed their relationship ended before Marissa and I were born in 1947 and that they never saw each other after that. As for the blood, we're hoping Juan Ignacio will help get a sample, but that's not a sure thing."

"What was your feel about Miguel? Did you feel he could be your father?"

"I don't know. The one thing that stuck in my head is that he's tall. Ofelia's short. Maybe Marissa and I got that tall gene from Miguel. And he has brown eyes like us. Ofelia's eyes are green. But otherwise, I didn't feel a particular connection. I mean, he's an Argentine gentleman. I may be too American to judge."

Vanessa headed for the door. "One step forward. You found your mother against all odds. Perhaps we need to bring the Ofelia Mystery Circle back to take advantage of our various brains."

"That's what Charlie said the other day."

"I want to hear all about Charlie, but I really need to get to my meeting. I'll give you a call later."

"Great, and thanks again for taking care of things here while I was away."

Seeing Vanessa out the door, Teri decided it was time to get off her butt and start moving on her preliminary dissertation proposal. With a new sense of determination, she headed to the Bateman College Library, where she spent several hours rediscovering there was very little written on the topic of third-culture kids. *That could be positive or negative for my research plan: if the literature is limited but rich, I could focus more energy on creating an original project; but if it's too limited, I may have trouble putting together a convincing proposal. Either way, I will have to dig further. It may just be that the topic hasn't reached academic journals, and I will have to expand my search to other types of source material. In any case, I'm done for the day.*

By the time she arrived home, Teri was ready to take off her shoes and plop down in front of the television with a glass of wine. It was starting to get dark outside, just in time for the five o'clock news. Then the phone rang.

Feeling comfortable in her chair, Teri was tempted to let the call go to voicemail. She could call whoever it was back at her leisure. Then it occurred to her that it might be Jack, so she got up to answer. It wasn't Jack, it was her older sister Pat. Teri immediately felt guilty she hadn't been in touch since returning from Ireland. As soon as she heard Pat's voice, she began to ramble.

"Oh my God, Pat, Hi. I'm so sorry I haven't called. I got back from Ireland a couple of weeks ago and had to take another quick trip to Buenos Aires. So much has been going on."

Pat laughed, "Don't worry about that. I wasn't calling to yell at you. I figured you would have a lot of catching up to do after three weeks away. Of course, I'm interested in hearing about your trip and time with Ofelia, but I actually called to share something I ran across you might find interesting."

"Something to do with the parents?"

Still angry at the deception that characterized her childhood, Teri had a problem with referring to Pete and Susan Addison as their shared parents but thought it was cold to speak of them as Pat's parents alone, so she referred to them as "the parents" rather than "our parents." She knew Pat would understand.

If Pat noticed, she didn't say anything. Instead, she went on with her reason for calling.

"This may be nothing, but I ran across a handwritten note on the back of a document I found in one of Dad's books. The paper was torn in half and folded into the shape of a bookmark. It looks very casually constructed. I would never have noticed it."

"What does it say? Why did it catch your attention?"

"To be perfectly honest, as I go through Mom and Dad's stuff since we've learned about their double life in Argentina, I keep an eye out for anything out of the ordinary. And for the most part, I've seen nothing."

"I suspect they were trained to be careful and not leave anything that would expose what they were doing. I'll bet the letters between Susan and Ofelia were a serious violation of the rules of the spy game."

"You were lucky to have two mothers who cared so much about you, Teri. It was to your benefit that they were willing to put themselves in danger with their coded messages. Otherwise, you and your friends would never have discovered the truth about your birth mother."

"But Pat, what was on the paper you found?"

"I honestly don't know what it means. It may or may not be anything, but if it is, it's definitely written in some kind of shorthand or code. It includes a string of letters. Some of the letters are capitalized, and some are in lowercase. I don't have a clue as to what they mean. What I can tell you for sure is that it was written by Dad. I know his handwriting, and he wrote it."

"What about the paper it's written on? What's on the other side? What's the book you found it in? What's on the page the marker was in?"

"Wow, Teri, you are quite the detective these days! It's in a copy of *Moby Dick*. I doubt I can figure out what page it was in, somewhere towards the end of the book. It never occurred to me to pay attention to that. The handwritten stuff is on the back of what looks like an old phone bill."

"It's my training. Anthropologists learn a lot from the context where things are found. Wait, I just thought of something. Is the phone bill from Argentina or the States? What's the date on the bill? This all sounds interesting, Pat. I'm trying to figure out how to have you send it to me safely."

"That's not a problem; I can send it to you by FedEx. That way, I can insure it and send it overnight. Do you want me to send the book too?"

"That would be perfect. Just let me know what it costs, and I'll reimburse you immediately."

"Don't be silly. I can afford it. I'm as interested as you to discover what it all means."

"Thank you for being such a good sister to me. And Pat, I have a quick question. Did you forget Spanish when we moved back to the States?"

"I did, and I didn't. I know you've been concerned about forgetting Spanish, but you have to remember it was your first language, along with English, but English was mostly spoken in our home. I learned Spanish as a second language. English was always my first language. I think those two processes use different parts of your brain."

"That's a really interesting way to think about it. It might just be that the part of my brain that could retain my first language wasn't used after we moved back to the States."

As Pat ended the call, Teri apologized to Chomsky for disturbing his rest. He had climbed onto her lap during the call, but she needed to go to the other side of the room to actually hang the phone up from her end. *These portable phones are handy, but I wish they could come up with one that doesn't need to be connected to its phone bed to stay charged.*

"Sorry Chom. Wow, this could be really interesting. I mean, it could be totally unconnected to Peter Addison's work or my life. But I'm still excited. I think I miss the Ofelia Mystery Circle, the fun of deciphering coded messages with my friends. Should I call Jack to tell him about it?"

Ultimately, Teri decided to wait to see what it was before sharing with Jack or anyone else. She felt sad but feared disturbing Jack. Before he left to help his parents, it would've been her first move, and Jack would have welcomed it. Now she felt the need to weigh their way of being together against his family's needs. She would wait, but first, she put her shoes back on and went out again…this time to pick up a candy bar. Chocolate was just what she needed to write the perfect letter to Jack.

Chapter 26

October 20, 1986

Dear Jack,

I started writing this a few days ago, and I know we've spoken on the phone since, so some of it is old news. But so much is going on. I will finish and catch you up to speed as of today, October 20th.

I recently returned from my trip to Argentina, and what a trip it was! I am so fortunate to have the money (and free time) to do all of this traveling. I don't question the expense because it has brought me closer to understanding who I am. At the same time, I find myself already missing you so much. No one else has the power to relieve me of my craziness, although Vanessa comes close sometimes.

I know you're consumed with caring for your family and hope you find your brother so he can take some of that burden from you. Not that you will ever call it a burden or stop being there throughout your father's hospital stay. I've decided to write instead of calling you as it seems like every time I do that, it's a bad time. And, of course, there is no pressure; just know that I love you and am thinking good thoughts and sending white light for a positive outcome for your dad.

So, my trip to Argentina was pretty amazing. First, I believe it brought Marissa and me closer, which makes me happy. By that, I mean she seems to be less guarded with me than before, and we agree on ways to move forward. Meeting Miguel Martínez was amazing and a real driver for both Marissa and me. He's a sweet, likable man, and Ofelia was right when she said we could be proud to have him as a father. Of course, that's something we may never learn one way or the other, but let me share the gut evidence. That's probably the wrong word because neither of us got a gut feeling about him. With such a short visit, he was hard to read. As Juan Ignacio had told us, Miguel is not well and seems to suffer from memory issues. However, he remembers Ofelia and recognizes our resemblance to her. In fact, when we first met him, he mistook Marissa for her. Physically, he's tall and has dark brown eyes like Marissa and me. You haven't met Ofelia, but she is quite short with green eyes. When we left, Marissa and I decided to look into finding a way to determine paternity. We spoke with a geneticist Marissa knows who told us there are blood tests that could come close. It's not simply the old ABO blood type comparison, but I guess even this test has a margin of error. The major block is getting a blood sample from Miguel. Juan Ignacio, ever protective of him and his privacy, says he might be able to help, but needs to think it over.

I only stayed in Argentina for a few days, spending two more with Marissa and a couple more with Juan Ignacio, who took me to the airport. I really enjoyed both visits and when I was at Marissa's, I got to spend a little time with Sylvita and Raoul, Ofelia's cousin, and her husband, who raised Marissa. I also got to meet Ofelia's cousin Che, who is VERY guarded. He tried to answer some of my questions. I think he is a kind man. It turns out that he was the guy who gave me a wounded bird in a paper bag when I was a kid. Not sure I ever told you about that. He said he and I served as couriers for Ofelia!

Now I'm home, hoping to get some work done on my dissertation proposal. I did a library search on third-culture kids and came up with very little, but this is a pretty new concept so it just may be that the best places to look are more casual than journal publications.

Oh, and I almost forgot, my sister Pat is sending me some writing she found in Pete Addison's things that looks coded.

Anyway, I will be busy but will never stop wishing you were here. I miss you.

Love,

Teri

Chapter 27

As she returned from mailing the letter to Jack, Teri praised herself for not being as pushy as she would've liked. She understood his need to be there for his parents but also wished he would include her, so they could operate and present themselves as a couple in all of their worlds. If this was a test, she was determined not to fail it. Once again, she collapsed in her chair, where she remained until she fell asleep.

Although a bit stiff when she woke up the next morning, Teri was raring to go. Energized, she had things to do. Time to move forward with her dissertation proposal. Teri's mind settled on Grace, the woman she had met on the plane to Ireland who knew and identified with the third-culture kid concept. Perhaps Grace could lead her to other sources. Armed with her cup of coffee, Teri dug out Grace's contact information and dialed the number. Grace answered the phone immediately.

"Hi, Grace. This is Teri Addison. Do you remember me from our conversation about third-culture kids on the flight to Dublin last month?"

"Oh yes, Teri, of course, I remember you. I still feel like I just got off the plane and have been running around like a chicken with its head cut off since. Oh, that's a terrible metaphor. I apologize."

"I completely understand that feeling. Do you have a minute now? I'll get right to the point. I'm hoping you can help me locate anything that might qualify as a written source related to TCKs."

"I'm not sure I can help with sources. I know not much has been published about third-culture kids, and what I've seen shows we're still missing a clear definition."

Puzzled, Teri asked, "Doesn't it refer to people who spend their childhoods in a culture that's different from that of their parents? I was under the impression the third culture is really the culture of childhood, which can be different from the adult culture in different countries."

"I think that's true, but there are so many variables, and I know there are arguments over who qualifies and who doesn't. Like in some cases, people think the child has to spend a certain amount of time in that position to qualify. And there are definitely differences in the experiences of children who only spend their very early years in those second cultures, like you, from third-culture kids who spend their entire childhood, or later childhood."

"Grace, I've been planning to make this the topic of my doctoral dissertation and figured there would be some existing literature to hang my hypotheses on. Do you think that's out there?"

"I don't know Teri. It sounds, to me, like a frustrating ride, but all dissertation research should be hard, I guess."

"I'm starting to think I may be too close to this to be objective. I mean, I'm drawn to the topic because I am pretty sure I qualify as a TCK."

"Okay, but what do you want to learn about the phenomenon?"

"To be perfectly honest, I want to explore what parts of an adult's approach to life can be explained as a result of being a third-culture kid."

"You want to determine causality?"

"I guess so. I hadn't thought about it that way."

"Honestly, Teri, I think you're going to have trouble with that. I mean, just in your situation, aren't there a million causes for how you end up being as an adult? How do you sort them from the cross-cultural circumstances of your childhood? Also, if you look at third-culture kids who spend only a short period in that situation, how do you compare them with third-culture kids who spend their whole childhood there? I suspect you would have to go into a lot of general child development literature to even get started."

Teri was silent for what seemed like a long time. Grace continued,

"I don't want to discourage you, but maybe you can work backward and begin with a personality characteristic you see as defining for you. Not that I'm suggesting your dissertation is a self-analysis project, but it could possibly give you a way of thinking about whether the TCK experience was causal."

"Can I ask this question of you, Grace? How would you describe the most notable outcome of your experience as a third-culture kid?"

"Just off the top of my head, I can come up with two things: my interest in being drawn to people who are different from me and my comfort with being in unfamiliar places. I've always been adventurous and eager to try new things. I believe my childhood experiences prepared me to deal with cultural differences and not be afraid."

"I think I share some of that, but, well, are you comfortable in your own skin? Do you ever feel like an outsider?"

"Not really, Teri. But when I think about it, I have to give my parents credit. I always felt secure with them no matter where we lived."

"One more thing. Have you had trouble remembering the different languages you learned in the other countries where you spent your childhood years?"

"If you're asking me if I'm multi-lingual, the answer is no. I was never anywhere long enough, but I do think I have a broader ability to learn how to pronounce new languages than a lot of people I've known over the years. I've often wondered if I learned how to use my mouth and throat in a lot of ways as a young child. But I certainly don't remember much unless I'm using a language routinely."

"Thank you, Grace, you've given me a lot to think about."

"Glad I could be of help. Good luck with your research, and please let me know what you come up with."

"Will do. I think I'll be making some important decisions soon, thanks to your help."

After hanging up the phone, Teri decided to take a walk with Gordon in Josh Woods. She had always done her best thinking there, and Grace had stimulated her focus.

Once in the woods, Gordon ran off to visit his favorite spots before joining her as she climbed the rocks to reach her log.

This could be a painful exercise, but I know the negative things that define me: my fear of abandonment and my inability to trust other people completely. And you don't need a deep psychological analysis to get at causality for these feelings. I never felt loved by the Addisons, especially as compared with their other children, their real children, as I came to learn. But they kept me and brought me to the States, where I experienced what I thought was a typical American childhood. I was so young; why would I feel abandoned? I wasn't abused or neglected; why would I stop trusting them?

Teri sat on her log for a long time and tried to relive scenes from her early life. As she thought about that time, her memories were mostly about her relationship with Ofelia and her friends, especially Juan Ignacio. Where were Susan and Pete and her four older siblings? The other kids were so much older than her; they were in school all day and playing with their friends the rest of the time. Pete Addison was always at work and if he had any free time with the children, he spent it doing boy things with his sons. Susan was also working and being with other people. Teri couldn't remember being included in family events; she was always told she was too young. She was always left with Ofelia. That was why she didn't have family memories. In retrospect, this made sense. She was Ofelia's child, not the Addison's. Then, the Addisons moved to the States without Ofelia, and Teri always felt alone; but by that time, she didn't expect anything different. The habits had already been established.

I get all of that, but was I thinking in such sophisticated terms like that I had been abandoned and had to take care of myself? I don't think so. I think I was always terrified they would drop me off on a street corner and leave me there. I'm not sure that isn't what I fear, at some level, today.

Putting herself into that sad headspace, Teri closed her eyes and immediately had a flashback to a moment when she was about five years old when they were still in Buenos Aires. She overheard Pete and Susan arguing over what they would do with her if they had to leave Argentina suddenly. Pete argued for leaving her behind. He used the word expendable. Teri wondered what that word meant but was afraid to ask. Susan said they couldn't do that, and Pete slapped her across the face. He said they would do whatever he chose to do and that she didn't have the power to change that.

Oh my God, I remember that. It wasn't the first time I saw him hit Susan, but it scared me to death to think I would be abandoned. I ran to find Ofelia and asked her if I was expendable and what that meant. She took me in her arms and told me she would never abandon me, but the following year, she did exactly that. At the age of six, I learned not to trust anyone.

Teri opened her eyes suddenly. Gordon had come up and was looking at her with his head on her knee. "I do trust you, Gordon." She said aloud, then looked to see if anyone was around to hear her.

But in retrospect, that was probably the year Ofelia planted all of the clues, along with Susan, so that we could reconnect in the future. And we almost didn't! I was too young and Susan was probably too scared, but she and Ofelia did care enough about me. They deserve my retrospective trust. I'll probably never completely recover my ability to trust or to worry about being abandoned, but these came from my unique life experience, not because I was a third-culture kid. I need to come up with another dissertation topic.

Teri breathed a sigh of relief as those words went through her mind. She had to focus on what was in front of her now. She was going to speak with her advisor about taking more time.

Chapter 28

Walking home from the woods, Teri was surprised at how relieved she felt. She had been unaware of how her academic obligation had been adding stress to everything else she was dealing with. She had somehow come to believe checking that off her list by just doing it was the answer, but that wasn't how it worked this time. No, she needed time and clarity to come up with a better dissertation topic, one that would give her a break from the complexity of her life history. One part of being an anthropologist she had always enjoyed was that it covered topics that had previously been foreign to her. Her dissertation research should be totally intriguing because she knew from what other people had told her over the years that it was probably the most finitely judged piece of work she would ever have to produce.

No matter how much Teri wished things were different, she was still too immersed in sorting out her childhood issues, and they were where her intellectual energy would be focused until she learned more. She had to take the chance that Rosalie would understand and continue to support her. She was pretty certain she could continue her teaching job at Bateson. They liked her there and would probably have to pay more if she had the doctorate anyway.

With these thoughts in mind, Teri was happy to see the FedEx package from Pat had arrived and was sitting on the main table in the apartment building foyer. Upstairs in her apartment, Teri tore into it, remembering the excitement of opening the box from Juan Ignacio containing their childhood treasures he sent her last year. Of course this was different, but Teri still hoped it would contribute to uncovering some of the mystery surrounding what went down in Argentina.

As Pat had described, the package included a copy of *Moby Dick* and a strip of folded paper on which someone had written letters and numbers. According to Pat, the handwriting was definitely that of Pete Addison, and Teri couldn't argue with her assessment. It also included a note from Pat describing where in the book she had first located the bookmark, or at least approximately where it was in the story. Teri had never read *Moby Dick*. All she knew was that it was about a sea captain's obsession with a whale and took place in the South Atlantic Ocean. The paper's location in the book would have no significance for her. She remembered Pete as a man who loved those old male-oriented classics. And the writing made little sense, although there had to be a way to decode it. Trying not to be discouraged, Teri thought of the Ofelia Mystery Circle again. Vanessa and Cliff were in town, but as far as she knew, Charlie was back in California, and, of course, Jack wasn't available.

I wonder if I can share this with everyone long-distance? I can at least bring it up with Vanessa.

Putting the paper aside, Teri called her advisor. Her decision to put off coming up with a new dissertation topic would weigh on her until she had a chance to explain her reasoning to Rosalie Osborne. While she feared being told they couldn't wait any longer, that the university and Anthropology department had rules about such things, she felt ready to take her chances. Her sanity had to take precedence and there was just too much else occupying her mind. Rosalie answered the phone but was in the middle of a meeting and couldn't talk. They made a date to speak later in the evening.

At least I've taken a step. I wish I could've gotten this conversation over with right away. So be it. What can I do to make the day go by faster?

The answer was that she could take a walk to Anneke's, her favorite deli, where all the food was comfort food. It was mid-afternoon, and Anneke's was pretty empty, so she and Anneke actually had a little opportunity to chat. Just hearing Anneke's voice gave her comfort. Teri returned home carrying boxes of homemade macaroni and cheese, coleslaw, and a double chocolate brownie. Teri smiled as she thought that there was enough for at least two meals.

As she approached her apartment door, her phone began to ring and she rushed to pick it up. It was Marissa.

"Hola Teri, I hope this is a good time for you."

"Hi Marissa, it's always a good time when you call. I have some news that might interest you."

"As do I. Let me start."

"Okay."

"I will start by telling you I recently learned that Mateo is a private detective who was in Ireland in search of Ofelia."

"What?!"

"Yes, it was not a chance encounter at the Matchmaker's Ball, but as it turned out, he was not using me to find her. His job was to find her and report back to his client, and that was all."

"It was just a coincidence that you two were matched up? That's too much of a coincidence!"

"It wasn't a coincidence that we were both there, but the matching up had mostly to do with our interviews, and both being Argentine. Anyway, I've gotten to know him and trust what he has told me."

Teri heard something in Marissa's voice that caused her to slow down. "Did he tell you who the client was?"

"Yes, he was hired by Paolo Fuente's ex-wife to locate Ofelia. She had come across a notable bequest in his will for Ofelia and wanted to know who she was. When they couldn't locate her in Argentina, they reached out to Mateo's international private investigation agency."

"Does Ofelia know about any of this?"

"Mateo is no longer working for the ex-wife and doesn't know what she's done with this information. He assured me that she did not intend to harm Ofelia but, as I mentioned before, wanted to know who she was."

"And, I presume she now knows Ofelia has changed her identity and moved to another country. Wouldn't that increase her curiosity? Wouldn't that place Ofelia in danger? I don't like the sound of this."

"I agree Teri, which is why I bring this up to you. I'm also curious as to why Paolo would include Ofelia in his will. Do you think he wonders if we are his children? I think we need to tell Ofelia."

"As far as I can tell, Paolo has played no role in our lives, but he could certainly care about Ofelia. From what Che told us, he seems to have been involved in her life, at least in the background. In any case, I was going to reach out to her about Tomás's burial. I can speak with her about this as well. Oh, that reminds me, my sister Pat sent me what looks like a note written in code she found in Pete Addison's effects. I was thinking of asking Ofelia if she's familiar with the code from her days in the underground. I'll try to reach her later. There's so much going on. My head is dizzy!"

"I appreciate your making that call, Teri. I look forward to hearing what she tells you. Oh, by the way, has Juan Ignacio made a decision about obtaining a blood sample from Miguel?"

"If he has, he hasn't told me. I know it's jumping to conclusions with no evidence but just having Paolo in the picture now makes me even more interested in determining our paternity. I promise I'll get back to you as soon as I speak with Ofelia. I will try calling her as soon as I hang up."

As promised, Teri called Ofelia and immediately announced that she had a number of topics to discuss.

"Are these serious topics I will need to think over?"

"Yes, most of them are serious topics."

"Would it be possible for you to come here for another visit to have this discussion? I would prefer to speak about important issues in person."

Although she understood Ofelia's need for secrecy, Teri hadn't considered traveling to Ireland again so soon. She decided to put off making the travel arrangements for at least a week. Looking at her pets and thinking about leaving them again, she realized they weren't the only ones who needed to experience some normalcy. She was honestly beginning to miss her old routines.

This is so funny. I wish I was back teaching and walking in the woods. I, who have always been drawn to new adventures and change, miss the structure of my previous life.

She told Ofelia she would get back to her once her plans were in place, but she had a few things to do at home before she could get away.

Newly determined to slow down her brain, Teri poured herself a glass of wine and sat down to watch the nightly news on television. Almost surprised she had been out of touch for such a long time, she decided to pay close attention and learned that on the previous day, the U.S. Government had shut down due to disputes between President Reagan and the House of Representatives; Keith Richards of the Rolling Stones organized a concert to honor rock and roll legend Chuck Berry; and the U.S. performed a Nuclear Test at the Nevada Test Site. Meanwhile, the World Series was about to begin and the Senate approved an immigration bill prohibiting hiring of illegal aliens but offering immunity to illegals who entered the country prior to 1982.

Not feeling any calmer, Teri switched the channel to watch a couple of sitcom reruns as she ate her deli food. She could feel Gordon and the cats relax around her. When she went to bed that night, she slept well. She had not even noticed that Rosalie didn't call.

Well-rested the following morning, Teri decided that speaking with Rosalie was the one thing she needed to do to clear her current to-do list.

Rosalie apologized, "I'm sorry I didn't return the call last night. There's a lot going on here, and all meetings seem to take forever. I'm glad you picked up the ball."

"I'm not sure that's what I've been doing, Rosalie. I'm calling to tell you I need more time. I did some research on third-culture kids and have come to the conclusion it's not a good study for me."

"Oh?"

"Two reasons: there just isn't much out there about it so not much to hang my hat on. But more importantly, I don't think I can be objective. I could be off base, but I've come to the conclusion I can't sort that from other parts of my early childhood experience."

"Do you have another topic in mind?"

"That's the thing, Rosalie, I don't and I don't think I can give anything the attention it requires until more of my family stuff is resolved. I'm just too caught up to concentrate on something new. So, I'm wondering if I can get an extension."

"I don't know, Teri, you've been extending your dissertation research for a long time. I want to be supportive, but I will probably have to pull some strings."

"I understand and am willing to pay the piper, but I really can't do it now."

"I'll do what I can. I've always believed you would be an asset to our discipline."

"Thank you."

Teri hung up the phone, broke down, and cried. Realizing she may have just destroyed her chance to accomplish the goal she had spent so many years pursuing, earning her Ph.D. in Anthropology, she was overwhelmed with a feeling of devastation.

What am I doing? It feels like finding the truth about my childhood, finding my mother and sister, will never be enough. It's so much work, and I feel increasingly overwhelmed and lonely. Even Jack is no longer with me.

Her moment of wallowing in self-pity notwithstanding, Teri went back to her typical way of dealing with things—using her logical mind to solve a puzzle. Picking up the phone again, she dialed Vanessa's number.

"Hey Nessa, any interest in reviving the Ofelia Mystery Circle?"

PART 4

October 31 – November 17, 1986

Chapter 29

"Thank you for meeting me at the airport, Ofelia. I feel as if I've been in the air a lot recently. And the rest of my time has been spent either here or in Argentina!"

"I understand and appreciate that you were able to make these travel arrangements so quickly. Was it just ten days ago when you consented to come here? I'm the one who has to thank you, Teresa. You've launched a new chapter in all of our lives. And I'm thrilled to be with you again so soon. I know there are many important subjects to cover, and I may be as anxious as you to address your questions and, despite all odds, bring our lives to a normal place, whatever that means. I take responsibility for our family's difficulties. I was the one who started it all when I was a young girl."

"Ofelia, you were exactly that, a young girl. Now we're all adults with life skills we didn't have all those years ago. I believe that, together, we can pull ourselves out of whatever's left to be resolved."

Settling down with a cup of tea, Teri said,

"I don't think I ever expected to visit Ireland in my life, and now I will have been here twice in one month!"

Ofelia laughed, "Life does throw curveballs, doesn't it?"

"It sure does, like you using that term, where on earth did you pick up that phrase?"

"I don't know. Words and phrases just pop into my head sometimes. You know, I lived with the American Addisons for six years. I probably learned a lot of American slang there, and now in Northern Ireland for the past eight years where British and Irish slang probably slipped in. Who knows?"

"You have lived a rich life, Ofelia."

"Yes, I suppose that's true. My mother would marvel at all I've experienced. So, what do you want to talk about? What do you want to tell me? I know you've been back to Buenos Aires. Have you met Sylvita and Raoul? Have you met Che?"

"I have met them all and feel proud to be part of this family. They are fine, caring people. I envy Marissa for having them in her life throughout her childhood."

Ofelia looked sad. "I know, and I'm sorry you got stuck with the Addisons. I guess that's the luck of the draw. Another Americanism, I believe. The other side of this coin was that I was there to play a large role in your early life, whereas I hardly saw Marissa."

"I feel fortunate to have had you in my early childhood. I never felt the Addisons cared much for me. I used to think it was because I came along so much later than their real children, and they weren't interested in raising another one. You were the only one who really cared, and when I lost you when we moved to the States, I felt truly alone."

"I know, I wish I could make it up to you, but I comforted myself with the belief that Susan cared for you. You would never have found me this past year if that wasn't the case. She and I established our communication codes hoping the world would be a better, safer place in the future and we could be reunited. Unfortunately, she died before Pete, so you had to be the great detective."

"Did Pete hate me? Why couldn't she tell him?"

"Pete was a ruthless man, which is probably why he was so valuable to the American and British secret services. He took you in to raise you as part of his family because that was how they could quickly establish themselves in Buenos Aires and, honestly, because including me in their household was part of the deal struck by the Argentine resistance movement. You and I provided him with cover and access he would've had trouble getting otherwise. In the wake of the World War, all foreigners were suspect, often for good reason. You know, of course, Perón welcomed many Nazis who escaped Germany after Hitler lost the War."

"I've thought for a long time that the mean German man who lived next door to us was a Nazi."

"You were correct. Al found Pete and Susan a home in that neighborhood precisely to be near him. He was an important Nazi, and with our help, the Allies found and arrested him for his war crimes. It was a big deal when he was taken out. Unfortunately, it was so big, it focused attention on the Addisons and Perón's people became suspicious. That was why the Addisons had to leave the country so suddenly."

"I never knew that. I never knew why we moved to the United States then, but I was only a little girl. Was that when you and Susan began to set up your secret communication?"

"Yes."

"I'm impressed with how complex it was, how many paths you created to sharing information, my first-grade reading book, the calendar, even the treasure box Juan Ignacio and I buried in the back yard. I've been wondering, you dug that up, added a few things, and reburied it didn't you?"

"Yes. I wanted Susan and you to find these things and understand that you had not been forgotten."

"I appreciate that. It was tough after we moved to the States. I always thought both Pete and Susan could've cared less about me. I'm glad to learn she cared."

"Susan was not a strong woman. Pete totally dominated her, so she had to do things he disapproved of on the sly."

"I recently had a flashback of overhearing them arguing. Pete said he wanted to leave me behind in Argentina, that I was expendable. You might remember when that happened because I ran to you and asked you what expendable meant. I was crying because I saw him hit Susan when she argued with him. I know I had seen him hit her before, but this scared me because they were arguing about me."

"I do remember, Teri. That was shortly before Susan and I started talking about making sure you remained safe and establishing a way to communicate. Pete wasn't a particularly nice man, but in the end, he probably saved my life when he worked with Al to get me out of Argentina during President Videla's Dirty War when I was clearly in danger."

"He was involved with that? I didn't know. And I have to give him credit; he never disowned me and left me as much money as his other children. Without that, I wouldn't be here now."

"I believe Pete was a man of his generation who did the best he could with what he had to work with. So, let's change the subject; what do you want to tell me?"

Teri looked at Ofelia seriously, "I'm sorry, I will need to start with sad news of your brother Tomás. He has recently passed away."

Ofelia sat up straight in her chair and closed her eyes.

"It's been so long since I heard from him or about him. He lived a very violent life. Please tell me, how did he die?"

"I don't know the details, but he was murdered in prison."

"Of course, how else? I always expected him to come to a sad end and at the same time, hoped he would care enough to rescue me from my mother. I have fond memories of our early childhood together. It was me and Tomás against the world. Then he left and became enamored with the dark side of Perón. Even when we all learned Perón was as crooked as the rest and didn't care about us decamisados, the poor people he called his shirtless ones, Tomás used his fists and weapons to protect that man. But still, I feel sad for my brother. May he rest in peace."

"Sylvita and Che want to bury his remains with the family. Che has apparently claimed them. They want to know if you will attend the funeral."

Ofelia put her head in her hands, then lifted it and said, "I would like to say goodbye to my brother and be with my family. It may be possible, but I will need to check with Al Watson. Before Al opened the door to our reunion, I would have said there was no way. Now I think he must believe the world is safer for me, but I haven't asked him that question."

"Is that something you will do now?"

"I can try. I can't speak about how Al and I communicate, but I can tell you there's a formal process we haven't strayed from since I came to Ireland. I have not spoken directly with him since I arrived here."

"Not in eight years? Wow!" Teri paused, "Okay, let me move on to another topic you may find interesting."

Ofelia smiled, "You already have my attention."

"Remember Mateo?"

"The man Marissa was matched with in Lisdoonvarna?"

"Yes. It turns out he is a private investigator who was hired to find you."

"What?! How do you know this? This could be dangerous."

"We know this because he and Marissa have fallen in love, and he told her so there would be no secrets between them."

"I'm trying to imagine such a relationship. Why haven't I heard about this? Who hired him to find me?"

"Well, from what Marissa told me, he was hired by Paolo Fuente's former wife because she discovered Paolo has included a generous bequest to you in his will. She hired Mateo's private investigation firm to find out who you are. He discovered Ofelia Cruz disappeared from Argentina in 1978 and that you have been living in Northern Ireland as Brigid Alvarez."

"All of this shocks me. So, it wasn't an accident that Mateo came into my room at the B and B in Oranmore. I'm assuming Paolo is still alive? But why would he include me in his will? Why haven't these people contacted me?"

"It's my best guess that it might be too soon. I mean, if Paolo's ex-wife was snooping around in his private papers, she might not want him to know. Mateo assured Marissa the wife isn't interested in harming you."

"Yes, of course, but her knowing who and where I am opens up the possibility that I can be found by other people who do not wish me well. I will definitely need to speak with Al about this."

Ofelia started to stand up, then saw an expression on Teri's face that indicated she wasn't finished.

"Is there more?"

Teri stood up and walked toward the bedroom where she had dropped her bags. "Just one more thing."

She took out the strip of paper with Pete Addison's writing and returned to the living room.

"This may be something or nothing. It looks like it's written in code, but I've had no luck playing around with it and wondered if you can figure it out."

Teri had copied the numbers and letters to another piece of paper but handed the original to Ofelia.

Ofelia glanced at the paper. "I have no idea, Teri. It looks like a model number you might find on the back of a television or something like that. But let me take a closer look. You never know."

Putting the paper aside, Ofelia changed the subject,

"How long can you stay here? It usually takes a few days for me to contact Al Watson and I will have to work some of the time, but you're welcome to stay as long as you like."

"If you don't mind, I would like to stay until you know whether you'll be able to attend Tomás' funeral so that can be planned. I'm also interested in hearing what Al tells you about whether you're safe to return to Argentina. Do you think he'll reveal why he opened the door for us to be reunited? And to be perfectly honest, I want to be with you when the family comes together."

"You're planning another visit to Argentina?"

"I want to be part of our family."

Chapter 30

As it turned out, Teri didn't have to wait long for Ofelia to meet with Al. As far as he was concerned, things were falling into place nicely.

Al knew he had launched a new chapter in the Ofelia story when he gave the twins her contact information. He had subsequently heard from his colleague Brian Mullin that Ofelia had brought her daughters to the Matchmaker's Ball, and they were spending a few weeks together in Ireland. Learning of their visit, Al was not surprised when Ofelia requested a face-to-face meeting, the first after all these years. She was undoubtedly hoping to hear his assurance that it would be safe for her to return to Argentina.

While Ofelia had played a small role in Al's ongoing secret service activities in Ireland, mostly as a courier, he had been careful not to use her for anything of major importance. He didn't know her well, and although she had been an effective underground agent in Argentina, he wasn't sure she would be loyal to Britain in opposition to the Argentine interest in the Falkland Islands, or as they stubbornly insisted on calling them, Las Islas Malvinas. Britain had rightfully won the war in 1982, and most of the island's inhabitants were British citizens, but many Argentines refused to acknowledge their loss, and it continued to be a contentious subject. While the Argentine underground worked closely with the British and American secret services during and after World War II, they weren't on the same page with respect to the Falklands. As far as the Argentine underground was concerned, they were still at war.

Although his meeting with Ofelia was his only reason for being there, Al lied that he had other pressing business in Belfast and arranged to meet her there in two days. Hanging up the phone, he called Brian into the office. Brian was the one person he worked with who had gotten to know Ofelia over the past few years. Since they were once selected as king and queen of the Matchmaker's Ball, there was never any question about their association.

Brian stepped into Al's office to find him packing a briefcase.

"What's up, Al? How can I help you?"

"I have to finish some things around here immediately so I can get to Belfast to meet with your friend Brigid, AKA Ofelia Cruz, the day after tomorrow. I'm hoping you can join us."

"Sure, Al, but what's going on? Have you stopped avoiding face-to-face meetings with her? Oh, does this have to do with your getting her together with her long-lost daughters?"

"That's definitely part of it. Sit down, and I'll explain. I think I may have found a way to obtain information about the identities of one or more of the Falkland Island traitors."

"The Falklands haven't been part of my portfolio. Who are the Falkland Island traitors?"

"Okay, let me catch you up. For a long time, we've had intelligence that there are documents identifying British traitors living in the Falklands who work undercover with the Argentines to undermine and weaken the Falkland government and its ties to Great Britain. It's well-known that former president Videla started the Falklands War to distract his people from their failing economy. He lost the war and the presidency, but as with the criminal Nazis who were allowed by Perón to hide in Argentina, the government has so far succeeded in protecting the Falkland Island traitors' identities."

"Is your source reliable?"

"I think so. My source is a Peronista I paid well. He told me he had seen the documents in the possession of a former friend and colleague of Perón named Miguel Martínez. Martínez disappeared in 1975 after his family was murdered by Videla's people."

"What does this have to do with Ofelia? Does she have a connection with Miguel Martínez?"

"Exactly, a very close historical connection. She was once Martínez' mistress, and he is the likely father of the twins."

"Ah, now some of this is coming together. You reconnected her with her daughters, who you think may connect you with their father."

"Bingo! But I have to be very careful. If either Ofelia or her daughters know of his whereabouts, they would probably not be willing to share that information with anyone. Martínez has been in hiding for the past eleven years, and people on both sides would like to find him. He was close to Perón for many years and undoubtedly has access to secrets Perón's followers and enemies, who still hold power in Argentina, would like to control."

"I'm assuming you won't be bringing his name up in your meeting with Ofelia."

"You are correct. Ofelia called this meeting, not me. She wants to know if she can safely return to Argentina. It's my understanding that her brother, a long-time follower of the most violent Peronistas, was recently murdered in prison. When we opened the door to her meeting her daughters, we gave her a taste of the possibility that it would be safe for her to return to Argentina. Her desire to be with her family could ignite that hope at this sad time. She has trusted me to keep her safe so far. I believe I can motivate her to go."

"Are you saying you can guarantee her safety if she returns to Argentina now?"

"Brian, you know I can't guarantee anyone's safety at any time, especially in a politically volatile country. I do believe there is greater stability under the current president, Alfonsín, than there was under Videla, who was determined to wipe out anyone he saw as a threat, such as Ofelia and the whole underground community. I don't want to see her harmed, but my purpose for sending her back is selfish. I want to find Miguel Martínez, and I believe if he's alive, following these women is my best chance of locating him. It may be a long shot, but at the moment, it's the only shot I have. I've been looking for those documents for a while now. This is the closest I've gotten."

"Why do you want me at the meeting with Ofelia?"

"I know you're fond of her, Brian, and I'm thinking you could go along to Argentina as my promise to her she won't be in danger, and you'll be around to protect her."

"To be her bodyguard!? I can't imagine that will be reassuring to her."

"I'm thinking more of her "backup"—just tell her you'll be in the country, and she can call on you if something comes up. That gives us an excuse for you to be there. Of course, you'll watch her when she doesn't know you're watching."

"Don't you have anyone in Argentina to do this, Al? It's not my territory. My Spanish is rocky, and I've never even been to the country."

"I do know someone there who might help, but at the moment, you're the only one who's up to speed on this. Listen, just come to the meeting with Ofelia and decide then. Okay?"

"Okay. But will you tell me who your in-country help is in case something comes up?"

"I'm hesitant to bring him into this. He's a prominent Argentine from a wealthy family with deep historical roots. I think his ancestry in Argentina goes back to the early 19th Century when local strongmen called caudillos ruled the provinces. These folks are Argentine aristocracy. This man has had access to the inner sanctums of every Argentine government and has played a serious role in helping us accomplish our goals. Still, he only helps when he sees what we're doing as being in his country's interest. He's a profound patriot but, at the same time, an independent thinker. I believe that's one reason he has never run for office. He clearly prefers to participate in the background and stay out of politics. His name is Paolo Fuentes. I got to know him during the first Perón administration. He's a very powerful guy."

"Where does he stand on the Falklands?"

"Haven't asked and don't think I will. I don't ever want to cross this guy; he's just too valuable an asset. So, push comes to shove, I'm hoping we can accomplish our goal of getting hold of the Falkland traitor documents without bringing Paolo into the picture."

"You don't think he'll find out what you're doing?"

"I'm sure he will find out, but unless we step on his toes too hard, he'll let us be, or he'll find a way to thwart us. I suspect Paolo would like to know where Miguel Martínez is hiding as much as us."

"Then maybe you can trade that information?"

"You're jumping way ahead, Son, but yeah, that has crossed my mind."

Chapter 31

As Ofelia told Teri, she didn't completely trust Al, or anyone else for that matter. However, she knew Al could make things happen for her if he saw it as advantageous to his agenda, whatever that might be at a given time. Ofelia walked into the meeting with this in mind, and the knowledge that she had a few things, bits of information, he might be interested in. Once they were eye to eye, she would decide what to share and what to hold back.

Ofelia was already in the hotel room when Al and Brian arrived. If she was surprised to see Brian, she didn't reveal that reaction. She acted as if this was a normal get-together. Al was impressed. He'd been told Ofelia was a good actress, but her lack of affect came across as a kneejerk response. He almost regretted not using her more during her time in Northern Ireland.

"Thank you for agreeing to meet on such short notice, Al."

"I was going to be here anyway, but I'm glad to be of service and am anxious to hear what you want from me."

As she watched him say these words, Ofelia knew without a doubt that he was lying. Why would he wonder? But she could play this game too.

"Well, I guess I have two items on my agenda. First, I'm interested in why you opened the door to connecting me with my daughters. I've been assuming it's because of the new Argentine administration that doesn't care about me and the work I did to undermine Perón. I'm assuming you believe it's safe for me to return to my home and have a relationship with my family. Is this correct?"

Al smiled. "Of course. I would never have opened that door if I thought you or they were still in danger. But you know, I wasn't the one who opened the door; your daughters figured things out. Very intelligent young ladies; take after their mother. But to be perfectly honest, I have no idea how they found me, let alone my connection with your disappearance."

"I don't know exactly either, Al. But as you say, they are very impressive women."

"So, to answer your question, I do believe it's safer for you to return to Argentina now the Alfonsín administration is in place and Videla, with his disgusting Dirty War, is out of power. Are you interested in going back there? I've been under the impression you've settled into your new life here comfortably."

"Yes, it's been alright, but it's not my home. And, as you are probably aware, my brother Tomás recently passed away, and I would like to be with my family for his funeral."

"My condolences, Ofelia. I didn't know of his passing. Of course, I understand why you want to share this sad time with your family. I know you've been in touch with your daughters." Smiling at Brian, he added, "Brian tells me they are both quite charming. Have you been in direct contact with other members of your family?"

"Thank you. I agree that they are both charming and intelligent. But to answer your question, I have not had direct contact with anyone besides my daughters. I've been looking forward to your assurance that they will remain safe from harm."

"Of course. So, is there a date set for the funeral?"

"I believe it will be set when the family hears of my availability."

"Well, as Americans like to say, as far as I'm concerned, you're free to go anytime. Would you like my office to make travel arrangements? Are you thinking about moving back permanently right away or making two trips, one for the funeral and another for the move?"

Ofelia scratched her head. "I think I would prefer to do this in two trips. We'd like to bury my brother within the next few weeks, and it will take more time than that to arrange for the permanent move."

"We can make those arrangements, the first trip next week? The following week?"

"Give me a week to tell my employers, but perhaps late next week would work. How about November 13th? I'll need to make arrangements with my family as well. I can't tell you how happy this makes me." Ofelia laughed nervously. "I'm not sure how I will adjust to not fearing for my safety."

"Brian, would you be available to escort Ofelia to Argentina during this time frame?"

Brian nodded, "Anything for my queen."

Acting as if this were a new thought, Al said, "Perhaps you could stick around for a while after Ofelia arrives to get the lay of the land."

Turning to Ofelia, he added, "He wouldn't have to be in your way, Ofelia, but could serve as a safety back-up in case you need it."

Standing up, Ofelia smiled, "Sure, it would be nice to have you as backup, Brian. And Al, please let me know about the travel arrangements as soon as possible, and I will pack my bags."

As she opened the door to leave, Ofelia's mind raced with all the lies Al had just told her. *Teri and Marissa would never have found me if he hadn't given them my phone number; of course, he knew Tomás had died in prison; and why does he want Brian to follow me to Argentina? These are petty lies, so what's really going on? If it's about my safety, why now? Alfonsín has been in power for almost five years. No, this has to have something to do with wanting me there, but what can that be?*

On the spot, Ofelia decided to do a little of her own snooping. "Before I go, do you know anything about a fellow named Mateo Roca?"

"Name doesn't ring a bell. Who is he?"

"Brian, you may remember him from Lisdoonvarna. He was the man my daughter Marissa was matched with there."

"Oh yes, the Argentine. Seemed like a nice fella."

"Marissa apparently agrees and has entered into a romantic relationship with him. But she has recently discovered that he was there to find me."

"And accidentally fell in love with your daughter?"

"I know it sounds fishy. I don't know the details, but she discovered he's a private investigator who was hired by Paolo Fuentes' former wife because they found a copy of his will that left me some money. Do you know anything about this? I know you and Paolo worked together to get me out of the country back in 1978. Are you still in touch with him?"

Al looked surprised by this news and said as much.

"I haven't heard much from Paolo recently and have never heard of this Mateo. I wonder if Paolo knows his ex-wife has done this. It's been a while since we were in touch."

"Well, I must be going. Thank you again for meeting me on such short notice, Al. I look forward to hearing about my travel plans. It was nice seeing you outside of Lisdoonvarna, Brian. I guess I'll be seeing you in Argentina!"

As she walked out the door, Ofelia thought, *At least he isn't involved with Mateo. Knowing that makes me worry less for Marissa.*

Closing the door, Al turned to Brian, "I think we need to check into the Mateo Roca piece. Paolo may not know what the ex-wife is up to, but I don't want to leave any stone unturned. Paolo and I will disagree about The Falklands, but he's usually realistic. I don't know why the Argentines cling to the hope the Falklands will miraculously become their Malvinas. It is so completely a British territory."

Chapter 32

It was late in the evening when Ofelia finally returned to her house. The traffic had been terrible, with many stops along the way, but Ofelia barely noticed as she turned all she had learned from Al over and over in her mind. By the time she arrived, she had made more than one decision regarding how she would move forward.

Holding the book she had been reading, Teri rose to meet Ofelia at the door.

Ofelia smiled, "I see you're reading Carl Sagan's novel *Contact*. I've been curious about it. Are you finding it enjoyable?"

"I can't put it down. I was first drawn to it because he's such an approachable scientist, and I thought I would learn things about astronomy. That's been true, but now I'm totally caught up with the characters and the story."

"It sounds fascinating, discovering ways to communicate with other intelligent life."

"You can have it when I'm finished. How was your meeting with Al? Wait, I haven't even given you a minute to take off your coat. Have you eaten? I threw together a veggie stew."

"Thank you, Teresa. I would love some. Haven't eaten anything in hours."

Teri went into the kitchen to heat up the stew while Ofelia flopped herself down and took off her shoes.

Teri called out from the kitchen, "It should be warm in a few minutes. Is there anything else I can get you? A glass of wine?"

"I would love a glass of Malbec. Alas, it's hard to find real Argentine Malbec here, but it's better than anything else."

"Coming up!"

"This is perfect, thank you. Now I can tell you what I have learned today."

"I'm all ears."

"I'll start with the answer to your question. Al has given me the go-ahead to return to Argentina."

"That's wonderful news! Does he guarantee your safety?"

"I guess he said that, but I don't really trust him to be completely honest. He offered to help me go back twice, first for a visit to attend Tomás' funeral soon, then later for a more permanent return, giving me time to make arrangements. Apparently, Brian, remember Brian from the Matchmaker's Ball? Brian will be in Argentina and will serve as protection."

"Really? Brian works for MI6?"

"I thought I told you. He and I were couriers for Al when we met at Lisdoonvarna. It helped that we'd been selected as king and queen a few years back."

"Makes sense. I'm curious, does Al know Mateo?"

"He says no, and I actually believe that, unlike much else I heard from him."

"So, what are you worried about?"

"I'm not worried because I think I can take care of things, but Al was clearly lying to me. I just don't trust him, so I need to figure out a way to take advantage of what he offers but take control of everything else."

"I'm sorry to be asking these questions, but you seem to trust him for some things, like not knowing Mateo and helping get you back to Argentina. What am I missing?"

"I don't trust why he's doing this. I don't believe he facilitated our reunion and has now decided I'll be safe without an ulterior motive. I'm always a little suspicious, or at least cautious around people who never seem to doubt themselves. Overconfidence makes me think the person is hiding something that could be harmful. And, like many people in our secret world, Al almost always has an ulterior motive. Kindness, for its own sake, doesn't run in his bloodstream. As for Mateo, I just got the impression Al was taken by surprise."

"So, where do we go from here?"

"You don't have to be involved. It might be dangerous. No one even knows you're here with me now, and I can keep you out of it if I stop telling you what I learn from this minute forward."

"Ofelia, there's no way you can push me away now. I finally have my family. Say no more about excluding me. What's our next step?"

Ofelia smiled, "You remind me of myself at a younger age, always wanting to be in the middle of the action, taking foolish chances."

"Ha Ha! I'm thirty-nine, not a young teenager like you when you became enmeshed in this world. But I'm not afraid to take chances to ensure your safety. I would probably be a tiny bit less reckless than you were. I am certainly less innocent."

"No adult is less innocent than I was. I was fortunate to be with older people who cared about me. At least some of them cared, anyway. I know I was used, but I knew what I was getting into, and we all shared the conviction we were doing what we could for the most noble of causes. We were saving our country from ruin." Ofelia paused, "Obviously, the fight goes on. I must admit, I'm hoping to get back into it in my home country. I miss the action."

Looking at Teri, she added, "I'm only fifty-seven."

"Okay, so what's our next step?"

"I told Al I wanted to make two trips to Argentina: the first in the next week or so to attend Tomás' funeral and a second later on to move myself and my belongings to a permanent home in Argentina. But I've decided to stay in Argentina after the first trip and find out what's going on with Al. At some level, I continue to feel momentarily useful; but ultimately dispensable to him. Somehow, after all these years, he's come up with a reason to send me back to Argentina, to connect with you and Marissa and resume my previous life. Just looking at his face when we met convinced me of this. I would appreciate your help in deciding what to take on my one and only trip; and perhaps to help me make that trip."

"I'm definitely willing to do both of those things. We can pack boxes to send in my name, so you won't need to leave anything you care about behind. I can also travel with you when you go to the funeral if you like. Perhaps tonight we should call Marissa and tell her the news. She can begin making living arrangements for you."

"That would be fine, but I need to wait for Al's office to arrange my flight. He said they'll pay for both trips, but since I will only be using one, I should let MI6 pay for it. And I think it would be a good idea for me to leave the British Isles before making him suspicious."

"Are you up-to-date with your passport?"

"Believe it or not, Ofelia Cruz and Brigid Alvarez are both ready to go passport-wise. You must remember, I've spent the past several years working for the postal service here."

"That's great! Have you done this with leaving the country in mind all these years?"

"Oh yes. I've always hoped to return to Argentina."

"Will Al's people be making a flight reservation for Brigid or Ofelia?"

"I suspect it will be for Brigid. I should be hearing the details within a day or two. Meanwhile, I have a week to make decisions and pack. I like the idea of sending things I want to keep to you and maybe Marissa, as well. My colleagues at the post office will completely understand my wanting to send things to my daughters, although they may wonder why I've never done so before. I can tell them I'm finally doing a bit of house cleaning and think it's time to pass a few family things to you two now that you are adults."

The following day, Ofelia received word that Al's office had made the flight reservations. She would travel from Dublin to Buenos Aires on Thursday, November 13, as Brigid Alvarez.

As they made preparations, Teri and Ofelia became increasingly comfortable with their developing relationship. They reminisced fondly about Teri's childhood years, and Ofelia told her some of what she was doing with the Addisons. Teri was fascinated to hear those stories with the ears of an adult who understood what was happening in the country historically.

One day, as Ofelia was leafing through and destroying documents she had kept over the years, she turned to Teri and asked what exactly had triggered her curiosity and led her to even think about decoding the random communications she and Susan Addison had created.

"You must have been very motivated to do all of that detective work."

"I was very motivated. I discovered the letter you wrote to Susan asking for help to get out of Argentina that had been written three years after Susan died. I found the letter in Pete's effects shortly after he passed away last year. It definitely sparked my curiosity. Prior to that, I had no idea you were all working for the secret services, but mostly, I wondered why the letter was so obviously written in code."

"That was very clever of you."

"Thank you, but I have to give credit to the fact that I teach a college course in anthropological linguistics. Anthropologists look at all language as code."

"Really?"

"Yes, so both reading and listening are acts of decoding. Most of the time, we just figure what we see and hear is what we get. People usually intend their communications to be what they seem. But in this case, it didn't make sense, so it got my attention. I was also suspicious of my ability to understand the Spanish language. So, I reached out to a group of smart people, some of whom are fluent in Spanish, to help me with the decoding. That was the famous Ofelia Mystery Circle."

"It sounds like anthropologists are good detectives." Ofelia laughed, "Wait, there is a mystery circle named for me?! Why haven't I heard of this before?"

"This is the first time we've had the opportunity to just talk about things. This is the first time you and I have been alone together and the first time you've asked me about how this all came about. I think our last get-together with Marissa was partly to get to know each other and, from Marissa's and my point of view, to learn about your life and why you did what you did. As painful as it was for me, I believe you made the correct decision."

Ofelia's eyes began to tear up. "I will never feel good about it, but have accepted that it was necessary. I don't know if I expected to see you or Marissa again, Teresa, but am so happy this has occurred, and you seem to accept my explanations. Whatever his motivation, Al has made our relationships possible."

"You're going to get me crying again. I'm just happy to have my mother and sister in my life. There was always something missing before, and I had a lifelong inability to commit to anything or anyone."

"What about Jack?"

"Jack came into my life in the middle of this process. I don't think I could've done it without him. He is such an extraordinary man."

"I look forward to meeting him."

"I hope that can happen soon, but at the moment, I don't even know when I'll be seeing him again. His family needs him in Michigan, and I understand that, but it's definitely keeping him from his work and me. Anyway, your questions about the decoding remind me of the mysterious jottings of Pete Addison on the back of the phone bill. Have you had a chance to look at it?"

"I'm sorry Teri, I just ran across it. I forgot; so much has been going on. Here it is."

Teri glanced at the scrap of paper.

"I was hoping you might recognize the code if that's what it is. Oh wait, I had forgotten it was written on the back of a phone bill and thought it might help to see the phone numbers and dates on the bill."

Ofelia laughed, "You are a good detective, Teri. This might help us think about when Pete wrote the note. At least it tells us that he wrote it after the dates of his phone calls."

Teri turned the paper over.

"This was clearly a recent phone bill. He died in August of last year, 1985, and the long-distance calls here are from May and June."

"So, the note on the back was something he was thinking about last year, just before he passed. That gives us a little something to work with."

Teri continued to look closely at the phone bill.

"I wasn't aware he was still in the spy business so recently. He made a lot of long-distance calls. I wonder who he was calling."

"Let's take a look."

Ofelia opened a drawer and pulled out a booklet.

"This should give us at least where he was calling. It's a listing of country codes. The only ones I recognize off the top of my head are +54 for Argentina and +44 for Great Britain. Isn't it interesting that those numbers are so similar? And it looks like he made more than one call to both places during that month. Let's make a list of the codes.

This has the potential to help us connect the note on the back of this page. Can you write them down as I look them up?"

"Sure."

"It looks like he made a couple of calls to the United Kingdom and Argentina, and one each to +56, +31, +353 and two calls to +500."

Ofelia paused, then continued.

"I know +353 is Ireland. Let me see, +56 is Chile, and +31 is The Netherlands; all understandable, but +500 appears to be an outlier. How interesting, that's the Falkland Islands code. Who on earth did he know there?"

Teri looked up as Ofelia answered her own question,

"This was 1985? He must have been helping the Brits dig dirt on Falkland Islands politics."

"But why? I thought the British won that war in 1982."

Ofelia laughed, "I'm afraid we will never acknowledge the British right to our Islas Malvinas. It's unlikely we'll ever call them the Falklands. They belong to us historically—going back to the 1493 papal bulls and Treaty of Tordesillas that give us sovereignty because of their location off our eastern coast. Even later on, Perón was almost successful in taking them back. In any case, that issue is still fresh for most Argentinians."

"Like everyone, I heard a little about the Falklands War a few years ago, but it sounded like the Brits won it without much effort. I didn't realize it was still an issue."

"Oh yes. It is a national pride issue, despite the fact that the British have pretty much occupied it since 1833. Most people who live there are British citizens."

Teri laughed. "So, Pete Addison had a finger in that pot too. I wonder whose side he was on?"

"I suspect he was working with the Brits. It may be that the coded note would give us a clue. I promise I will take a look at it in the next few days. There's just so much to do."

"You're right about that. My head is spinning. Actually, this is reminding me I need to call my friend Vanessa to let her know I'll be away longer than I originally thought. She's been caring for my dog and cats. I only hope she can continue for a few extra weeks. In fact, now that I know we'll be leaving here on November 13, I should give her a call right away."

Chapter 33

Leaving Ofelia to go through drawers in her bedroom, Teri picked up the living room phone and called Vanessa, who answered immediately. "Teri, you're a mind reader! I was going to call you tomorrow. I just heard from Jack. He's coming home to Mariel for a long weekend next week and is, of course, hoping to see you here. He said he didn't know how to reach you in Ireland directly."

Teri's brain was racing. "What great news! But wait, is his father okay?"

"He didn't say. He really didn't say much of anything except he wants to see you and has a few business things to attend to. Charlie is in town and I think they have a meeting scheduled with the Nevarez Foundation."

"When will he arrive?"

"Saturday, November fifteenth. He said he plans to be here until a few days after the weekend.

"This is a bit of a dilemma for me. I'm supposed to be taking Ofelia to Argentina on the previous Thursday, the thirteenth. But I really want to see Jack. Ironically, I was calling to ask you to extend your pet care for a week or two. I know I can make this work, let me talk to Ofelia and get back to you."

"Of course, I could extend the pet care, but I have to tell you, Gordon and the kitties really miss you." Vanessa paused. "Listen, I don't want to pressure you but I hope making it work includes your being here for Jack next week. I definitely had a feeling he needs major TLC only you can provide."

"Let me talk to Ofelia. I'll call you back within the hour."

Walking into the bedroom, Teri said, "I have a problem. I think I need to go home to Mariel for a few days next week."

"Oh? Your friend can't extend her pet care? You don't need to worry about me. I can go to Argentina by myself. Perhaps you can travel again in time for Tomás' funeral. We don't have a definite date yet anyway."

"That isn't the problem. Jack will be there for just a few days and I really want to see him. So, I'm thinking of an alternative plan."

"I'm listening."

"Why don't you come to the U.S. with me? You can meet Jack and see how I live there. I could even bring together the folks who are around from our original Ofelia Mystery Circle. I know they would all enjoy meeting you."

"Can we trade our tickets in? I would love to visit your home in the States. I've never been there. And I would love to meet Jack. But I can't stay for a long time."

Teri smiled. "Of course. I still want to go to Argentina with you and attend the memorial service for your brother. I know I can switch my flight to Newark or New York City, but are you okay with changing yours? Obviously, Al and his people would figure out that you went to the U.S. rather than Argentina."

"I don't care what they find out. Al knows where you live. If they ask, I'll tell him I decided to meet with you before going to Buenos Aires for the funeral. I can tell them we will be traveling together from New York to Buenos Aires later. What can they do to me? I believe Al is only interested in getting me to Argentina for whatever reason. A few days sooner or later should make no difference to him. I'll just say you called, invited me to visit your home in New York, and we decided to travel to the funeral together." Ofelia smiled, "This will be a great adventure!"

"Yes, it reminds me of some of the fantasy adventures you created for Juan Ignacio and me when I was small, but this time, we actually make tracks. Let me call Vanessa and the airlines so we can both change our flight plans. Shall we call Marissa to tell her of our new schedule as well?"

"Of course."

Changing plans gave both Teri and Ofelia a feeling of purpose as they carefully packed Ofelia's belongings. They had decided to prepare two cartons to send to Marissa and Teri, respectively. They would carry the rest in their luggage on the plane. Knowing she would not be back for anything, Ofelia felt it was a great opportunity to get rid of things she had accumulated over the years that she no longer cared about. Even then, she was surprised to find objects she had forgotten but still valued.

"This is harder than I expected. I spent so much of my life living in other people's houses, I never thought of myself as one who gets attached to things." Looking around her little house, Ofelia said. "I've been bored a lot of the time here, but have also found something I never had before."

"What's that?"

"Occasional feelings of peace and belonging. All the time I've been here, I've longed for the excitement of my previous life, but some of the time I've enjoyed this domestic life and being part of a community. I will miss this place."

Teri looked up, "I completely understand that feeling. Until the last year or two, I never felt like I belonged anywhere."

"What changed last year?"

"I found community with my friends. I have to give our search for you a lot of credit. Then I found you and Marissa."

"I'm the lucky one, Teresa, that you and Marissa have forgiven and embraced me. As they say around here, this is the first day of the rest of our lives and I am optimistic."

"Getting back to business here. Are you getting close to deciding what will go into each box, what we'll carry on the plane, what you'll leave behind? I see the piles are becoming more reasonable. Since we're leaving Thursday, I think it would be good to have them ready to send on Monday. That gives us a few days through the weekend. By the way, have you thought about what you're going to say to little Marti and Meghan about leaving here?"

"As you know, I've invited them for a farewell visit on Sunday after church. But haven't thought beyond that. I obviously can't tell them I won't be back. I'm definitely going to miss my little charges. Perhaps I can do something special with them before we go."

Thinking about how it felt when Ofelia left her as a child, Teri's mind was clicking. "Maybe we can throw them a little party. I'll be happy to help."

"Yes, that's a lovely idea."

"Let's make it a tea party. We can have tea and their favorite pastries. Do you know what they are? This could make it a special occasion they will remember fondly."

"Great idea. I can make them a traditional Irish Tea Cake with strawberries and cream."

"That sounds like something I would love. Let's do it! Or shall we get it from the bakery?"

"No, we can bake it ourselves. It's quite simple. Of course, now I've added something else to the job jar!"

"I know you've told the girls' mother and the post office you'll be away for a while visiting family in Argentina, but what about your house? Obviously, you'll have to put it on the market at some point."

"This house is a rental, Teri, and I'm paid up; but I will contact the owner from Argentina to let him do what he wants with it. As far as the rest goes, I hope to come back at least to visit once we solve the mystery of why Al wants me in Argentina. I know this will come as a surprise but I'm ready to live my life as openly as I can."

Ofelia went back to going through a box that had been lying under a pile of linens in her bedroom closet. It was filled with bric-a-brac she had little interest in, and she was about to put the entire box into the toss pile when she ran across a locket with an etched red flower that resembled a bird's head on the front. Putting the rest of the box aside, she took out the locket and stared at it for a long time. This caught Teri's attention.

"How pretty! I don't think I ever remember you wearing jewelry. May I take a look?"

Ofelia handed it to Teri. It appeared to be gold, but the etched flower was almost flame-colored.

Ofelia had a faraway expression on her face when she said, "The flower is a Ceibo tree blossom, a kapok, the national flower of Argentina. Miguel Martínez gave this to me the last time I saw him. I don't know why I kept it, but I sometimes wore it under my shirt."

"That's so sweet. Wait, the Ceibo, isn't that the tree in Juan Ignacio's backyard where we buried our treasure box?"

Ofelia continued to look lost in thought. "Yes, you're right. It's very common in Barrio Buenasuerte and a lot of other parts of Buenos Aires. I've always been drawn to it. I think I told you and Marissa that some of the people I worked with when I was young nicknamed me *Anahí* because I reminded them of the brave Guarani girl legend says was the source of the Ceibo tree."

"And Miguel gave that to you as a gift. Did he know of that connection?"

"He wasn't part of that group at all. No, I think he gave it to me because he knew how much I loved those flowers."

Touched, Teri thought this would be a good time to tell Ofelia that she and Marissa had met Miguel and Juan Ignacio had been caring for him for the past eleven years. Then she thought better of it. She and Marissa had agreed to protect Juan Ignacio's involvement and Miguel's whereabouts from everyone, at least until they were able to find out if he was their father.

Back in the present, Ofelia put the locket aside and said, "You know, that would be a great gift for Marti and Meghan at our tea party."

"But there's only one locket."

"No, I will hold onto this one, but I can give them each a special piece of jewelry. Please remind me. Before Sunday I need to bake a cake and find the perfect lockets. Our days are certainly filling up."

As planned, Ofelia and Teri spent Saturday shopping and baking. Teri felt like she was in heaven. Every place they went in the village, people embraced her as Brigid's lookalike daughter. She was beginning to understand why Ofelia was so fond of her village. It seemed like a sort of Camelot the horrible Irish Troubles had left behind. With the help of the jeweler, they found two slightly different charm bracelets for the girls, both of which were started with small medallion charms imprinted with their names.

Returning home with the necessary ingredients, Teri and Ofelia learned they were compatible in the kitchen. When Teri pointed that out, Ofelia looked at her seriously,

"I had you as my child for your first six years. I don't want to dismiss what you have learned since then, but you were always with me when I prepared food."

"You know, you're right. I always wanted to be with you, even when you were doing housework, so I tried to make myself useful."

"That was a special time."

"As is this! Our time together with Marissa was wonderful, but this has been spectacular. I guess it's true what they say about everyone secretly wanting to be an only child."

"This will happen with Marissa as well, Teresa, but she and I have a different set of issues to resolve. I believe the time the three of us were together was as good as it could have been, given you had so many questions. But now, we will have the rest of our lives. I feel very blessed."

***

Since they were flying out from Dublin, Teri and Ofelia spent the night at a hotel near the airport. This time, it was a daytime flight and they needed to be at the airport quite early in the morning of the 13th. Teri napped throughout the flight. When she opened her eyes, she saw Ofelia jotting things in a small notebook. Not wanting to be nosy, Teri didn't ask what she was writing, but Ofelia told her anyway,

"I've been working on decoding Pete's string of letters and numbers."

"Any luck?"

"Not really. I didn't expect to figure it out. If you recall, the codes Susan and I used were invented connections we thought you would be able to recognize. In secret communications circles, no formula lasts for very long."

"But there has to be a way to figure out what he wrote!"

"Of course there is; we just haven't come up with it yet. If the code is any good, it won't be easy, but we can try."

Having lost a few hours due to flying west, they arrived in Newark, NJ, at midday. There, they changed to a commuter plane that took them to Ithaca, where Vanessa was awaiting their arrival.

Chapter 34

Ofelia listened quietly as Teri and Vanessa chatted in the front seat of the car.

"Have you spoken with Jack yet?"

"I tried once, but he wasn't available to have much of a conversation. That's how it's been for a while."

"I wouldn't be discouraged, Teri. When I spoke with him last week, I had the feeling he was catching a rare moment by himself. I know he's anxious to see you."

"I'm not discouraged, Nessa. It seems like he's surrounded by people all the time up there. I just can't wait to see him! I'll be picking him up at the airport on Saturday morning. That's as far as our conversation went. I could tell he was worn out. I think they located his brother, but he has to go into rehab, so that's just another thing on Jack's plate. What a nightmare! I'm determined to provide him with a respite from all of that noise."

Hearing Ofelia snoring softly in the backseat, Teri said, "He knows Ofelia is here with me and is excited to meet her. He also said that he's really happy we still have two apartments."

"Ha Ha! So what are your plans for Ofelia while you're here?"

"I don't know exactly. I really want you and Cliff to get to know her. She is an extraordinary woman."

"That was evident from the complexity of the coding system she came up with. I feel like we got to know her mind in some ways."

"Yes, and I would love to bring together our Ofelia Mystery Circle with her as guest of honor. I think she would like that. You know, we've been trying to decode a line of letters Pete Addison wrote on the back of a phone bill before he died."

"What?"

"My sister Pat found it in one of his boxes. It looked like he was using it as a bookmark. She thought it might have some meaning and sent it to me just before I went to Ireland. Ofelia and I looked at it, but the only thing we determined was that he had recently made phone calls to a number of countries, including Great Britain, Ireland, Argentina, and, of all places, the Falkland Islands."

"So you think the coded word is somehow related to one or more of these calls?"

"Possibly. I'm a little slow, but it surprised me that he was still in the Secret Service biz as recently as last year, just before he died."

"Or, he could simply be calling his friends?"

Teri laughed, "I'm sorry. It's hard for me to imagine Pete having friends. Oh, here we are. I'm really happy to be home."

"Prepare yourself for an enthusiastic greeting from your biggest fan, Gordon!"

Vanessa had changed the sheets, figuring they would be ready for a nap after the long flight. Teri settled Ofelia in her bedroom and went downstairs to bring their luggage up. Saying goodbye to Vanessa, who needed to get over to the campus to teach a class, Teri then went to Jack's apartment, where she cleaned up a bit as well. She had decided to spend the night in his bed, giving Ofelia privacy and warming it up for his arrival the next day.

By morning, Ofelia had settled into the apartment and become Gordon's third favorite person. The cats were even more enthusiastic, seeing her lap as one of the best they had ever encountered.

Teri enjoyed showing Ofelia around her little town, food shopping, and walking in the woods with Gordon. Teri also proudly gave Ofelia a tour of the Bateson College campus where she introduced her mother to fellow faculty and students she had taught. As they were leaving, she heard Vanessa call out,

"Teri, Ofelia, wait, look who's here!"

Teri turned around and saw Vanessa walking towards them with Charlie. Throwing her arms around him, she said, "I'm so happy to see you, and I want to introduce you to my mother, Ofelia Cruz. Mamá, my dear friend, Charlie Elliot."

Charlie reached out a hand and said, "This is such a pleasure, Ofelia. We all feel as if we got to know you last year."

Teri explained, "Charlie was part of the famous Ofelia Mystery Circle. Without his help, we wouldn't have been able to decode your communications with Susan."

Ofelia smiled, "I've heard many good things about you and am grateful. Without you, I wouldn't be here with my wonderful daughter."

"Mamá, Charlie's also a brilliant scholar."

"That's very kind of you, Teri, but please don't create unrealistic expectations I'll be unable to live up to."

Ofelia jumped in, "Don't ever doubt your ability to accomplish any goals you set for yourself. That's the key to a successful life. One thing I've learned about my daughter here is that she has no ability to be dishonest. If she says this about you, it is true."

Charlie smiled, "I'm already convinced I would like to have many long conversations with you, Ofelia. How long will you be here? Teri, I suspect it's not a coincidence that you are here at the same time as Jack. He and I are meeting with the Nevarez Foundation on Monday, but I believe he's arriving tomorrow."

"Correct on all counts, Charlie. And to answer your first question, Ofelia and I will be here for a week, then we're headed to Argentina. Ofelia's brother, my Uncle Tomás, passed away recently. We'll combine a family reunion in Argentina with a memorial service."

"I'm sorry for your loss but glad I was finally able to make your acquaintance, Ofelia. I will be here through the end of next week as well. Perhaps we can get together before we all go our separate ways?"

Teri said, "Actually, Charlie, we hope to bring the Ofelia Mystery Circle together."

"Is there a particular purpose for this meeting, or just a fun social event?"

"Well, we do have a bit of an agenda. First, Ofelia wants to meet you all, and I suspect the feeling is mutual. Decoding her communications was central to our work together for all those months last year, and I'm sure everyone has questions. And secondly, Ofelia and I have another decoding project we thought you might be able to help us with. I'm thinking, if everyone's on board, we could do this Monday evening?"

"Jack and I are meeting with the Nevarez Foundation folks on Monday morning, but I'm free after that."

"What about you and Cliff, Vanessa? Does Monday evening work for you?"

"Absolutely! And I would like to host at my old apartment where we met last year. I haven't been ready to give it up yet. Now I have to run to my next class. Teri, let's talk later about snacks and such."

"See you later, gators."

As they walked away, Ofelia said, "I am so happy to see how settled you are in this place you have made your home. It's comfortable, and I really like your friends. But I do have a question—what's a gator?"

"Ha Ha..it refers to an alligator, you know, the very large reptile that lives in rivers and terrorizes people. The song line is 'See you later,

Alligator, After a While, Crocodile.' I think the songwriter came up with those references because they rhymed, but it became something people say."

Ofelia laughed, "I have much to learn about my daughter's life!"

Teri hugged her mother. "Let's call Marissa and tell her what's going on and make a date to bury Tomás."

Chapter 35

Teri didn't sleep well the night of the fourteenth. She was both excited and anxious about seeing Jack. When she tried to analyze her concerns, it came down to her fear of losing him. Had it always been an experiment for them? Coming from such different cultures? Throughout the night, she tossed and turned, thinking. *Have we been living in a bubble? He's had to immerse himself in his family situation, where it seems like he's been made to feel responsible for everything. Will that change his ability to move forward with his life plans? Will that negatively impact our ability to make a life together?*

When she finally woke up in Jack's bed, she went to her apartment, where she found Ofelia already dressed and making coffee.

"Good morning, Teresa. Will you join me for some coffee? I can also make eggs or something else for you. What time will you leave to pick Jack up at the airport?"

Pleased Ofelia seemed so comfortable in her apartment, Teri said, "Thank you. I need to take Gordon out to the back for a minute. I'll feed him and the cats when I return; then, I should probably get going. Maybe a piece of toast, and I'll definitely grab a cup of coffee for the drive. I'm sorry to leave you alone."

"Actually, I've decided to spend my time alone to help set up the Ofelia Mystery Circle event. I'm going to identify some ways I've known to create written codes. Perhaps the group can try some of them out and see what we come up with. It's good to have a little quiet time to think about this. I will begin with the premise that Pete Addison was never a creative person. I suspect he used a known formula."

"That would be wonderful, Ofelia. I agree with something you said before. The best code is one that both parties to the communication agree on. Now, if we only knew who his intended audience was!"

"Well, my dear, we have to start somewhere. Now you must get going. Drive safely. I look forward to your return and meeting your Jack. I think I can figure out how to feed your pets."

While she continued to worry about how Jack may have changed, by the time she arrived at the airport, Teri was simply happy to see him. He held her tightly as she held him. All he brought was a backpack, so they were able to quickly get to the car and drive home. During their hour-long drive, Teri babbled about all that had happened since they had last seen each other. While he seemed sincerely interested with her news, Jack uncharacteristically answered in monosyllables when she asked about his family situation.

Stopping at a diner along the highway, they ate pancakes and talked about his meeting with Nevarez. Teri was happy to hear he was still planning to continue with his research project. Their lack of communication over the past several weeks had made her fear he would have to abandon that along with their relationship. Waiting for a second cup of coffee, Teri got up to use the restroom. When she returned, Jack began to open up.

"I know this has been a difficult time for you, Teri."

"Not worse than for you."

"This is one time I must agree with you. It has been really tough for my family. I will tell you all the gory details in due time, but first, I need to tell you nothing has changed my feelings for you and the life I hope we can have together. Being away from you and the stability you bring to my life has been horrible."

"Oh, Jack, I've missed you so much!"

"Please don't ever doubt my love for you, Teri."

"I love you too, Jack. We'd better get back on the road, or I may make an embarrassing scene in this diner."

When they arrived at the apartment, Jack said, "I'm looking forward to meeting Ofelia, but really need to take a nap and have a shower first. Do you mind?"

"Nope, and I'm going to join you."

Jack smiled, "As I hoped."

A few hours later, Teri and Jack walked down the hall to Teri's apartment. Seeing Teri and Jack's happy faces, Ofelia knew things had gone well between them.

Jack said, "It's a pleasure to meet you, Ofelia. Needless to say, I've heard a lot about you these past several months."

"As I have about you, Jack, the pleasure is mine. And Teresa, I believe I have come up with a plan for your deciphering party."

Jack looked at Teri. "A deciphering party?"

Teri said, "Oh, I forgot to mention, we're going to have an Ofelia Mystery Circle get-together Monday evening. I hope that works for you. I know you and Charlie will be meeting with the Nevarez Foundation people earlier in the day and thought it would be better to do this after your meeting. We ran into Charlie on campus yesterday, and he's on board. And this time, our guest of honor, Ofelia Cruz, will be joining us."

"Wouldn't miss it for the world. Ofelia, you will be impressed with this meeting of great minds! It'll be great to catch up with everyone."

The following few days sailed by. Jack and Charlie met to talk about the next phase of their research and to plan an agenda for the meeting with their Nevarez Foundation sponsors. Knowing their sponsors were anxious to have a timeline for data collection and report writing, Jack and Charlie had been unsure of how to approach the Foundation with the fact that Jack had to deal with an ongoing family situation in the Upper Peninsula of Michigan. In the end, they decided not to mention it but pointed out that they would conduct the field research in Argentina, at times together and at times separately. In reality, Charlie would be playing a larger role than they had originally expected.

Teri couldn't have been happier. Here she was, living in her happy place with her mother and the man she loved. At night, Ofelia had the apartment to herself, and Teri got to sleep cuddled up with Jack. During the days while Jack and Charlie planned, Teri and Ofelia helped Marissa organize their Argentine family reunion by phone.

On Monday afternoon, Teri, Ofelia, and Vanessa bought snacks and cleaned Vanessa's old condo apartment. Since she and Cliff married, Vanessa had not spent much time there and, although she claimed to have plans to sell it, everyone doubted she would ever let it go. She just had to figure out what to use it for. This was the perfect place to have a Mystery Circle reunion. When people arrived early Monday evening, they found a beautiful fire in the stone fireplace, comfortable chairs all around, and a dining room table covered with delicious munchies.

The group began the meeting by chatting about their lives and asking Ofelia polite questions. After about a half hour, Teri decided to move things forward.

"I know we could spend hours chatting, but we actually have a mystery to solve."

Cliff spoke up. "I'm probably the one here who is most out of the loop, but I understand we'll be trying to untangle a coded message."

"That's the plan, and this time we have Ofelia to help us think things through."

"I'm good with that, Teri, but I'm wondering if you can explain what we're looking for? Can you give us the background context of this piece of the puzzle?"

Teri looked at Ofelia. "Do you want to do that, or shall I?"

"Why don't you explain as you see it? I will contribute if I feel the need."

"Alright. So, as you all know, the parents I grew up with, Peter and Susan Addison, worked for the British and American Secret Services when we were living in Buenos Aires. Ofelia, my birth mother, lived with us disguised as the Addison's live-in maid. The previous Mystery Circle was dedicated to decoding messages Ofelia and Susan created as the Addisons moved me with their family to the United States. They did this so I might one day discover the truth about who I was."

Teri began to tear up. *When will this stop being so painful?*

Sensing her discomfort, Jack stepped in. "I think you told us before that you discovered your first clues in boxes containing Pete and Susan Addison's belongings. Now, the new mystery comes from another of his boxes your sister, the Addison's daughter Pat, recently shared with you."

"Yes, thanks for getting me back on task."

Everyone laughed, and Teri continued.

"So, this message is a more traditional-looking thing. It's basically a string of capital and lower-case letters. From what Ofelia has told me, this type of coding is based on letters and numbers replacing other letters and numbers that are meaningful. And oh, I almost forgot, Pat found the message written on the back of a telephone bill that seemed like it was being used as a bookmark. The phone bill covered calls from mid-May to mid-June of last year, 1985, just a few months before Pete died."

Charlie asked, "Is there any meaning to the book or the page the bookmark was found?"

"Hard to say, Charlie. The book is *Moby Dick*. We're unsure what page it was marking as Pat pulled it out to read to me over the phone. She believes it was at the beginning of a chapter towards the end of the book, but that's all we know."

"What about the phone bill? Besides telling you when the message was written—I mean, I'm assuming it had to have been after the end of June when he would have received the bill—Is there anything on the bill itself that could have motivated him to write that message?"

"That is the million-dollar question. We looked up the international country codes for the calls he made. He made several calls to Great Britain, Ireland, Argentina, and Chile, all places he would've had professional contacts, although I had no idea he was still in the spy business by then. It could just have been social calls to old acquaintances. I don't recall Pete having friends, but I certainly didn't know much about his personal life. So, it's possible if there's a connection between the message and one of the calls. But the plot became a bit thicker when we discovered that he also made a call or two to the Falkland Islands."

Vanessa asked, "Interesting coincidence that the message was in a book that takes place in the South Atlantic. Isn't that where the Falkland Islands are located?"

"Wow! I never thought of that!"

"But, Teri, why would it make a difference that he made those particular calls? How are the Falklands different from the other places"?

"They aren't, not on the face of it, but as you all probably know, the Falkland Islands have been a point of contention between the Argentine and British governments for centuries."

"Oh yes, I've never figured out why the Brits want it. Isn't it near the eastern coast of Argentina in the South Atlantic Ocean?

"Can't answer that question, but I know they fought a war over it in 1982, and the Brits won."

Ofelia spoke up for the first time. "We Argentines will never accept that verdict. Las Malvinas Islas will always belong to our country. They were given to us as part of the Tordesillas Treaty and papal bulls of 1493."

Teri said, "As you can see, this remains an emotional issue between the two countries."

Cliff asked, "What does it mean that Pete Addison had a phone conversation with someone in those islands last year?"

"A second million-dollar question. It may mean nothing important. It may mean he had a friend who lives there and they were talking about the weather, but as I said before, I don't remember Pete as a person who had friends. I just think it's worth exploring."

Teri passed individual sheets of paper to everyone in the room. They each had a copy of the message: **KJSjcuM**

Cliff was the first to lift his head and ask, "What do we do now?"

Laughing, Teri said, "You mean you can't decipher it just by looking at it?"

They all laughed, then Cliff repeated the question. "I get these figures have to be replaced with letters and/or numbers that have meaning, but perhaps you can give us an idea of how to explore. On the face of it, it could be a million different codes."

"Ofelia has decoding experience and volunteered to give us a few hints. But the reality is, we don't know. If we don't come up with anything, we're no worse off than when we started, right?"

Ofelia started. "This may be a shot in the dark, but I recall Pete and Susan often used a particular replacement code. We always tried to change them up, but let me try. If nothing else It might give you a sense of how people did these. They almost always involved more than one step."

Everyone in the group was fascinated as they watched Ofelia's mind work. Charlie couldn't help thinking how she had been initiated into a secret world of intrigue at such a young age.

Ofelia continued, "It's been a long time, but if I recall correctly, you go back and forth between letters and numbers in this system. So, if we apply that to this message, **KJSjcuM**, we can begin by changing the letters to numbers. Can someone write the letters of the English alphabet across the top of a piece of paper? Okay, then write their numerical place in the alphabet underneath, so A is 1, B is 2, and so on."

Vanessa walked out of the room and returned with a chalkboard easel. "Let's do this together." She wrote the letters of the alphabet across the top, then added the numbers directly below.

A	B	C	D	E	F	G	H	I	J	K	L	M
1	2	3	4	5	6	7	8	9	10	11	12	13

N	O	P	Q	R	S	T	U	V	W	X	Y	Z
14	15	16	17	18	19	20	21	22	23	24	25	26

Charlie started. "Okay, so the first step involves finding the replacement formula. Let's begin with replacing the K with the number eleven."

"Vanessa, do you mind writing these down on the board:

K	J	S	H	A	S	M
11	10	19	8	1	19	13

"Okay, Ofelia, what next?"

"Let's begin with the simplest possibility. Ignoring the numbers, can anyone come up with a meaningful sentence or phrase whose words begin with these letters?"

They all stared at them silently.

Charlie was again the first to say something. "I think we need to look at them differently. Remember the way we interpreted clues in your first-grade reader, the <u>Mamá</u> book. We had to step outside the box and view it from another angle."

Ofelia smiled at the reference to the way she and Susan Addison set up their coded communication all those years ago. Then she spoke up, "One of the things we used to do was code capital letters differently from lowercase letters."

"How differently?"

"Well, for one thing, when we translated the letters to numbers, we would add one number if the letter was in caps and two if the letter was lowercase."

"That gives us something to try. Vanessa, do you mind doing the two ways on the board?"

"Okay, but give me instructions. I'm a little lost here."

"Our coded message is: **K J S j c u M**

Let's just start with its numerical equivalent: **11 10 19 10 3 21 13**

Are you following so far?"

They all nodded. "Now I will try to sort by whether the letters are caps or lowercase. The first three letters **K J S** are capitalized in this code, so the rule is to subtract one, which means if these are intended to be capital letters, the first three are JIR. The second three letters are lowercase, so if we subtract two from each, we come up with has., and the final letter, being a cap, we subtract one, so the letter is L. Put it all together, and we get **JIRhasL**."

They were all silent, staring at the words in front of them. Finally, Vanessa said aloud, "I'm still puzzled, but it looks like a real message. I think we broke the code because it says someone with the initials **JIR** has something."

But Teri and Ofelia immediately knew what it meant. **JIR** had to be Juan Ignacio Ramón. And while Ofelia tried to figure out why Juan Ignacio would be involved with Peter Addison, Teri knew. This had something to do with Miguel. This involved two people she cared about. She decided not to say anything to anyone. It was possible that Pete received this message when he was ill and never shared it with anyone in Argentina. After all, Teri had seen Juan Ignacio and Miguel recently, and both seemed alright. She couldn't even share this with Ofelia. They had yet to tell her about her and Marissa's meeting with Miguel.

Teri decided to put an end to the meeting.

"I think we cracked the code, thanks to Ofelia's great memory. Now it's just a matter of figuring out what it's referring to. I, for one, am really tired. Maybe we can go our separate ways and think about this mystery in our leisure time."

Vanessa looked at her curiously. Teri didn't set aside unanswered questions so easily, but she also respected her right to privacy. Teri would tell her when she was ready.

"I agree, Teri. I have spent what little brain I have for the moment but I will be happy to think further when I have the time. I hate to say it, but I need to get my beauty sleep, for tomorrow is a busy teaching day for me."

As people began getting up from their chairs, she said, "Please take food. We have enough here to feed an army."

Chapter 36

The rest of the Mystery Circle participants took their cues from Vanessa. They could tell Teri and Ofelia had been notably affected by the message they decoded, and although they were curious, knew it was best to leave them alone with their thoughts. Even Jack left Teri and Ofelia so they could speak privately. Entering her apartment, Teri went into the kitchen and poured herself a glass of wine. Calling out to Ofelia, she asked if there was anything she could get her. Ofelia said she would join Teri and have a glass of wine as well.

Settling across each other in the living room, Ofelia sipped her drink lightly.

"I guess Chianti is a good Italian wine, but I cannot tell you how much I look forward to the best wine in the world, Argentine Malbec."

Teri laughed, "I have to agree. And I have never had any Malbec, from the cheapest at the corner grocery store to the finest, most expensive at a restaurant, I didn't love."

Ofelia got down to business. "I could tell you understood the message. What would you suppose Juan Ignacio has? What do you think the L stands for?"

"I don't know, Ofelia. And I'm puzzled as to why Pete Addison was writing about him. Of course, they knew each other; we lived next door to the Ramóns all those years, but only when Juan Ignacio was a young child. What do you think?"

"I knew him later than that. I worked for his family until he went off to college. He was always a bit secretive but a good man."

"He's a wonderful man. I've spent a lot of time with him since we reconnected last year and have grown to feel the same closeness we shared as children. You know, he was the one who remembered the treasure box you helped us bury in the backyard when we were kids. That was a major contribution to our ability to solve the mystery of you, Marissa, and me."

Ofelia smiled. "You two were so adorable and always thick as thieves as children with your secret this and secret that. Will you tell him about this message? Maybe Juan Ignacio can solve this mystery as well."

"I will, Ofelia, and I will probably explain all of this to Jack, but I would otherwise prefer to keep it between us until we know more."

"I agree, Teresa. Our family reunion will be emotional enough without adding more drama, at least for the moment."

Teri laughed, "I'm starting to believe drama is our family's second name." Standing up, she said, "I'm off to Jack's. I hope you sleep well. I'll see you in the morning when I come in to feed the cats. Gordon will be staying overnight with us, so you won't have to worry about him."

"I've hardly seen your dog since I've been here, Teri. It's my impression he lives with Jack as much as he can."

"I guess that's true; those two really love one another."

"As is obvious do you and Jack. I'm very happy for you."

"Thank you. I feel really blessed."

Walking down the corridor, Teri decided to tell Jack everything she'd been experiencing. While Ofelia and Marissa each were aware of some of the puzzle pieces regarding Miguel Martínez, she was the only one who had been in Juan Ignacio's confidence. Teri didn't feel she had the right to share that information with her mother and sister until she spoke with Juan Ignacio, but she knew Jack would listen and support her. She knew she could trust him to be there for her and to provide clear-headed advice.

On her way down the hall, Teri ran into Jack and Gordon, heading towards the stairwell. She joined them for a walk around the neighborhood.

As they walked, Jack said nothing to prod her into talking about the message. Knowing he could read her like a book and already figured she had learned something from the decoded message, she also knew he would wait for her to start that conversation. Instead, he told her more about his and Charlie's meeting with the Nevarez Foundation that morning.

"I wish I could be completely honest with everyone about this."

"From what you and Charlie said before, I had the feeling the Foundation folks were comfortable with you two sharing the field research more equally."

"They are obviously okay with any amount of time Charlie spends in the field. They rightfully consider him to contribute a huge amount to our work there, but I can't help worrying that my family situation will make it hard for me to spend extensive time periods in Argentina, and this is supposed to be MY audition for the job with Nevarez. I mean, the fact that I've roped a big name like Charlie into sharing the field load gives me prestige, but I need to be the one doing the bulk of the work."

"Jack, is it primarily a perception problem for you? I mean, you and Charlie can be conferring and analyzing as you go along, and of course, you will be the report's primary author."

"I guess perception is part of it. I don't want Nevarez to wonder if I'm actually the guy who has done this."

"I get that, but Charlie will never try to steal your thunder. And, the reality is that it IS your study, your idea, everything. You can do this!"

Jack stopped and put his arms around her. "Thank you, Teri. I sometimes forget how you make things better for me. I wish I could figure a way to keep you by my side all the time."

"Me too, Jack. I've come to realize how much I depend on you. I suppose that's not a good thing, feeling dependent?"

"I think it's great when we feel the same way."

"I hate to bring this up, but do you have any idea when your father will be better and you'll be free to resume your life here?"

"Unfortunately, I can't answer that yet. My father seems to be better, but the rest of the family has to make decisions about moving forward. My brother Tyler's in rehab for his drug and alcohol addictions. He can't be counted on, even after he leaves the program. And my mother can't get it into her head that I need to have my own life that doesn't revolve around daily care for her and my father after he comes home."

"Are the doctors saying your father will need home care from a medical professional?"

"There are cultural issues around that. But it's probably true."

"I hadn't thought of that. I wonder if you could explore finding a culturally appropriate care situation?"

"I know the hospital administration includes people with Native healing backgrounds. My sister Nola told me she's been approached by one doctor in particular who specializes in herbal medicine and medically-related religious practices."

"Oh my God, Jack, I totally forgot about your sister."

"She's been a lifesaver. I couldn't be here today without her help, but I can't ask her to take the reins. She has seven young children and is overwhelmed most of the time. She really doesn't have the time or energy to run two households, but I will definitely follow up with the person she was talking to. Anyway, totally changing the subject, what did Ofelia think of the Ofelia Mystery Circle? It had to be a bit weird for her."

By this time, they were walking up the five flights to Jack's apartment. "I think she found it intriguing. Do you mind waiting until we're in the apartment? There are some things I want to share with you privately."

"Of course, anything I can offer you before we settle in?"

"No thanks, I'm good. The walk was perfect. Just what I needed to clear my head. Now I'm going to spill some things that have to remain between us. At least for the moment, we can't share this with anyone."

"Not Ofelia or Marissa?"

"Not even them. Although both of them know some of what I'm going to tell you. The code revealed Juan Ignacio to be the subject of the message. JIR are his initials, Juan Ignacio Ramón. And if you recall, the next word was 'has.' The only part I don't know is the last word, which obviously starts with the letter L. Ofelia and I both got this part, but neither of us has any idea why Pete Addison would be writing Juan Ignacio's name in such a message. I mean, we knew they knew each other all those years ago when we were next-door neighbors, but since then?"

"Is it possible Pete wasn't the author of the coded message but that he received it from one of the people he spoke with on the phone? Do you think it's possible that Pete never told whatever this is about to anyone after he deciphered it? Or maybe, he didn't even decipher it. This took place shortly before he died of natural causes. It was of natural causes?"

"Yes, he had a bad heart. Died of heart failure."

"So maybe he received this message and never did anything with it."

"That's possible. The phone bill was from last year, and as far as I can tell, Juan Ignacio has been okay since then. So, if he was involved in something Pete's cohort uncovered, he hasn't been harmed by it."

"Yet?"

"Yes, yet."

"What else are you worried about?

"It's about Miguel Martínez."

"I know Juan Ignacio took you and Marissa to see him last month and that he's been in hiding for several years. Do you think Juan Ignacio HAS something someone wants from Miguel Martínez? The thing that begins with **L**? Does this mean Juan Ignacio and Miguel are in mortal danger? You need to tell Juan Ignacio about this. It sounds really serious, but I can't help wondering why it's taken so long. I mean, Miguel went into hiding eleven years ago, ten years before Pete wrote the message."

"These are all legitimate concerns, Jack, and I can't help wondering why Miguel's family was murdered. I know he was an old friend of Perón's, but he worked in several Argentine governments after Perón was exiled. He seemed to have succeeded in keeping his head down as a numbers-crunching bureaucrat for a very long time—from 1955 until 1975. So why did they go after him then? What did he possess or know that was important enough to murder an innocent family?"

"From what I've heard, Videla was throwing people out of airplanes just because he disliked them. He seemed to enjoy murder."

"I know, but I'm interested in the timing. Miguel had been so successful in staying out of the fray. Something had to have triggered Videla to go after him."

"And you think this message is connected?"

"I don't know, but I would love to learn what the **L** stands for."

"I understand your wanting to know, Teri, but if this is that big a deal, everything you know has the potential to put you in danger. The Videla administration has been out of power since 1982, yet this message was sent in 1985. Someone doesn't want Juan Ignacio to have possession of the mysterious L. I know this is asking a lot, but is it possible for you to pass this on to Juan Ignacio and let it go?"

"Oh, Jack, I will definitely pass it on to Juan Ignacio, but I'm not sure I can let it go. Miguel may be my father!"

"This has been so amazing, Teri, I almost forgot. And you're still waiting on Juan Ignacio to help determine whether he is or not. Do you think this information will impact Juan Ignacio's willingness to get the blood sample?"

"I don't know, but I've been hoping Ofelia can help with that."

"You said Ofelia doesn't know you and Marissa met Miguel."

"That's true, but I intend to ask Juan Ignacio if we can take her to see him."

"Do you think he'll go along with that?"

"I'm pretty sure Juan Ignacio thinks Miguel is fading. I mean, he let us visit, and of course, he knows Ofelia and Miguel were fond of each other back in the day. You also need to remember that Juan Ignacio, like me, grew up with Ofelia. There's a lot of personal attachment."

"This is so much to absorb, Teri."

"There's been a lot of political turmoil and government turnover since 1975. Why would anyone care about the whereabouts of a former Peronist bureaucrat? I know some Argentines are anti-Perón, but he remains a hero to many others."

"Perhaps time heals wounds. I mean, Ofelia, who worked underground to overthrow just about all of Argentina's governments, has been given the go-ahead to return safely."

"Yes, by a British secret service agent she doesn't trust."

"Do you think the message says Juan Ignacio has something in his possession Miguel's enemies want?"

"Yes. Juan Ignacio has been taking care of Miguel since he escaped in 1975. It's now 1986, and he has been well hidden. No one has seen or heard from Miguel for the past eleven years. I think it's possible Miguel took something into hiding his enemies would like to have, something he gave to Juan Ignacio for safekeeping."

"If that's it, it starts with the letter L."

Jack put his arms around Teri and held her tight. She reciprocated, and they stayed like that for a long time. When he stepped away, he gave her a look that completely absorbed her eyes and her heart. Then he said,

"Teri Addison, you are the love of my life, and I would do just about anything to protect you from harm except ask you to be any different than you are. Whatever you decide to do, I'm by your side. I can only ask you to be careful and to call on me at any time. I love you, I trust you, and I respect you, and I may have never mentioned this to you before, but I intend, if I'm very lucky, to spend the rest of my life with you and make beautiful babies."

Speechless, Teri burst into tears.

PART 5

October 18 – November 26, 1986

Chapter 37

Driving Jack to the airport Tuesday morning, Teri promised to be careful and keep him informed as best she could. He did the same, but they both knew there would be times when their family issues would prevent their being together again as soon as they would have liked. Teri expected to have to stay in Argentina for at least a couple of weeks. Ofelia's reunion with the family had to take precedence. Teri didn't want to interfere with what was going to be an emotional time for them all, so she decided to wait to speak with Juan Ignacio until the following Sunday, after the family memorial service for Tomás.

Waiting was difficult, but there was no way she would feel it would be safe to communicate with him about her concerns regarding the coded message by phone or letter. She also had two other agendas for their conversation and no idea whether the coded message would make him more or less open to either or both. She hoped Juan Ignacio would be okay with informing Ofelia of his current relationship with Miguel. Killing two birds with one stone, once that was done, Teri believed Ofelia could convince Juan Ignacio and/or Miguel to help obtain his blood sample. As far as she knew, Juan Ignacio hadn't yet decided about the blood, but she was optimistic. Knowing that Ofelia, who Juan Ignacio had always loved, would want to see Miguel and knowing Ofelia and Miguel could be Teri and Marissa's birth parents might bring out his sentimental side. Teri could only hope.

Meanwhile, she and Ofelia were on their way to Argentina. While they were pumped about what lay ahead, they both fell asleep right away and only woke up when they arrived in Texas, where they would change planes to the even longer overnight flight to Buenos Aires. The layover time was two hours, so they decided to walk around and do a little airport shopping to exercise their stiff legs. After a while, they found a sit-down restaurant, figuring the food would probably be better than anything the airline would serve. As they waited to order, Teri got up to use the restroom while Ofelia sipped on a glass of water.

As she returned to their table, Teri called out, "Look who I ran into, Brigid!"

Ofelia was only slightly surprised that Teri was accompanied by Al Watson's associate, Brian Mullin. The mop of red hair was the first part she saw. She had figured it was only a matter of time before Al and Brian would catch up with her, but this was pretty impressive.

Without blinking, Ofelia stood up and, with a smile on her face, shook his hand.

"What a lovely surprise, Brian; what brings you to Texas?"

Brian loved the game and was impressed with Ofelia's aplomb.

"Well, I'm on my way to Buenos Aires, and this is apparently the American's favorite airline hub. What about you two lovely ladies?"

"It would appear we will be on the same flight. Small world. Would you like to join us for dinner? Boarding begins in about forty-five minutes."

"Thank you, I would enjoy that."

As it turned out, their seats for the remainder of the flight were in different sections of the plane. Knowing how uncomfortable the long flight could be, Ofelia and Teri had splurged on first-class tickets while Brian was in the only slightly less roomy business section. The following morning, Ofelia and Teri saw Brian climb into a hotel limousine.

As they watched the limousine drive away, Teri asked, "What do you make of Brian being here?"

"Well, I guess he and Al did their homework and figured out where we were. Now, Brian will follow me around, pretending to have my back."

"Are you worried?"

"A little. I wish I could figure out if there's a connection with Juan Ignacio. I can't help thinking Al has something to do with the message. I would hate to make trouble for Juan Ignacio by leading Brian to him."

"I know Juan Ignacio is looking forward to seeing you, and we have plans to visit, but maybe I should go by myself first. I can tell him about the coded message and let him decide how to move forward."

"Good idea. Let's take one step at a time."

Not that she wanted Brian snooping around, but Teri was happy to have an excuse to have her first conversation with Juan Ignacio privately. She was anxious to include Ofelia in the conversation but couldn't be open and honest until Juan Ignacio consented to letting her know about Miguel and his whereabouts.

Meanwhile, she and Ofelia could focus on their family reunion. Teri knew it was going to be strange for her. She was the only non-Argentinian, non-Porteño, in the family; a family with whom she shared genes, but no real history, except for Ofelia. It was a crazy situation all around.

The two-hour drive to Punta Lapiz was dominated by Ofelia and Sylvita, who sat in the back seat with Raoul and went back and forth sobbing and talking non-stop. Teri didn't hear Raoul say a word, nor could she understand the two happy women. Yet, she couldn't help but smile; there was such a feeling of joy in the car. She could also tell Marissa was experiencing it in the same way. Here were her two mothers, the one who raised her so lovingly and the one who gave birth to her, having a great time talking about old times and catching up with each other's lives. For a moment, Teri was envious of Marissa, but quickly snapped out of it. *There's no reason to envy Marissa or anyone else. Finally, at age thirty-nine, I'm in a car with my mother and sister on our way to a family reunion; and when the reunion's over, I will go home to Jack, the man with whom I will spend the rest of my life.*

Since it would only be attended by the immediate family, they were able to make the funeral arrangements on short notice. Sylvita had asked their parish priest to help with a brief mass for Tomás' soul, but since he had already been cremated, they could hold on to his remains until there was an agreement regarding what to do with them.

When they arrived in Punta Lapiz, the women went their separate ways. Ofelia would stay with Sylvita and Raoul, while Teri would bunk with Marissa. The first thing they did after arriving at Marissa's house was take her dog Lobito to a local park, where he could run freely and play with other dogs. Sitting on a bench together, the twins started to catch up.

Teri began, "It's wonderful to see Ofelia and Sylvita together. I didn't understand a lot of what they were saying; they were talking so fast, but I could tell it was happy talk."

"Yes. I believe they were very close as children. It's almost as if they're picking up where they left off. Teri, you must tell me, is that glow on your face entirely due to our family reunion, or is there something else?"

"Well, a lot of it is because I'm happy to be here. Some may just be because I'm very tired from the trip, but you are correct in seeing that I'm in a good place. I had a wonderful time with Jack, and I guess I'm still feeling the glow."

"I'm happy for you, Teri; perhaps my favorite researcher will someday become my brother-in-law."

"And what about you, Marissa? Are you still seeing Mateo?"

"Yes, I am. And I completely trust him despite Che's concerns about how we met."

"Have you learned any more about Paolo's role in all of this?"

"Mateo assures me he was hired by Paolo's ex-wife without Paolo's knowledge. She didn't tell him what she would be doing with the information he provided. When he told her he had found Ofelia in Ireland, his work was done. Teri, have you told Ofelia about this?"

"Yes, I have, and she is sincerely surprised Paolo would include her in his will."

"Another mystery. I wonder what Ofelia will do with this information."

"Oh, Marissa, there's so much going on I need to share with you!"

"Yes?"

"I know I haven't had time to give you these details, but if you recall, while Ofelia and I were in Mariel this past week, we had a meeting of the Ofelia Mystery Circle, my friends who helped figure out the secret communications between Ofelia and Susan. This time, Ofelia was with us."

"That must have been fun for her and for everyone to meet her in person."

"It was, but there was also a purpose for the meeting. Remember I told you my sister Pat found a scrap of paper in Pete Addison's stuff with what looked like something written in code?"

"Did you engage the skills of your friends to decipher it?"

"Yes, and Ofelia played a big role in that. As it turned out, they used a familiar code. Pete was close to death and was probably not up to complicated messaging. In any case, Ofelia and I both determined that the message referred to Juan Ignacio."

"Oh, my goodness. Is he in danger?"

"I honestly don't know. It's hard to tell whether the message was ever sent to someone else. In fact, the way it came to us, we couldn't tell whether Pete was simply copying something someone else sent him or if he was preparing the message to do the sending. We tend to think that if he intended to send it to someone, he may not have done so since Juan Ignacio has been fine (at least we believe so) since Pete wrote the coded message around June 1985."

"What does the message say?"

"Simply that JIR has L."

"And that means?"

"That Juan Ignacio Ramón has something that starts with an L."

"You're certain?"

"Ofelia and I agree, but we could be wrong."

"And no one knows what the L stands for?"

"Ofelia and I, and now Jack and you, are the only ones who recognized his initials, but we haven't come up with what L stands for. I have plans to visit Juan Ignacio next week after the funeral and will tell him about the message. I suspect he'll know what the L is and will hopefully tell me, but if he doesn't, I have to respect that."

"I was hoping to go with you to speak with Juan Ignacio about Miguel, but perhaps I should wait for you to have the first conversation privately."

"I think so, Marissa. I'm also planning to suggest that we tell Ofelia about Miguel, hoping he'll allow her to see him."

"Does Ofelia know we've met Miguel?"

"No. I haven't told her. It really hinges on Juan Ignacio. I have to believe he'll be open to such a reunion. I'd love it to include you and me as well. Maybe seeing us all together would motivate Juan Ignacio to enable the blood sampling too."

"This all sounds lovely, Teri, but we don't know what a reunion between Ofelia and Miguel would spark. There may be anger or excitement that could impact his failing health."

"I know. I guess I'm just hoping it would be a happy occasion, but as I said before, it all hinges on Juan Ignacio. He holds all of the cards here. Oh, and one more thing I forgot to mention. Remember Brian, the red-headed guy at the Matchmaker's Ball?"

"The one who turned out to be Al Watson's crony?"

"That's the one. Anyway, he showed up at the airport yesterday and is here in Buenos Aires."

"Huh?!"

"Apparently, when Ofelia met with Al to make travel plans to return to Argentina, he decided to send Brian along to keep an eye on things, basically to protect her. Ofelia didn't inform Al when she changed plans and came to New York with me, so it was kind of a surprise to see that he had caught up with her so quickly. On the other hand, they're all spies, so they are schooled in sneaking around."

"Are you worried he's here following her around?"

"I guess that depends on what role Al has been playing. Remember, I thought my parents, the Addisons, had long ago retired from the spy game, and I guess I thought the same about Al. In any case, would you mind if I go back to your house and take a long nap before we meet the rest of the family for supper?"

"Of course, Teri. I need to go to my mother's house to help prepare for the feast."

"Please wake me up in time for the festivities!"

Chapter 38

The family dinner was delightful. Like Teri, Ofelia had spent the late afternoon napping, followed by helping Sylvita and Marissa prepare their traditional dishes. Che showed up just as they were setting the table. He had taken the night off from his work at the tango club and walked in carrying a huge bouquet of flowers. Ofelia threw her arms around him and burst into tears. Che also had tears in his eyes as he hugged her back closely.

Stepping away, he smiled broadly and said, "You look as young as ever, Ofelita."

Doubting his sincerity but happy with his warmth, she replied, "As do you, Querido Primo, we have so much to talk about."

It was a beautiful moment as everyone in the room knew of their close lifetime relationship and the extent to which Che had been devoted to Ofelia's well-being. Watching them together, it was clear that from Ofelia's point of view, Che, not Tomás, was her closest relative, her true brother.

As they sat down to eat, Ofelia couldn't stop talking about how nothing in Ireland could compare with homemade empanadas with ingredients from Argentina and the best wine in the world. After dinner, they sat outdoors, passing around a cup of yerba mate. Ofelia took a moment to speak with Che privately.

"I haven't wanted to interrupt our reunion with noise, Che, but there are some things I need to tell you and ask you."

Che agreed. "Let's take a walk. I'm sure no one will object."

Ofelia began, "Are you in touch with Paolo Fuentes?"

"Only indirectly, Ofelia. I did a bit of investigating and learned Paolo's ex-wife indeed hired Marissa's friend Mateo Roca to find you, but there is no more to it."

"That must make Marissa happy. Have you told her?"

"No, I didn't want her to know I was looking into this matter. I honestly don't know what I would've done if it turned out to be more sinister."

"She does seem to be in love with this man. Perhaps we can suggest that she invite him to a family event so they will both know he's in the clear." Ofelia laughed, "Poor Marissa to have been born into such a suspicious family."

Che laughed as well. "Your daughters are lovely women, and it's wonderful to be with family. I'm not sure I ever expected such a good outcome. So, tell me what concerns you."

"I don't want to compromise your position in the movement by asking you to reveal things I don't need to know, Che. I have never known exactly how I was able to leave the country safely back in 1978, but I do know you played a role. Can you tell me now?"

"I played a small role, Ofelia. I got you through this border and a few others on this side of the world, but the rest was in other hands."

"Did you know Al Watson?"

"No, and until recently, I had not heard his name. For many reasons, this cannot be shared with anyone. I was contacted through a member of PpV and asked to play the small role I played. I knew a man in Bolivia. They knew I could get you to Point A. I didn't ask, but it once slipped that Paolo was involved."

"Do you think Paolo is still involved?"

"Of course, Ofelia, Paolo has always been involved in everything that goes on, but I'm too low on the totem pole to know what he believes or what he does."

"What do you think?"

"It doesn't matter what I think."

"Che, this is me. Please tell me what you think."

Che looked closely at his cousin. "I think Paolo is a very successful man who cares about our country's well-being. He is also very secretive, wealthy, and connected enough to protect all of his secrets. And what about you? He obviously cares about you. You must know him better than me."

"I don't know him, Che. I haven't seen Paolo in close to forty years. I'm shocked to be included in his will. I was a teenager with a big crush, and he was kind to me."

Even after all these years, Ofelia didn't want to admit that she had a sexual relationship with Paolo. Che had wondered, but didn't feel comfortable asking; yet, he was also not telling her he was often in touch with people around Paolo Fuentes and knew exactly what side he was on at all times. Paolo was always on the side of Argentina and what was best for the country.

Ofelia changed the subject.

"I don't know if you heard about the coded message Teresa's sister from the Addisons discovered."

"No, what is this?"

"Shortly before he passed, Pete Addison left a coded message on the back of a telephone bill."

"What did it say?" Che chuckled, "I'm assuming you decoded it."

"Of course, at least most of it. It says "Juan Ignacio Ramón has *L*"

"What is L?"

"That's a good question. Teresa is close to Juan Ignacio and will be seeing him next week. She intends to share this information with him, and perhaps he will tell her."

"I would be interested. Did you learn anything else from the message?"

"This is only speculation, but it was written on the back of a telephone bill dated late June of last year, shortly before Señor Addison passed away. We checked out the country codes and came to the conclusion that he was probably still active in the Secret Services. He had made recent calls to Argentina, Chile, Great Britain, Ireland, and Las Islas Malvinas."

"Las Islas Malvinas?"

"Yes"

"This could be important information. Do you have access to the original phone bill with the message?"

"Teresa has that. I can ask her if she will show it to you, perhaps after the funeral. I don't want to alarm her before she meets with Juan Ignacio. I think we should get back to the family now."

Che agreed. He would wait to inform Paolo until he had all of the information.

Chapter 39

After a long discussion, the family decided to deposit Tomás' ashes in the Rio De La Plata. No one felt they had ever gotten to know him well but collectively decided he had spent his adult life following the tides of their country's sad recent history. Once the decision was made, they shared a few happy stories of childhood games and events, for which Ofelia was grateful. She had loved her older brother and although he had abandoned her when she needed him most, forgave him as she realized he was also still a child when he made so many stupid life decisions. No one chose to speak about his decision to join the most violent of Perón's supporters and to remain faithful to that cause well after Perón's true nature had been revealed.

The following day, Teri took a train to Buenos Aires to meet with Juan Ignacio.

Greeting her as she climbed into his car, Juan Ignacio smiled, "I must admit I was surprised to hear you would be back so soon and that Ofelia is with you. This is wonderful news! I almost expected her to come with you today."

"She's anxious to see you, too, but we decided I should meet with you first. We have some important decisions to make. As you requested, I haven't told her about Miguel, but I am hoping you will give me permission or tell her yourself."

Juan Ignacio tried to make light of her request, replying, "All this as you get into the car!"

"All this and more, Juan Ignacio. I hate to jump into it, but there's a lot of serious shit going on that involves you."

"The traffic is terrible, Teresa. Let me get us to my house safely, and I promise I will take everything you ask seriously. But first, please tell me, how was the funeral for Ofelia's brother? I'll bet Ofelia's happy to be home after all these years."

"Okay, I will hold off for a bit. Ofelia is thrilled to be back in Argentina. She was content with her quiet life in Ireland, but not happy if you know what I mean. It's obvious that she's very fond of her cousins, Sylvita and Che. The funeral was a bit strange. No one had seen Tomás for years, and they were all appalled at his violent life's work. But I think they did a good job of focusing on some early memories and, I don't know, bringing him back to his family. They ended up throwing his cremains into the Rio de la Plata after a long discussion of what they thought he might enjoy in the afterlife. It was actually very touching."

"And what about you, Teri? Did you enjoy being with your family?"

"I did, but have to admit, I always feel like the outsider. They try to include me, but everyone mostly speaks to each other in Spanish—very rapidly, in my opinion. I suspect I will always be the family Yanqui."

Juan Ignacio pulled into his driveway, stopped the car, turned to Teri, and said, "Estamos aqui!"

Teri laughed, "Yes, I do understand that we are here."

Sitting across from Teri in his living room with a sandwich and cup of mate, Juan Ignacio began. "I'm ready to have our serious conversation. I will begin with conversational Spanish. Dígame, por favor. Please tell me."

Teri opened her handbag, pulled out the original copy of Pete Addison's phone bill message, and handed it to Juan Ignacio. He looked at both the front and back of the paper with a puzzled expression.

"What is this? Why would I be interested in an old telephone bill?"

"Your name is written in code on the back of the bill."

"Now, you have my attention. What is this?"

"This is one of Pete Addison's last telephone bills prior to his death last year. He had obviously written something in code on the back of it. When we deciphered the code, it said 'JIR has L.' Those are your initials. I thought I should share this with you."

Juan Ignacio studied both sides of the paper intently and looked up at Teri.

"Do you know any more about this?"

"All I can say is what Ofelia and I have deduced. We looked at the country codes of calls he made that month and saw that they included Argentina, Great Britain, Ireland, Chile, Bolivia, and the Falkland Islands. I was never close to Pete, but I assumed he had retired from the Secret Service long before he passed away. However, I know these are some of the places he had worked with in the past. The only thing that stuck out to me were the two calls to the Falkland Islands."

"Why those in particular?"

"I don't know. It just seemed odd until I thought about the battle between Argentina and Great Britain over their ownership. Obviously, by last year, the war had been fought, and Argentina lost, but whenever I ride through the streets of Buenos Aires, there are billboards and graffiti indicating that at least some Porteños disagree with that decision."

"That's an understatement."

"One more thing. We can't tell whether this was a message he received during one of those calls or one he intended to send out. If it's the latter, he may or may not have done so. In any case, I do believe you're the JIR and that someone was telling someone else that you have L. Obviously, you don't have to tell me one way or the other, but both Ofelia and I wanted you to be aware of this."

Juan Ignacio sat quietly for a few minutes. Then he said,

"Thank you for telling me, Teri. I need to think about this."

"Is there anything I can do to help? I promise I can be discreet and obviously will not be sharing this information with anyone else except Ofelia, who was with me when we deciphered the code."

"Have you told Marissa?"

"Yes, and Jack."

Juan Ignacio put his head in his hands, then looked up again.

"I would like to see Ofelia."

"She wants to see you too, Juan Ignacio, and I'm sure she understands much more than me. If you like, I'll call and see if she can catch a train down later today or tomorrow."

Juan Ignacio nodded.

Teri picked up the phone and then put it down.

"Will you tell her about Miguel, Juan Ignacio? You know this is important to me and Marissa."

"I understand, Teri. I've been conflicted about that. I haven't wanted to open the door to more people knowing his whereabouts. I need to think. The message you decoded makes me fear it may be too late. Please call Ofelia. I promise I will decide once I have the opportunity to speak with her."

Chapter 40

Ofelia had been anxiously awaiting Teri's call from Juan Ignacio's house. After they spoke, Ofelia explained to Sylvita that she had to make a quick trip to Buenos Aires. Sylvita feared this signaled a return to the dangerous world Ofelia had inhabited for all those years; but also knew it was best not to protest. Ofelia appreciated that about her cousin. Although she wanted her life to be simpler than before in Argentina, and a bit more exciting than her eight years in Ireland, this was important.

Juan Ignacio met her at the train station alone. He wanted to have a private conversation with Ofelia, and they would speak in the car.

He began immediately. "Teri told me about the message you and she decoded. Do you have any thoughts about its origin?"

"Juan Ignacio, I know as much as you about that, although I'm assuming Teresa shared our belief that it has something to do with Las Islas Malvinas. I must ask you, what is the L it says you have?"

Juan Ignacio laughed ironically, "I knew you would get right to the crux of the matter, Ofelia. Before I decide whether to answer, I need to know who you work for. Are you in the employ of the British Secret Services now? If you are, our conversation ends here. I will always be fond of you, Ofelia, but I am an Argentine patriot."

"I understand why you ask this question since I was basically rescued and protected by the British Secret Service, but I, too, am an Argentine patriot and would never do anything to harm my country's interests. During my eight years in Ireland, I was barely involved with that world. The man who brought me to the British Isles, Al Watson, occasionally asked me to pass sealed messages to other couriers, but I don't believe I was ever trusted with valuable information. Living in Northern Ireland, I've been kept aware of the Irish political situation, but until this came up, barely registered what was happening in Argentina."

"Are you in touch with Al Watson now?"

Ofelia laughed, "Not from my side. He agreed to allow me, first, to meet my daughters and now, to move back to Argentina, but I don't trust him at all. Which reminds me, he sent one of his agents, a tall redheaded man named Brian Mullin, to follow me around. He claims it's for my protection. What a joke."

"Have you seen this Brian since you arrived?"

"I saw him on the plane and at the airport, but not since. But Juan Ignacio, you must know I am very skilled at being aware of my surroundings."

"I don't doubt that Ofelia, but I don't have those skills, and I'm going to trust you to help me. We have to make sure you aren't being followed."

"¡Digame! Tell me!"

"For the past eleven years, I have been responsible for hiding the whereabouts of Miguel Martínez."

"What?!!"

"You know Miguel's son Manuel was my lover for many years?"

"I don't know if I was aware of that. I only knew Manuel as a young child. Please go on."

"I understand all of this was happening in 1975, a few years before you were forced to leave Argentina, but I'm assuming you knew Manuel and the rest of Miguel's family were murdered by the Videla thugs, and that he disappeared."

"Yes, I did know that. Most people believed he was also murdered and his remains would never be found. I think it has been assumed he was thrown out of an airplane into the ocean along with other Videla enemies. What a relief to hear he's alive!"

"The rumors around this have enabled him to be successfully hidden."

"He's alive, and you know where he is hiding?!"

"Yes. Manuel knew they were gunning for Miguel. He begged me to protect his father, so I found a place where he has lived since."

Ofelia said, "I, too, was hearing rumors that he and his family were being targeted, but Miguel was such an innocent, kind-hearted soul. He never believed them. I went to see him, to warn him. He laughed and assured me that Perón and his people would always take care of him. He had survived more than one change in administration and gave credit for his survival to Perón even though Perón was long dead by that time. Now you tell me Miguel is still living."

Tears began forming in the corners of Ofelia's eyes. "Can you take me to him, Juan Ignacio?"

"I can, Ofelia, but I first need to tell you a few more things. Then you can decide if you want to be involved further."

"Alright"

Juan Ignacio sat up straight, "You know I have never been directly involved with PpV or any part of the resistance movement, not even against Perón."

"I wasn't sure, but have never heard that you were."

"I have been sympathetic to the cause of doing what I could to make Argentina a safe, prosperous nation, but until this came up, I never joined any movement. As a homosexual man in our macho culture, I have always felt vulnerable. I have stayed on my side of the road and simply did my work as a banker. Everything I've done to help Miguel has been personal, not political. I don't know how to do any of that."

"That?"

"The kind of undercover work you spent your life doing. I don't even know what to call it."

"Is there something you want to tell me, Juan Ignacio? Is there something you think I can help you with?"

"I don't know what the **L** in the message stands for. When he first went into hiding, Miguel entrusted me with a packet of documents. He told me they were important government documents and that it would be dangerous for me to read them, so I hid them without reading. I honestly have no idea what's in that packet. Now you tell me it has something to do with Las Malvinas. That is already more than I want to know."

"Unfortunately, having these documents in your possession, whether you've read them or not, places you in danger, Juan Ignacio. Seeing your name associated with L, whatever that refers to, should make you nervous. To answer your previous question, I can help you deal with this problem, but you need to tell me everything. Do you understand? Please start at the beginning and tell me what you remember about the whole chain of events, starting with your being asked by Manuel to protect his father. I need names, dates, and what any and all people who've been involved might know. Will you trust me to take this over? Because if you don't, if you don't tell me everything, you and Miguel will be in serious danger. That message indicates that at least someone out there knows you're in possession of something they want."

"There's not much to say, Ofelia. A lot of it is an emotional blur for me. Manuel had been telling me his father's life was in danger for at least a year before he was murdered. I don't know their sources, but the family had been told Miguel was on Videla's enemies list. Manuel told me his father didn't believe he had done anything to deserve Videla's wrath, so he, Manuel, began to make plans to protect the family in case Miguel was taken and/or murdered."

"What did he do?"

"Well, for one thing, he made it clear that he would tell me nothing that would expose me, but he did make two arrangements. He managed to collect a large amount of money, which he gave me in case we needed to find a safe place to hide Miguel and the family. As a banker, I manage large amounts of money all the time, so it would not be a red flag. I have to add, Manuel and my personal relationship had never been an open one, for obvious reasons."

"And the second arrangement?"

"He asked me to care for his father, no matter what else happened. As it turned out, Miguel was not home when the murderers took the lives of Manuel, his mother, and his sister. The poor man came home from wherever he had been to find them lying dead throughout their house. The place was torn up. It looked like they had been searching for something. Miguel called me in tears, and I rushed over there, packed up a bag of his belongings, and drove as fast and as far away as I could. It was obvious they would be back to finish the job. To be perfectly honest, I'm not certain Miguel has recovered from the shock to this day."

"What a terrible experience for both of you!"

"I'm haunted every day by what I saw in that house, but I've been comforted by the fact that Miguel has been safe in my care. You understand why I haven't wanted to share his whereabouts with anyone?"

"I do understand that, but why did you confide in Teresa and Marissa? Why did you take them to meet Miguel?"

"They believe he's their father, and to tell you the truth, I had come to think no one is interested in finding Miguel anymore. Videla and his people are no longer in power, and Videla is in prison, hopefully for the rest of his life. I've also let my guard down a bit. Even if Miguel remains of interest, I would be the last person they would connect with him. Anyway, my connection with Teri is completely understandable. We were next-door neighbors as children who have recently found each other. Why would anyone suspect my taking her for a ride in the car? By the way, the people who run the place where he lives don't know who he is. All they know is that he is an elderly man with some medical needs who is financially secure enough to afford their services. You know, Ofelia, when all of this began, I had no idea why Videla would want to kill Miguel. I mean, I understood his history with Perón could be compromising, but he had survived all who came before Videla just by being a good bureaucrat. On the other hand, Videla, with his Dirty War, was just crazy, so who could figure him out? But, when I saw how they had torn up the house, the furniture broken, everything in pieces, I wondered if they were looking for something. When I discovered the documents sewn in the seam of a jacket, I came to the conclusion there was something important there. Miguel confirmed that when he recommended that I not read them for my safety."

"Did Miguel give you the documents? Where are they now?"

"As I mentioned previously, someone, perhaps Manuel, had sewn a packet of papers into the seam of a jacket. I first saw it when I helped Miguel unpack when he moved to the facility where he currently resides. Before that, we had kept most things packed up, so it was probably a few months later.

"Did Miguel tell you what it was?"

"Not exactly, just that I needed to hide it"

"And what have you done with it?"

"I have hidden it. Miguel asked me to keep it hidden. What do you think I should do?"

"Juan Ignacio, I know you're aware that many Argentines will never accept the idea of Las Islas Malvinas being part of Britain."

"Of course, they have belonged to us for centuries."

"And the Brits wanted them enough to invest in a war that cost them a lot of money. Even though they are now under British control as the Falkland Islands, I don't believe the war is over for either side. Now I'm wondering if there's something in those documents."

"Do you recommend that I destroy them?"

"Based on what you've told me today, probably, but first, I need to speak with Miguel. I would like to hear from his lips what they are and why they needed to be hidden."

Juan Ignacio smiled for the first time, "It may surprise you to hear, but your involvement takes a huge load off my shoulders and I know Miguel trusts you completely. He would like to see you for other reasons as well. He often speaks of you with affection."

"Will you arrange a meeting?"

"Yes." Opening the car door, he added, "Now we must speak with Teresa, who waits impatiently to hear what we've been talking about. I believe she will want to join us with Miguel."

Chapter 41

Brian entered the British Embassy, where he would have access to a secure phone line. He had not spoken with Al Watson since he discovered Ofelia had ditched her original flight to Buenos Aires. Although he'd been traveling from London, he and Al had coordinated his flight schedule to arrive in Buenos Aires at approximately the same time her flight was due to arrive from Dublin. The Buenos Aires airport was small enough for him to watch all arrivals in that period of time but she never showed up. He called Al to find out what was going on and heard curse words he had never heard before. Al had been particularly peeved when he learned she had possession of two different passports. How had that gotten past him?

Although her change of plans was inconvenient for him, Brian was secretly impressed. He had only known her as the lovely Brigid, the low-level courier for Al he danced with once a year at Lisdoonvarna. This Ofelia side of her was much more interesting, and Brian looked forward to matching wits.

Settling into a small windowless room, Brian picked up the phone and dialed an exclusive number. Al answered immediately. Unlike their earlier conversation, his voice conveyed his typical smooth self-control.

"Hello Brian, how are things on the other side of the pond?"

"Well, if you're asking about the weather, I can tell you I have never been so uncomfortable. It's summer here and the humidity is unbearable. I feel the need to change my shirt three or four times a day!"

"Sorry about that, Old Chum, but I'm more interested in what you've been doing, and what you've learned since we last spoke."

"Of course. Apparently, one of the daughters had been visiting our Brigid when we met with her in Belfast, a small bit of information she chose not to share with us."

"What has that to do with your mission?"

"Instead of flying directly to Argentina, using the ticket you provided, the two ladies took a flight to New York, where they stayed for about a week at the daughter's house."

"Ah, so this was her American daughter Teri."

"Yes. And Teri accompanied her to Buenos Aires where they are both currently residing. I actually ran into them at the Texas airport, where we were all changing planes. We shared a drink and had a nice chat. Since then, I've been keeping an eye on Ofelia."

"And, what have you found?"

"Specifically, she has been staying with relatives in a small town in Buenos Aires Province called Punta Lapiz."

"Has she done anything interesting?"

"It appears the entire family spent the first few days preparing and celebrating a memorial service for Ofelia's brother Tomás."

"So that wasn't a lie. Has she been staying close to home since then?"

"I haven't seen her today. Her daughter took a train to Buenos Aires to visit a friend in Barrio Buenasuerte and has yet to return, but I've been here and seen no sign of Brigid, I mean Ofelia. Do you think I should touch base with Señor Fuentes?"

"Not yet. I've already informed him I facilitated Ofelia's return to Argentina. When we learn more, I will be the one to contact him. He's a high-level player, way above your pay grade. And I'm still not certain what side he's on with respect to the Falklands. I am curious about his including Ofelia in his will. Ha Ha! But I doubt he would appreciate being asked about that."

"Anything else, Al?"

"Just keep doing what you're doing, Brian. Besides her family, it will be interesting to see who Ofelia reaches out to after all these years, and I like that you're keeping an eye on the daughters too. I wonder if they are also trying to find Miguel Martinez. Yes, I would suggest you follow up with the social activities of both daughters. I'm still not sure what the story with Mateo Roca is, and I can't help wondering if there isn't more to it beyond his courtship of Ofelia's daughter. At some point, I will probably ask Paolo about him. And, it occurs to me that Teri doesn't live in Argentina and is unlikely to have many friends there, so who could she be visiting with? Might come up with something."

Brian hung up the phone, thinking, *Al is so full of himself; he's the only one who's good enough to speak with Paolo Fuentes? What's he hiding I can't do as well? Well, at least I know what I should do next.*

Chapter 42

Teri had been waiting impatiently as Ofelia and Juan Ignacio sat talking in the car. The fact that their conversation stretched over an hour gave her hope that Juan Ignacio had decided to bring Ofelia into his confidence regarding Miguel and the coded message. As she opened the door, Teri couldn't help beginning her greeting with, "Well??" Then became tongue-tied.

All three laughed out loud, in part simply to relieve the stress they'd been experiencing.

Ofelia came right to the point, "Juan Ignacio and I have decided it's time to visit Miguel."

Teri smiled broadly. "This is great news. When do you plan to go? Shall I tell Marissa? Should we all visit him together?"

Juan Ignacio jumped in. "Oh no, Teri. Seeing Ofelia will be a large enough shock for Miguel. Let's save the family reunion for the next time."

"I understand. When do you plan to go? Soon I hope."

Juan Ignacio said, "If it's alright with Ofelia, I would like to go out there tomorrow. We need to explain what's happening, and its potential danger to Miguel. We may have to move him again, maybe even out of the country."

Ofelia nodded, "I'm happy to go as soon as possible. I need to see Miguel for myself to assess his state of mind so I can think about the best way to move forward. I know it will be a shock for him to see me after all these years."

"How many years has it been, Ofelia? When we were there last month, Miguel said he had seen you before he left Buenos Aires in 1975."

Ofelia fingered the locket hanging from her neck. "I did see him that year. I went to warn him that he was in danger, that it had come to my attention that he was a person of interest to Videla. He laughed it off. Then he told me he had always loved me and gave me this gift."

Teri turned to Juan Ignacio, "Can't you see how important the blood sample is for us, Juan Ignacio?"

"What blood sample?" Ofelia asked.

"If we can obtain a blood sample from Miguel, Marissa and I can find out for sure if he's our father."

Looking again at Juan Ignacio, Teri continued, "Please help us with this. Marissa knows a scientist with access to a laboratory where his blood and ours can be analyzed easily. You're the only one who can ask Miguel for his permission. They have medical staff where he lives and experts who draw blood from many of the residents when they need to assess certain health issues. Most of the residents appear to be elderly or in poor health there."

Juan Ignacio threw up his hands. "I was resisting this as a violation of his privacy, but it seems like a reasonable request at this point. I have been overly protective, but it's starting to feel possible that you are his family, and who has more rights than family? I suppose if it's determined that he's not your father, we go back to the way things were before."

Teri said, "So, you two will visit Miguel tomorrow. Is it alright if I stay at your house until you come back, Juan Ignacio?"

"Of course. Now I must call the residence to let them know we'll be visiting. I have no obligation to do so, but I feel it's a courtesy so neither Miguel nor his medical caregivers will be surprised."

"Will you tell them Ofelia is joining you?"

"I think not. Let's make that a surprise. I'm just hoping he recognizes you, Ofelia. Last time, he mistook Marissa for you."

"I find that very flattering. How did you introduce her and Teri?"

"We told him the truth, that they are your daughters."

Ofelia couldn't help smiling. Just hearing those words put a song in her heart.

The next morning, Teri watched Juan Ignacio and Ofelia as they drove off, wondering if she would be able to concentrate on anything until she saw them again and heard their news. Her only plan for the day was to give Marissa a call. She knew Marissa would be as anxious to learn about the outcome of the Ofelia-Miguel reunion as she was. She also wanted to make sure Marissa's professor would be available to do the HLA blood test in a timely manner. *Oh please, Miguel, don't refuse the blood draw; surely that's a routine part of life there.*

Teri picked up the phone to call Marissa, who was anxious to hear her news.

"I barely believe I can say these words, Marissa. Ofelia and Juan Ignacio just left. They're on their way to see Miguel."

"That's great to hear. Will Juan Ignacio be asking for Miguel's blood sample?"

"As a matter of fact, that's one reason I wanted to speak with you right away. I don't know if there's a time constraint around testing blood, and I want to make sure we do this correctly."

"I'll speak with Professor Seguro today. I'm so pleased Juan Ignacio has consented to help us. Did Ofelia convince him?"

"I guess so. They sat in his car in the driveway, talking privately for more than an hour. By the time they were done, there was a notable change in Juan Ignacio."

"What change?"

"I had the feeling he was worried after I told him about the coded message. I think Ofelia convinced him she had the skills and knowledge to manage things from now on. He was clearly taking care of Miguel for personal reasons. He doesn't have a background in the secret world Ofelia was schooled in. I don't know; it just seemed like he let Ofelia take over, and whatever she thought was best was the way things would be. I'm not sure I can describe it differently."

Marissa was silent for a minute or two, then she said,

"I feel I've been out of the loop."

"You seriously know everything I know at this point."

"Do you know the meaning of **L**?"

"No, but I'm willing to bet Juan Ignacio knows and has told Ofelia. Hey, can you join me here for the next couple of days? We can both be here when Ofelia and Juan Ignacio return. Hopefully, they'll have the blood sample in hand, and we can hand-carry it back to the lab as soon as possible."

"I probably can do that. First, I need to make excuses to my mother and Mateo. We had plans for this evening."

"You can wait to come tomorrow, Marissa. Juan Ignacio and Ofelia will surely spend the night at Miguel's place."

"Hmmm. I'll let you know."

Chapter 43

Marissa canceled her date with Mateo and joined Teri in Buenos Aires. Unable to reach her mother by phone, she walked to Sylvita and Raoul's house. When she arrived, she found her mother on the phone trying to make a medical center appointment for Raoul, who had been exhibiting signs of influenza.

Sylvita hung up the phone, looking harried. "I need to take your father to the medical center immediately for an official diagnosis. Otherwise, we will have to wait for a week to get him the medicine he needs. Can you believe this?!"

"How can I help?"

"Do you mind going into the bedroom and helping him get ready? Che is with him. All you need to do is make sure he's properly dressed and has his current medications to show them. He is very weak, but Che can help get him into the car. I'll take care of things after that."

"Of course. Are you sure you don't want me to come with you?"

"That won't be necessary, Marissita. But, did you come over for a reason?"

"You have enough on your plate, Mamá. I came to tell you I will be out of town for a few days. I was coming to ask your help with Lobito, but I can find someone else."

Hearing the last part of this conversation, Che stepped out of the bedroom and said, "I can care for your dog for a couple of days."

"Thank you, Che. Ofelia and Teri are with Juan Ignacio. They've invited me to join them."

About to say more, Marissa stopped, not remembering what Che knew and didn't know.

Che smiled, "Is this about the mysterious coded message? Don't worry; Ofelia told me all about it."

"It is, in part, and I promise we will soon know and be able to share what I hope will be exciting news."

"How enticing! I look forward to learning more."

Sylvita called out from the bedroom, "It's time. We need to get this man to the doctor."

Raoul was obviously having trouble breathing and was laboring as he walked. Both Marissa and Che once again offered to accompany Sylvita to the medical center, but she said it was unnecessary; there were always wheelchairs at the door.

Che turned to Marissa, "Shall I come to your house for dog care instructions?"

"Probably."

As they walked, Che apologized for his skepticism about Mateo.

"I suppose my professional life has made me suspicious of everyone. Mateo seems to be a gentleman, and I'm glad to see you happy."

Marissa laughed, "I was annoyed at first, but as I think about it, all that's happened with our family surely warrants checking into new acquaintances. Especially when we meet them at Matchmaker's Balls in a foreign country."

"I continue to be intrigued at the thought of Paolo Fuentes including Ofelia in his will. Has Mateo told you any more about this?"

"No, I don't believe he was told more than what we've already heard."

"Has he had further contact with Paolo's former wife?"

"Not that I know. Sorry to be such a poor source of information, Che. I must admit, I wonder if Ofelia is telling us all she can about her past relationship with Paolo. She says she hasn't seen him in many years, so why would he remember her in his current will?"

"What do you think, Marissa?"

Marissa turned red, "Please don't share this with anyone, but I think it's possible that Paolo is Teri's and my father, and somehow, he knows that. Of course, this is pure speculation, but Ofelia told us she was in a sexual relationship with him at the same time as the one with Miguel Martínez."

It was Che's turn to blush. "I wondered but never knew that. So, she told you."

"That's one of the reasons Teri and I are so anxious to get blood for a paternity test from Miguel. If it comes out negative and Ofelia is telling the truth that there were only two men in her life at the time, Paolo becomes the top candidate. Either way, we really want to know."

"I understand. Now, where do you keep the dog food?"

Chapter 44

Getting off the phone with Al, Brian decided to follow Teri before heading back up to Punta Lapís to track Ofelia and Marissa. Although he had presumed it would be a dead end, the house in Barrio Buenasuerte was close by. It might be interesting to see who Teri was visiting. He knew Teri had lived in Buenos Aires as a young child and figured it must be a childhood friend or acquaintance. As he drove by the house, he noted a car parked in the driveway with two people conversing intently in the front seat. For the next half hour, he drove around the neighborhood, passing the house every ten minutes or so. During his last revolution, he was rewarded to see Ofelia and a younger man get out of the car and go into the house. It was turning dark, so he watched the house for another hour, then decided they would probably be spending the night there. Brian found a place to park where he could keep an eye on the place, grabbed some food at a small supermercado around the corner, and settled in for the night.

The following morning, Brian was rewarded once again when he saw Ofelia and the same young man get into the car and drive off. He followed them for a few hours until they arrived at a gated residential complex southwest of Buenos Aires. Along the highway, there had been enough traffic for him to comfortably stay hidden and keep them generally in view at the same time. However, when they arrived at the entrance to the complex, he decided not to follow and continued driving out of their sight.

Stopping at a restaurant in the next town, Brian pretended to be a lost British tourist and used his poor Spanish skills to charm his waitress.

"Café con leche, por favor."

Hearing his questionable accent, the waitress smiled and said in perfect English, "You aren't from around here, I gather."

This was perfect. Brian smiled back at her and said, "How can you tell?"

"Where are you from in the British Isles?"

"London, how about you? And how did you end up here?"

"I'm from York, couldn't you tell from my northern accent? And to answer your second question, long story, but I have to work. What can I get you besides coffee?"

"I'd love a sandwich. Do you serve sándwich de miga? "

The waitress smiled, "Sí Señor. Toasted?"

"Please."

"You know, it's rumored that sándwich de miga was created to serve British businessmen who missed their crustless cucumber sandwiches."

"That could describe me, I guess."

The waitress looked around to see if she was being watched, then said, "So, what brings you to this remote part of Argentina?"

"Believe it or not, I'm looking for a quiet residence for my elderly mother. I had heard there was a good residential complex in this area. Could it be the one I passed down the road from here?"

"Casa de Lobo de Crin? Oh yes, it's a lovely place and extremely exclusive. Only very wealthy people live there. I believe many of the residents are elderly."

"Is it a place I could just walk in to obtain information, or would I need to make an appointment, do you think?"

"It is gated, so you would probably need an appointment. If you remind me before you leave, I can give you their phone number. We have a phone directory in our office in the back."

***

Armed with the phone number, Brian decided to return to Buenos Aires, where he could find the resources to investigate the residence. It was in such a remote area; he was already worried word would get out in the community that a tall, red-headed Englishman was asking about it.

In Buenos Aires, he went to a local library and looked up La Casa del Lobo de Chin and learned the name lobo de chin referred to a maned wolf, a species of animal found in South America that wasn't actually a wolf. Perhaps that indicated the residence itself wasn't what it appeared to be. In his profession, it was always wise to be skeptical, and this place was seriously remote. However, everything else he found indicated it was exactly what the waitress had told him: *a peaceful, luxurious residential community where wealthy people deposited their elderly or disabled relatives where they could live out their lives in a pleasant environment with the best of care.* Brian was drawn to its remoteness. It was unlikely people would simply run across such a place. The more he thought about it, the more he became convinced it would be the perfect place to hide Miguel Martínez.

Should he wait for Ofelia to return to Buenos Aires, or should he call Al now? Brian decided to wait. He was on a roll and annoyed at the way Al dismissed him, keeping him out of the loop and just giving him the minimal amount of information he would need to do "his part of the job." Then Al would go on to take credit for his hard work. No, this time, he would take the initiative and keep Al in the dark until HE was ready to share. This was big and perhaps the project that would lead to his rising status in the agency.

The following morning, Brian drove back to Barrio Buenasuerte, where he parked his car and took a walk around what appeared to be its perimeter. He liked the way the neighborhood seamlessly integrated homes with small stores and restaurants. As he ambled along the perfectly coordinated tree-lined streets with their well-manicured lawns, he pondered the meaning of its name, *Good Luck neighborhood. There has to be an interesting story behind that.*

Although a bit warm for his taste, it was a lovely summer day. Brian began to feel mellow. In that state of mind, he stepped into a coffee shop and struck up a conversation with customers who were curious about who he was and what he was doing in their part of town. He told them he had heard the son of an old friend of his parents lived here, but he was damned if he could remember the guy's name or exact address.

"I think the house is on Avenida Cuarenta. If I recall, my mother said he lived in a house that was second in from the corner."

The men he was talking with looked at each other, then one said, "Ah, that must be the banker, Juan Ignacio Ramón. He inherited that house when his parents passed away a few years ago."

"Gracias. I will go knock on his door and see if he remembers hearing of me."

Brian walked out of the shop grinning from ear to ear. He would bypass Al and call Paolo Fuentes directly.

Chapter 45

Neither Ofelia nor Juan Ignacio had noticed the car that followed them throughout their journey. Brian was a professional who knew how to slide in and out of traffic with minimal detection. In this case, he was helped by the fact that the roads they traversed were either well-traveled highways or lightly used curved mountain roads. In the former case, he could weave in and out while keeping an eye on Juan Ignacio's car; the mountain roads were even easier because there was nowhere to get off, so he could maintain a good distance.

Like her daughters, Ofelia was impressed with the beauty surrounding Miguel's residence, both inside and outside the building. She said as much to the caregiver, Natalia, who escorted them to Miguel's rooms.

After knocking, Natalia opened the front door with a key and asked Juan Ignacio and Ofelia to wait outside until she was certain Miguel was prepared for visitors.

"Buenos noches, Señor Martínez, tus visitantantes estan aqui."

Miguel greeted them with a warm smile as they entered the room,

"Hola, Juan Ignacio y quien es?"

Before Juan Ignacio had a chance to respond, Miguel stood up and walked to Ofelia with his arms open.

"Ofelia! Estás aqui!"

Ofelia hugged him back, and as they separated, he noticed she was wearing the locket he had given her the last time they'd seen each other. Pointing at it, he looked at Juan Ignacio and announced,

"You see, Juan Ignacio, I told you my Ofelia would come home to us."

Juan Ignacio nodded. "I will leave you two to reminisce." And walked out of the room thinking, *This is a man in love. Miguel will give Ofelia anything she asks.*

Miguel barely noticed Juan Ignacio leave the room and focused totally on Ofelia. Fingering the locket, he asked,

"I don't believe I've seen this on you before. When did I give it to you?"

"It was eleven years ago, in 1975, just before you and I went our separate ways."

"I know I came here, but where did you go?

"I went to Northern Ireland, where I lived until a short time ago."

"Were you also in hiding?"

"Yes. Like many of our acquaintances, I was targeted by Videla and his cronies."

"It's such a bad business, but I understand he is no longer el presidente."

"Es verdad, he is in prison for his crimes. Alfonsín is now our president. Let us hope he's a better leader than the rest."

"I've been isolated here, Ofelia. It is very peaceful. I do not miss the political intrigue of my past life."

"I'm happy for you, Miguel. I hope we can both live peaceful lives in our home country from now on."

Miguel smiled, "I believe I met your twin daughters the last time Juan Ignacio came to visit. They are lovely and so much like you. I must admit, perhaps in my old age, I had forgotten you had children."

"No Miguel, you hadn't forgotten. I never told anyone about my pregnancy. My daughters are in their late 30s now. They were born out of wedlock when I was a teenager. Do you remember when I left your family's employ when I was a nanny to your son and daughter?"

"How could I forget? It was a sad time in my life. Wait, are you telling me you think your daughters are my children?"

"I think it's a possibility since you and I were in a sexual relationship when I became pregnant."

"I understand why you never told me; that would have caused many problems with my wife. The truth is, I cannot be their father. I became infertile when I contracted mumps a few years before you came to work for us."

"After your children were born?"

"Yes, as a matter of fact, I contracted mumps from my children."

Ofelia closed her eyes and thought. *This means Paolo is their father. At least I won't have to ask HIM for a blood sample!*

"I wish it were true. As you know, I lost both of my children when Videla's people came looking for me. Since that day, I have wished I was the only one home when they came."

"I'm glad you're still among the living, Miguel, but it is so tragic that they killed your wife and children for no reason."

"I almost wish it were so, but they had their reasons, and it was my fault. They were looking for documents I had in my possession."

"How do you know this?"

"When I returned to my home, I found the dead bodies of my family and the house torn apart. They were clearly looking for something they never found. I knew they would be back for me and the documents. That was when I called Juan Ignacio. He saved my life."

"He told me your son was aware you might be in danger. Your son made arrangements to save you."

"Yes. This all remains painful. Can we speak of something else? Oh, here is Juan Ignacio. I have been a poor host. Can I offer you both a glass of wine?"

Juan Ignacio looked at Ofelia, who nodded. "Of course, we have been on a long car ride."

"How was the traffic?"

"We started early and avoided a lot of the commuter and highway traffic, and of course, it's always relaxing driving along the beautiful mountain and country roads."

Miguel poured three glasses of wine and handed two to his guests, saying,

"Juan Ignacio, did you know Ofelia thought I may have fathered her beautiful daughters?"

Juan Ignacio looked at Ofelia. "I did, Miguel. That was one of the reasons I brought them to meet you last month."

"I'm sorry to disappoint you. I'm even disappointed, but as I just explained to Ofelia, it wouldn't have been possible. I've been unable to father a child since I contracted mumps when Manuel and his sister were small."

"You're sure about that, Miguel?"

"Absolutely sure. My wife wanted more children and blamed me for not giving them to her."

"How sad for you."

"I was happy with my two children, and I must confess, was tired of being hounded by my wife. When she finally stopped, our sex life ended, which is one reason I became involved with you, Ofelia. She knew about it and didn't care. I had the happiest moments of my life with you. I'm only sorry if it caused you pain."

Ofelia smiled, "I learned long ago not to regret past decisions. I was unhappy when I first became pregnant. I was ill a lot of the time and totally unequipped for parenthood. But people who cared for me helped and allowed me to go on with my life—a life, I, as a young girl, was enjoying. I was also able to spend time with both of my daughters when they were young, and we are now reunited as adults."

"How wonderful, and I'm thrilled to be reunited with you as well. Perhaps you can visit me again?"

"I certainly hope so, Miguel, but I'm afraid I must return to our earlier conversation. It has come to our attention that there are bad people out there who are still interested in obtaining documents they believe you have hidden. I agree with you that the people who murdered your family were in search of something, likely to be those documents."

"Yes, but they are well hidden."

"These people are looking for you as well as the documents."

"Yes, but we are both well hidden."

"We discovered a coded message that identifies Juan Ignacio as the one who has them. This places him in danger."

Miguel looked at Juan Ignacio with a concerned expression. "Have you hidden them well?"

"So far, yes. It has been successful for two reasons so far. No one knew where you were, or even whether you were alive or dead, and no one knew anything about me or my role in this. Now someone knows my name. Can you tell us what these documents are? Can Ofelia and I destroy them, or are they too important?"

Miguel sat down and took a gulp of his wine. Looking at his visitors, he said, "I trust you both with my life, but I fear if I tell you anything, you become endangered. I have already been responsible for the deaths of my wife and children. I don't think I could bear it again."

Juan Ignacio took a deep breath. "Miguel, eleven years ago, you entrusted these documents to me, asking me to hide them in a secure location without looking through them. I did that. Now I must ask you to trust me again. Ofelia cannot help us without knowing what the documents are and why people are willing to commit murder to obtain them. Do you understand that, now that my name is connected with the documents, they suspect, or even know, I'm in possession of them? This means neither you nor I are safe at all. You are in hiding, but I have always been easy to find. When that happens, they will kill us both. You say you trust Ofelia with your life. Please give us permission to read the documents and decide what to do with them."

Miguel's face turned dark with confusion. Ofelia kneeled in front of him. Reaching behind her neck, she unclasped the locket chain and placed it in his hands.

"Will you give me permission to read the documents, Miguel?"

Looking up from the locket in his hand, he responded quietly, "Yes"

"Thank you. Will you allow me to destroy them at my discretion?"

Miguel looked first at Ofelia, then at Juan Ignacio, and took a deep breath. With that breath, his entire demeanor changed. He stopped crying, sat up straight, and exhaled loudly. When he spoke again, he was a different person, a man with confidence.

"If I recall, many of the documents in the packet I gave you are only of historical interest. Feel free to destroy those as there are probably other copies of them out there. But there is one document, a list of names, that has the potential to destroy people's lives."

"The people named on the list?"

"Yes, these are people who serve our country honorably but are seen as the enemy by some. We must protect them from being exposed."

Ofelia stepped in, "Miguel, please tell us what this is all about. We have the power to protect such patriots. Who are these people? How many are on the list?"

"If I recall, there are seven or eight names on the list. This may have been altered as the list was created several years ago. Some of them may be dead or moved on to other positions."

"Positions doing what?"

"They are government employees in various positions in Las Islas Malvinas."

"They are British Falkland Island government employees?"

"Yes, but they are secretly working to overthrow the Falklands Island government and restore the islands to their rightful place as part of Argentina."

Miguel bowed his head and covered his face with his hands.

"Now you know everything. Please be very careful, as I'm sure you will understand, many people would be willing to kill for that list, people on both sides of the conflict."

Ofelia looked at Miguel and took a breath, "Whew! This is certainly a lot to absorb, Miguel, but I can promise we will be alright. I don't want to alarm you, but I'm wondering if we need to find you another safe haven, at least for a short while?"

"I appreciate your concern, Ofelia, and am certainly uninterested in being harmed, but I'm also resistant to moving. As you may have noticed, I have chronic medical issues that require professional attention. They know me, and care for me here. I don't want to move."

"I understand. I think Juan Ignacio and I need to return to Buenos Aires and attend to the documents soon. I promise we will keep you informed. If there are any signs of trouble for you, we'll make sure you remain safe."

"As I said before, I trust you both with my life. Ofelia, seeing you has been the greatest pleasure of my time here, and I'm touched that you thought of wearing the locket I gave you."

"Believe it or not, I have often worn it over the years."

"That makes me even happier."

Looking at the locket in his hands, Miguel ran his finger over the etched flower. "I remember having this locket made especially for you. I wanted to give you a keepsake and remembered how much you love the Ceibo blossom. I've often thought it resembles a fiery dragon, so appropriate."

Miguel began to hand the locket back to Ofelia, but Ofelia held it in his hand. "Please, Miguel, hold on to this precious gift for me until we meet again."

Miguel smiled, "I will do that. This has been quite the visit! Please give my regards to your lovely daughters"

Chapter 46

Ofelia mused thoughtfully about Miguel on their return drive to Buenos Aires.

"I found it difficult to read Miguel. Teri and Marissa gave me the impression he was struggling with memory loss, but I didn't see that at all. I mean, he seems alert and has clear memories of the past and what has led him to live here. On the other hand, I had the sense that he didn't quite understand the seriousness of the current situation."

Juan Ignacio sighed, "I take responsibility for that, Ofelia. From the moment I took charge of his life, he has trusted me to protect him from harm. I think we both pretty much forgot about the documents. I know this may sound strange to you, but in the beginning, we made a deal. He protected me by not telling me what they were about, and I protected him by not telling him where they were hidden. It's been eleven years, and this is the first time we've spoken about them. As for his mental health, I don't know. What I do know is that he doesn't know that he is seriously ill with more than one debilitating condition."

"Are his doctors saying he will die soon?"

"Yes, and I was hoping his last months would be peaceful, but I guess that was too much to expect." Juan Ignacio smiled, "I think seeing you has made him very happy. He is always sweet, but in a sad way. Today, he is happier than I can remember. I don't believe I could have convinced him to give us permission to make decisions about the documents on my own. He clearly loves you and trusts you completely."

"I could tell he isn't well; he just seems weak. It makes me more determined to resolve this issue so he can continue to live a comfortable life. It may seem odd, given that our past relationship was built on a lie, but I believe we became fond of one another, and that has not changed. I have never regretted my belief that he was my daughters' father."

"And now you know he isn't."

"Yes"

Juan Ignacio could tell this part of the conversation was over. Ofelia needed to process what she had learned about their paternity, and it was none of his business.

The remainder of the drive to Buenos Aires was dominated by a conversation regarding what they had learned from Miguel and how they would move forward. Both Juan Ignacio and Ofelia were energized and happy Ofelia was taking the reins. She knew her way around political intrigue and was clearly enthusiastic about getting back into that world.

Arriving at Juan Ignacio's house, the travelers were surprised to be greeted by Marissa as well as Teri. Marissa had driven to Buenos Aires with hopes of being able to quickly pick up and deliver the blood sample to her professor's lab.

As they walked in the door, Teri asked, "You were able to obtain Miguel's permission?"

Ofelia said, "Actually, we didn't ask for it because he convinced us he couldn't be your father."

"Really?"

"He was apparently rendered sterile from a case of mumps he contracted from his children a few years before you were born."

Marissa said aloud what everyone was thinking, "So, Paolo Fuentes is our father."

Teri was the only one in the room who didn't have a strong opinion about Paolo Fuentes. Although she had heard Ofelia's story of the role he played in her early life, she wasn't aware of his family's deep historical roots and what that meant to the average Argentine. For Marissa, who had grown up learning the Fuentes family history as a school child, this new reality was almost incomprehensible. It was like being told she was the bastard child of royalty. Even Ofelia hadn't thought about what this could mean for her daughters until that moment.

Teri interrupted her thoughts, "So, now what? Should we contact him and ask for a blood sample to confirm?"

Ofelia smiled, "I tend to doubt that would get us very far. Paolo is one of the most powerful men in Argentina. He might take it as an attempt on our part to blackmail or at least demand money from him."

Teri glanced at Marissa, who continued to look as if she was in shock. Then she addressed Ofelia, "But what about the fact that he included you in his will, Ofelia? Doesn't that indicate you've been on his mind? Would it be totally weird for you to contact him?"

"I understand this is important to you and Marissa, but I need a little time to absorb what we've learned. Meanwhile, there are a few other important things Juan Ignacio and I need to attend to first."

"Okay, like what?"

"Juan Ignacio is in possession of important government documents."

"Is it dangerous for us to know what they are, Juan Ignacio?"

"Ah, Teri, I don't even know what they are; at least, I didn't know until Miguel told us about one of them. I have never read any of them; all I did was hide them."

Ofelia jumped in, "We would prefer to keep you two out of this for the moment. Juan Ignacio and I need to review them and decide what to do."

"Can you tell us if they have to do with the Falkland Islands? I'm just curious because that was what we figured from the phone bill."

"Teresa, you are your mother's daughter, having to know everything! Please give us a chance to study them. We'll do that today or tomorrow after Juan Ignacio retrieves them from the hiding place."

Marissa said, "What would you like us to do now? Should Teri and I stay here or return to Punta Lapiz? What can we tell Sylvita, Raoul, and Che? I know they will want to know."

Chapter 47

Ofelia Cruz was on Paolo Fuente's mind a lot these days. It seemed as if every time the phone rang, there was news of her, a woman he hadn't seen for at least thirty years. He first met her when she was a young girl with no fear, a lively intelligence, and a natural talent for successfully taking on any role that was asked of her. There was no doubt he was charmed by her and, although not proud of it, took advantage of her obvious crush on him. It was perhaps guilt that prompted him to follow her life and help her out when she got into trouble. And her troubles were notable. First, a teenage pregnancy resulted in out-of-wedlock twins, for God's sake, then having to escape the country during the Videla administration.

Oddly, after many years, her name came up again when Paolo's former wife revealed angrily that she had seen a copy of his will, a copy that included a bequest to Ofelia. Although she had no business looking into his financial affairs (Paolo had made certain she would be well-cared for despite the cessation of their marriage), she had gone ahead and hired a private investigator to track Ofelia. The investigator found her in Northern Ireland, where she appeared to be living a quiet life under another name. He told his ex she could have saved her money and simply asked him who she was. While he was annoyed with her actions, Paolo had long ago decided to avoid conflict with this woman. She was the mother of his two sons, and he wanted to maintain peace in the family. He told her, with a straight face, that Ofelia was someone he had worked with many years previously, a young woman he had simply wanted to help out. She had placed herself in danger many times to make Argentina a better, safer place to live. It was basically an act of charity he had forgotten, having included her in his will a long time ago. It was not necessary to tell his ex that he had, in fact, always kept eyes on Ofelia Cruz and played a major role in supporting her throughout her life, both in Argentina and Ireland.

Paolo's former wife seemed to accept his explanation at which time thoughts of Ofelia moved to the back of his mind. Then he received a message from Al Watson, the MI6 agent who sponsored Ofelia's escape to the British Isles eight years previously. Al's cryptic message indicated that two notable things had happened in the past year: Ofelia had been reunited with her twin daughters, something Al had facilitated, and Al had made the decision to allow her to return to Argentina, explaining that it seemed safe for her to make the move. Paolo was okay with her return and happy with the thought that Ofelia had a chance to live a good life with her daughters. With Videla out of power and recently imprisoned for life, Ofelia had no particular enemies in Argentina as far as Paolo knew.

All of this was fine. Then Paolo received a call from an agent working with Al Watson who said he believed he had followed Ofelia to the hiding place of Miguel Martínez. Martínez was a fugitive former Perón crony who had either been in hiding or dead for the past eleven years. It was evident from the conversation with this agent, Brian Mullin, that Al had supported Ofelia's return to Argentina, hoping she would lead him to Martínez. A bit of information Al had neglected to tell Paolo.

Paolo knew why Al didn't share this information because people on both sides had been looking for Martínez for years. It was well-known that Miguel went into hiding in possession of a list of Falkland Island government employees who were working to overthrow the currently British-controlled government from the inside and restore power to

Argentina. The British Secret Service and the Argentine resistance worked well together when it suited both interests. This was not one of those situations, and both sides were anxious to keep the other from obtaining that list.

Now it appeared that Ofelia was the key to finding Miguel and taking possession of the list. Paolo couldn't help thinking this confirmed the rumors he had heard 'on the street' that Miguel was the father of Ofelia's daughters. He was ashamed to have been part of it, but Ofelia had been placed in Miguel's family's employ with the specific mission of seducing Miguel for government secrets shortly before she became pregnant.

Although Paolo didn't know how she would react, he decided he had to reach out to Ofelia. She had always been a fierce patriot. He figured if he brought up Miguel's name and how important finding those documents would be to their country, she would help.

The best path to Ofelia would be through her cousin Che Delgado. Che had always been a loyal soldier who would protect Ofelia to the death. Paolo knew if he could get Che on his side, Ofelia would be open to listening to him. Paolo dialed Che's telephone number.

"Hola Che, this is Paolo Fuentes. I am hoping I find you well."

Che knew this was an important call. Paolo never called simply to chat.

"Hola Paolo. I have been thinking about calling you with news of Ofelia. She has moved back to Argentina."

"Yes, I did hear that, Che. Let me get right to the point. I also heard she may be in touch with Miguel Martínez."

Surprised and concerned to hear that Paolo, and who knew who else, would have heard such a thing; Che scrambled to take control of the conversation. Deep down, he knew that would be hopeless. With his overwhelming power, Paolo held all of the cards. Wondering what else

Paolo knew about all that was going on, Che decided to respond to this question and perhaps learn more.

"What you've heard is accurate, Paolo. May I ask the source of your information? Ofelia's first meeting with Miguel just occurred yesterday."

"Thank you for confirming. I heard about it from one of Al Watson's MI6 people, a fellow named Brian Mullin, who has apparently been sent to Argentina to follow Ofelia with hopes of leading him to Miguel. He followed her to a remote residential community in the Southern Pampas he believes may be where Miguel has been hiding. If he is correct, we need to find Miguel first."

"And you would like me to share this information with Ofelia?"

"More than that, Che, I would like to meet with her as soon as possible. There are several issues we need to discuss. Can you arrange such a meeting right away?"

"I will speak with her immediately. She is currently visiting with a friend in Buenos Aires. Would you be able to travel to that location?"

"I can be anywhere in Buenos Aires within a few hours. What is the address?"

"I don't have it at the moment, but will ask Ofelia when I call her. I will give it to you then. One more thing, there are people at this house who should not be involved."

"Don't worry about that, Che. I know how to be discreet, and I will also be on the lookout for Mr. Mullin."

"I will call you immediately after I speak with Ofelia."

"Gracias"

Che hung up the phone and called Ofelia at Juan Ignacio's house. She was shocked to hear Paolo knew she was in contact with Miguel. Everything was happening so fast. But she also trusted Paolo and knew neither he nor Che would ever do anything that would cause her harm.

Che told her Paolo was anxious to meet with her and was willing to drop everything to meet with her as soon as she was available.

"Did he speak with you about anything else, Che?"

"Just that he heard you were in Argentina to see Miguel Martínez and one of his sources of information was the MI6 agent, Brian Mullin, who apparently followed you and Juan Ignacio to Miguel's residence yesterday."

"¡Dio Mio! We had no idea! Of course, I will meet with him as soon as possible. Che, do you think it's safe to meet at Juan Ignacio's house, or should we find another place?"

"Definitely another place. Let me reach out to some of my PpV colleagues and get back to you. Actually, I have a better idea, there is a small backstage dressing room at my tango club. It can be accessed through a back alley, and one of the dancers, Pepper Murphy, lives in a building that backs into the alley on the other side. Even if Brian Mullin is following you to her apartment, he won't be able to follow you the rest of the way."

"How quickly can you make arrangements?"

"Let me call Pepper and get back to you. I believe she knows Teresa and Marissa."

"Really?!"

"That story can wait for another time. I will call Pepper to arrange a convenient time, then get back to you and Paolo."

Chapter 48

It was lunchtime. Brian was bored to tears and about ready to take a break from watching Juan Ignacio's house, which had been notably quiet throughout the morning; when Ofelia walked out the front door and stepped into a taxi cab that had just pulled up. Thankful he was already in his car, Brian followed the cab into the bustling commercial center of Buenos Aires, where Ofelia was let off in front of a popular shopping mall. He drove his car into the mall parking lot, hoping the mall itself wouldn't be too busy.

Although there were quite a few shoppers milling about, Brian had no trouble finding Ofelia where she was casually window shopping in front of a high-end women's boutique. It appeared she had plans to go clothes shopping. Lingering there for a while, she entered the store and walked around, as she chose a variety of outfits to take into a fitting room.

In an effort to remain undetected, Brian hid among hanging outfits some distance from the fitting room area. He had a good view and knew she would have to come out at some point. What he didn't know was that Ofelia would be meeting up with Pepper Murphy in the fitting room area where she would be outfitted with a new look including a blond wig, floppy hat, large sunglasses, and high heels. After a half hour, Brian asked a woman who worked there if she had seen his Argentine wife, who had entered a fitting room and disappeared. He was worried something had happened to her. He discovered there was no one there who fit her description. The saleswoman was amused, thinking his wife had successfully sneaked out to get away from him. Little did she know how close she was to the truth.

Meanwhile, Ofelia and Pepper left the mall and drove to Pepper's apartment, where they exited the building and walked to the back door of Che's tango club, where Paolo was waiting.

It was a surprisingly emotional meeting. Ofelia had not forgotten Paolo but had also never known the major role he played in her life after the twins were born. As they spoke, reminiscing and catching up, it became evident to her that he had cared for her and contributed to her well-being from the background to the present day. She was touched and decided to bring up what she had heard about his bequest.

"It's evident you've been my guardian angel, Paolo. I am very grateful for that, but I don't understand being included in your will."

"Ah, Ofelia, there are many reasons. I have always admired your fierce loyalty, your intelligence, and your fearlessness in action since you were that naive young girl. But you must understand, it is a small bequest I included in my will many years ago. I just wanted to acknowledge my admiration and make sure you could live in comfort when you are finally old, which from the looks of you, won't be happening for a long time. I have often thought about you and your beautiful ojos verdes."

Ofelia smiled. "You are too kind, Señor."

Paolo returned her smile. "Can we talk about Miguel Martínez and the documents in his possession?"

"Of course, Paolo. I know I don't have to ask you to make sure no harm comes to either Miguel or the gentleman who has been helping him."

"They will be protected from harm, Ofelia. Let me come to the point. Al Watson and I have worked together many times over the years when the interests of Argentina coincide with the interests of the British Secret Service. We are, of course, on different sides with regard to Las Islas Malvinas, but Al has not been certain where I stand. Now it's evident he knows Miguel is still alive and in possession of the documents. For some reason, he decided to turn you loose and facilitate your return to Argentina to find Miguel for him."

"Well, he succeeded, didn't he?"

"So please tell me, Ofelia, how is Miguel faring these days? I know, thanks to Al's agent, Mr. Mullin, that you have visited with him."

Ofelia didn't blink. "Yes, actually yesterday. He is not in good health. However, despite other things I have heard, his mind appears to be alright."

"What are your other sources, if I may ask?"

"My daughters met him a short while ago. They thought he exhibited signs of memory loss."

"Your daughters. Was this the first time they met their father?"

Once again, Ofelia didn't blink. "It was the first time they met Miguel, but he is not their father."

"I'm sorry for that assumption, Ofelia."

"That's alright, Paolo. Everyone who was around me at the time assumed the same thing because I was in Miguel's employ, and part of my job was to seduce him. My daughters and I also thought he must be their father. We discovered this week that he was sterile at the time."

"I thought he had children."

"Yes, the ones who were murdered by Videla's thugs when they broke into Miguel's home in search of the documents. According to Miguel, his children were the ones who brought home the mumps they gave to their father, which rendered him incapable of reproducing further."

"I know it's not my business, but is there another candidate for this honor?"

"Yes, there is."

Feeling he didn't have the right to probe further, Paolo changed the subject.

"I give you my word. No harm will come to any of you."

"I want to believe that, Paolo. I know you are a powerful man, but can't help fearing for my loved ones' safety. Can you tell me? I can't help wondering how you learned about what's been going on the past few days so quickly."

"I make it my business to learn things that concern me. In this case, I had more than one source, but Brian Mullin appears to have been put out by the way Al Watson has been treating him and decided to go over his head."

"Al has a habit of offending with his arrogance."

Paolo smiled, "Ofelia, do you have possession of the documents?"

"I do, but they are not on my person. I wanted to make sure they would remain safe until they are in your hands. But I do need to ask you a question."

"Anything."

"I went through them for the first time this morning. Most of the documents are covered with numbers neither of us could make heads nor tails of. Miguel left it entirely up to us to decide what to keep and what to destroy. He didn't believe any of them would be of interest at this point in time. Should we destroy them?"

"I could take a look at them if you want. I suspect if they were important enough to hide, they might reveal someone in the government cheating the public or their rivals. But that goes on all the time, and we would only have proof of a small part of the corruption that occurred all those years ago. I'm primarily interested in what else you found in that packet."

"That's what I figured. It's a list of eight names."

"Will you take me to retrieve it now?"

"Yes"

"Let me call my driver." Paolo looked at Ofelia to see if she was concerned and laughed. "He is always armed and can protect us from Brian Mullin if he's figured out where we are, which I tend to doubt."

"Brian followed me from the house to the mall, where I lost him. It's possible he has returned to Buenasuerte to watch the house."

Paolo laughed again, "Have you missed the cloak-and-dagger life you loved so much as a young girl?"

"I must admit, I've missed the excitement, but I may not be as fleet of foot as I was then. I'm not quite ready to be la abuelita who sits in her rocking chair knitting booties either, maybe something in- between."

"Perhaps I can find a position for you in my business. Would that be of interest?"

"Absolutely!"

"Will your daughters be at the house? I would like to meet them."

"Oh yes, Paolo, and they are dying to meet you!"

Chapter 49

Frustrated at losing sight of Ofelia, Brian was quickly convinced it was not an accident. She knew she was being followed. She had obviously set up the ruse to fool him and go to her destination without being detected. *Does she know I'm on her tail or just worried in general? But the most important question is, what is she hiding today? Why did she need to shake me off?*

Sitting on a bench in the middle of the mall, Brian pondered as his mind led him in two directions. *First, what do I know? Second, what should I do next?*

I know, or at least think I know, Ofelia has found Miguel Martínez and visited with him yesterday. If this is so, he probably told her about the documents. If he did, he had them at his residence and gave them to Ofelia when she visited, or he told her where they were hidden, where she could retrieve them, or he told her he had destroyed them. Actually, there is a fourth scenario where he denied knowing anything about them. I choose to believe Miguel told Ofelia where to find the documents. Why else would she avoid being followed? Then there is the role of Juan Ignacio Ramón. The message indicated he has the L. That has to be referring to the list of traitors. But today, he stayed home while Ofelia went to the mall by herself and disappeared. I need to go back to the Buenasuerte house and follow Juan Ignacio!

Arriving in the neighborhood, Brian parked a few streets away from the house and walked casually around the block. As he passed Juan Ignacio's house, he glanced down the driveway and saw the young man he presumed was Juan Ignacio carrying what appeared to be a trowel towards a large tree with vivid red blossoms in the backyard. Brian quickly concluded he was witnessing an important moment. Juan

Ignacio was either digging up or burying the hidden documents. This was Brian's opportunity to obtain the list. Deciding it was now or never, Brian fingered the small revolver he kept in the inner pocket of his jacket.

Brian purposefully walked up the driveway. Startled by the abrupt presence of the large red-headed stranger, Juan Ignacio was alarmed.

"Who are you? This is private property."

Brian smiled nervously. "My name is Brian Mullin; I'm a friend of Ofelia Cruz."

"She's not here. Shall I tell her you stopped by?"

Brian toyed with the gun.

"Actually, I'm more interested in what you're digging up back here."

"Somehow, that's hard for me to believe. I don't know you, and I think it's time for you to leave."

"I know you are Juan Ignacio Ramón, and you are in possession of a list I want. I work for the British Secret Services, and that list belongs to us."

"What list? I have no idea what you're talking about."

"I know you have it, and I may have to force you to give it to me. I don't want to hurt you, but this is important to my government."

Seeing Brian fidgeting with the inside pocket of his jacket, Juan Ignacio decided he had to keep him in the backyard and away from the house, away from Teri and Marissa. Sensing Brian was nervous, Juan Ignacio feared what might happen if he was startled. He needed to think fast and calm the man down. He decided his best chance was to keep the conversation going.

"Maybe if you tell me what the list is about, I will be able to help you."

Brian took the gun out of his pocket and aimed it at Juan Ignacio.

Just then, the backdoor flew open, and Teri emerged, calling out, "Juan Ignacio, what's taking so long?"

Stopping in her tracks, she said, "Brian, what are you doing here? Shit, what's with the gun?"

In an effort to regain face but still holding the revolver, Brian smiled at Teri, "Well, hello again, Teri. Please tell this gentleman I am here to protect you and your mother."

"Protect us from what? We're visiting our friend at his home, and my mother isn't even here."

Just then, a limousine pulled into the driveway. Brian, Juan Ignacio and Teri were riveted as they watched a large muscular man wearing a traditional limousine driver's livery step out of the driver's seat of the car. Without glancing at them, the driver opened the back door for Ofelia, then walked around to the other side of the car, where he opened the door for an elegantly dressed silver-haired man. When he turned to face the backyard, the first time he acknowledged the presence of other people, the driver already had taken a large pistol from his waistband he was aiming directly at Brian.

Realizing he was outnumbered and the driver had the capacity to disarm him with no difficulty, Brian put his small gun back into his pocket and tried to act as if he was simply dropping by. He began by greeting Ofelia, "Hello Brigid." Then he reached out a hand and introduced himself to Paolo. "I'm Brian Mullin, a friend from Ireland."

Paolo smiled as he shook Brian's hand. "It's nice to meet you in person, Brian. I'm Paolo Fuentes. I believe we've spoken on the phone recently, and I'm glad to have the opportunity to thank you for informing me about what's going on. You may tell Al Watson our business here is well in hand and you can be relieved of your surveillance services. Would you like me to make that call?"

Brian shook his head, "I'll let him know the next time we speak. It's nice to meet you, Paolo."

Giving Ofelia a quick hug, he said, "I suppose I shan't be dancing with you in Lisdoonvarna any time soon."

Ofelia smiled at him. "No Brian, I've come home."

Thankful that a potential disaster had been averted, they all watched as Brian walked down the driveway to the street.

Juan Ignacio led the group into the house through the back door. When they arrived in the living room, Ofelia took a deep breath and formally introduced Paolo to Teri, Marissa, and Juan Ignacio. She then walked across the room, where she picked up a large framed photograph of Miguel's son, Manuel. Removing the back, she retrieved a list of names, the list Juan Ignacio had been hiding.

Teri looked at Juan Ignacio, who was still holding the trowel. "If the list is here, what were you digging?"

Juan Ignacio laughed and pulled a package of flower seeds out of his pocket.

"Teri, after our phone conversation, I decided to plant lavender at the site of our treasure box burial to commemorate our reunion and that of your new family."

"Why lavender?"

"I don't know; I just thought the color would complement the bright red blossoms of the Ceibo tree.

Turning to Paolo, Juan Ignacio said, "I can't thank you and your driver enough for saving me from being killed for planting these seeds."

Paolo smiled at Juan Ignacio as he glanced at the names on the list. "You have saved the lives of eight brave Argentine patriots. I want you to be assured that your name will never be associated with any of this, and Miguel Martínez' whereabouts will remain a secret."

"I appreciate that, but how will you prevent Al Watson and Brian Mullin from pursuing Miguel?"

Paolo laughed, "I don't believe Brian will be reporting what just happened to Al. And, I will call Al and tell him this was all a dead end, that he was following Ofelia to a visit with an old family friend. He will probably not believe me; but is highly unlikely to challenge my view of things. He doesn't want to lose what value he gets from our relationship."

"Do you think we will succeed in reclaiming Las Islas Malvinas, Paolo?"

"In time, Juan Ignacio. I will probably not live to see that day, but perhaps you, Teresa, and Marissa will have that honor."

Even though they recognized what was going on as an important moment, Teri and Marissa were having a hard time paying attention. Instead, they found themselves whispering to each other as they focused on the tall, dignified man with warm brown eyes they knew to be their father.

When they heard their names, both looked up to see everyone looking at them.

Teri asked Marissa, "Is it time?"

Marissa responded, "You or me?"

Before Teri had a chance to answer, Marissa said, "Paolo, we believe you are our father, and we don't want to spend another day waiting for you to learn this on your own."

Paolo looked at Ofelia, then broke out in a dazzling smile. "I have been wondering since I heard your news about Miguel but didn't want to assume. I only wish I had known of this miracle sooner. Up until now, I have had two sons and could only wish for a daughter. Now I have two! But how will I ever tell you apart?"

Chapter 50

November 26, 1986

Dear Jack,

You're not going to believe what just happened!

Acknowledgments

I published my first novel, *The Other Side of a Tapestry* three years ago. The story was imagined as an alternative to my own early life and included some elements that were historically and personally accurate, but the story itself became increasingly fanciful as I wrote. In the end, I left many parts unresolved which apparently left more than one reader dissatisfied. *You've Found Her* has been written to tie up some of those loose ends, as well as to move the lives of some of its main characters forward. Both stories take place in the late 20th Century over brief periods of time. *You've Found Her* begins nine months after *The Other Side of a Tapestry*. I write all of this to explain that there is very little of my personal story in this book, which is a complete work of fiction. However, as such, it has given me the freedom to dig deeper into the minds and hearts of its three main characters to explore their different personalities and this book was written to serve both as a sequel to *Tapestry* and to stand alone as a family drama and character study.

A large number of people helped me to conceptualize and write *The Other Side of a Tapestry,* all of whom deserve my thanks because this book would not exist without the other. I didn't bother everyone in the same way as I wrote *You've Found Her* so my acknowledgement list will be shorter. I specifically want to thank the following people: Bronwen McInerney, Liz Smith, Bonnyeclaire Smith Stewart, Patricia Beynen, Emily Peña Murphey, and Donna Ursillo, who were kind enough to read and share their thoughts about manuscript drafts as they evolved; my sister, Diane Woodworth Liebert, who not only read and commented on more than one draft, but was always available to answer my questions about Buenos Aires and our family's life there; Bill Finan, whose editorial and moral support throughout my entire novel-writing career has been priceless; and Josh Bankes for creating the book's cover. As always, my husband Ray Basanta has played a huge role in helping me create this story. And finally, big thanks to Denise DeMarsh for putting me out of my misery by coming up with the perfect title.

About the Author

Lynn Woodworth Gregory was born in 1947 in New Rochelle NY; lived in Buenos Aires, Argentina between the ages of one and six during the post-World War II dictatorship of Juan Perón; and spent the remainder of her childhood in Norwalk CT. Her father was an international businessman who worked in the export-import field and their home was often visited by people from around the world. It was consequently not surprising that Lynn ended up with college degrees in Social and Cultural Anthropology and a professional career that revolved around research designed to learn about different cultures and ways to bridge gaps in cross-cultural communication. Throughout her forty-year career, she met and heard the stories of a variety of interesting people, many of whom, along with her own life experiences, inspired the creation of fictional characters and stories. *You've Found Her* is Dr. Gregory's third completed work of fiction. She currently lives in Philadelphia PA.

About the Author